UNDRESSING
STONE

HAZEL MANUEL

D1332875

INDEPENDENT INNOVATIVE INTERNATIONAL

Published by Cinnamon Press
Meirion House
Tanygrisiau
Blaenau Ffestiniog
Gwynedd
LL41 3SU
www.cinnamonpress.com

British Library Cataloguing in Publication Data. A CIP record for this book can be obtained from the British Library.

Designed and typeset in Garamond by Cinnamon Press. Cover
Adam Craig © Adam Craig from original artwork stone figu
'Scarface' © Kaplan69, Dreamstime.

Cinnamon Press is represented by Inpress and by the Welsh Bo
in Wales.
Printed in Poland.

The publisher acknowledges the support of the Welsh Books

Acknowledgements

Undressing Stone emerged from the earth and the trees and the stars and the soft cream limestone of a landscape steeped in sunshine and shadow, whose vines and sunflowers flare and fold with the seasons and whose secrets hide among the stories the locals tell, and those they don't. My novel owes its soul to a landscape as much as anything or anyone and as such I am so very grateful to have had the opportunity to immerse myself during its realisation in the beauty of rural France. I am a great believer in learning from genius, and very much enjoyed the research I did for this book. I acknowledge the influence of Auguste Rodin, Rainer Maria Rilke, Camille Claudel and David D'Angers, particularly in the development of Clotilde's character. On a more personal note, my heartfelt thanks to Connie, Jim, Ksenya, Nancy and Ruth, fellow Francophile adoptees who spent time with me in my rural idyll, and who encouraged, critiqued and inspired my story. Thank you also to the other members of Paris Scriptorium—those who regularly or occasionally offered honest feedback—invaluable to my story's journey. As ever I am grateful to Jan and Adam and all at Cinnamon Press for their unstinting support of my work. And of course to Pierre—qui comprend tres bien la folie de Sian. And to Willow—sydd bob amser wedi fy ysbrydoliaeth fwyaf a bob amser.

Hazel Manuel is a UK born CEO turned novelist whose writing follows on from a career in business. Having fallen in love with a French man she met in India, Hazel now lives and writes in France. Her fiction features strong female characters—complex women who are sometimes uncertain or vulnerable, but who nonetheless create spaces in which they can fully express their strength. You can find out more about Hazel and her work at www.hazelmanuel.net

I saw the angel in the marble
and carved until I set him free.

Michelangelo

UNDRESSING STONE

Prologue—Saint Vey, Rural France

'Never let the internet make a decision for you.' I can't remember now what Arwel had been talking about, but not wanting to do his bidding, that's exactly what I did. I, Sian Evans, a fifty-something divorcee, moved from Cardiff to Saint Vay—a four-house hamlet tucked away in a forgotten corner of ancient France, perfect for farmers, old people and escapees. I went because the internet told me to. And I loved the fact that Arwel was furious.

'Good grief Sian, how can you possibly move there?' He had been adamant that, living alone in rural France, I'd overdose or be eaten by French savages. At least there was no chance of the first occurrence, since I'd stopped taking my medication a month before and had no plans to resume. I didn't tell Arwel that, of course. My dear ex-husband, for reasons he would insist are motivated by my own good, would have been unimpressed. My shrink might have been less troubled—after all, it was partly his fault I went.

'Where is home?' That was the title of the online quiz that sent me here eleven months, three weeks and two days ago. The answer was France. *You're chic and sophisticated*, the quiz proclaimed once I'd answered questions like, *Which scene inspires you most?* (a picture of wine and cheese on a checked table-cloth) and, *Which celebrity would you date?* (I didn't recognise any of them). *You can be introverted, but you enjoy good food and fine wine. You understand that life is short but you know how to savour it.* I wasn't sure about the chic and sophisticated part, so Paris was out. Rural France it was.

Home. A small word but so cavernous. Home now is my little cottage, the garden and the field behind. I'm sitting on an old wooden bench sipping a glass of wine as I typically do at sunset, the scent of wet leaves and wood-smoke suffusing the usual tirade of buzzing, twittering and rustling. The meadow is a restless sea of live things: Crickets, gendarmes, chaffinches, pigeons, a little cat grey with a bent leg. Two big hares lope past occasionally, cocking their long ears at the slightest sound, but I haven't seen them tonight. And there are bats, small ones that fly out of the shadows at the turn of the day. All this makes it impossible to be alone. I don't feel restless. I'm at the still centre of it all or something like that.

The sun is setting. That isn't a metaphor, it's that time of evening when the trees turn black and spikey and the world takes on a melancholic air, as though it regrets the futility of the day's exertions and wants to wallow in self-pity. I like this time of day. Especially here. Strange to think it's always sunset somewhere. When I first arrived, I used to try to work out when the sun would set in Wales. And in India. I don't do that anymore. One sunset is all we can have at a time and it makes no sense to go chasing someone else's. Mine, this evening, is rather a dull affair, cold and not very colourful. *A glorious sunset,* people say. Since I arrived I've been hoping for one worthy of the term, the kind that people try to be poetic about. My sun has probably sunk behind the horizon now, it's hard to tell because it's cloudy. Again, not a metaphor. Although, being post-menopausal, I can see how some might say I protest to much on that front.

Eleven months is more than long enough to acquire habits. I've acquired plenty since I arrived. And they're not a French re-packaging of those I had in Cardiff. Back then, the first thing I'd do each morning was to dredge the night. Depending on how busy I'd been, this could take some time. Dreams, wakefulness, fears, worries, all the night-dwellers of an overactive mind would be excavated and picked over. I'd consider my discoveries, mistrustful, whatever we try to suppress will come out in our dreams. I don't need to do that anymore. These days, on waking or on hearing the dawn chorus—the countryside is so *effing* noisy—I note my mind's nocturnal output, and simply acknowledge it.

This morning, I woke with the birds, having left the shutters open. I lay in bed listening to amorous pigeons and twittery little things that were probably martins, competing with enthusiastic chaffinches, whose elaborate warbling ends with the proclamation *it's reeeeeal.* Truth birds. I stretched languidly, enjoying the warmth of my duvet in the early morning chill, and thought about coffee. It's then that it occurred to me: I was finally naked under my clothes.

PART ONE:
STONE

Chapter One

'So this is it then, you're going.'

There's nothing like Welsh rain, it's cold, its grey and, I swear, it's the wettest rain in the world. It was late spring and in spite of my half-hearted protests Arwel had insisted on driving me the twenty minutes through the deluge to the coach stop to wave me off. And to my surprise, considering we'd been divorced for years, we'd both got a bit tearful.

'I'm going, Arwel,' I'd replied swallowing hard and clutching my small leather backpack in front of me.

I glanced around at the huddle of teenagers in skinny-jeans, swarthy-looking men, elderly couples saying their good byes amid the diesel fumes of the already-running engine. No one was interested in me. I pulled my coat round me in the chilly morning air. Despite the hot tears which threatened to defy my fortitude, I'd thought I'd feel more. Here it was. I was moving to France. Arwel turned back to me and I pinned a bright smile on my face.

'It feels like I'm just going on holiday,' I said over the pounding of the rain on the bus-stand roof.

'Maybe you are, Sian.' He wasn't smiling.

'Arwel…'

I had no idea what I wanted to say to him, so maybe it was good that he cut in, his gloved hands clasping my shoulders.

'You've got nothing to prove, love. If it doesn't work out, come home.'

Arwel, I'm not your 'love', I felt like saying. But I didn't. And what did he mean by 'home'?

'That's very sweet of you, Arwel,' I said, hoping my sincerity outweighed the sarcasm.

After all, that's not what he'd said to our son at the start of *his* adventure, but then, everyone knows middle-aged women don't have adventures. I was gracious and let Arwel hug me tightly, his stubble grazing my cheek, before helping me onto the coach where I shuffled along the aisle behind two pony-tailed French boys. Once installed in a window-seat, my coat folded on the seat next to mine so that no one could join me, I sat looking back at Arwel, the collar of his coat turned up, miming a telephone call and mouthing the words 'stay in touch.' The engine shuddered, the coach lurched forward and I watched him through the rain-streaked glass as we left our stand to join the morning traffic, his dark form growing smaller and smaller, waving at me until we rounded a corner. *Effing hell, this really is it!* Did he feel the same sense of sudden panic? I shoved the thought away and turned to face the road ahead. *'I'm going to live in France,'* I repeated over and over in my mind. *'I'm going to live in France.'*

In the weeks before I'd left, Arwel had tried everything to make me change my mind. He'd invoked the gods of common sense, financial ruin, mental-breakdown, the wrath of my psychiatrist, maternal abandonment (that was the least plausible), even giving our marriage a second go (actually, *that* was the least plausible). Finally, for lack of any other options, he'd asked me out for a goodbye dinner.

Arwel and I had one of those rare divorces that ends in friendship. Of sorts. 'No reason not to keep things pleasant,' he'd said at the time. 'For Nate's sake at least.' I'd agreed. The divorce had been complicated, but not in the traditional sense —our house, our finances, our son—already a man, all were easily divided or incorporated into a new reality. It was complicated because I had no grounds for divorce.

'You're going to have to give me something to work with here, Sian,' my solicitor had said.

'But he's been a good husband and father,' I'd replied. 'I'm not going to lie and cite 'unreasonable behaviour' or whatever you call it, it wouldn't be right. And there's no-one else. On either side.' I crossed my fingers under the desk, although it wasn't exactly a lie. 'I want a divorce because I don't want to be married anymore.'

Arwel did all he could to convince me to stay, but in the end—and bizarrely, having realised that nothing was going to stop me from leaving—he helped me to fabricate some woes that I cited in the 'irretrievable breakdown' of our marriage. 'Just tell her I neglect you—never listen to you, always forget your birthday, never take you on holiday, that kind of thing.' None of it was true. But it was plausible. 'He never once remembered our wedding anniversary...' The solicitor wrote it all down with a look of distrust and I shoved away the memory of beautiful bunches of roses or gerberas arriving at my job to the envy of colleagues. Finally it was done. I was no longer Mrs Arwel Pritchard-Ellis, but plain old Sian Evans.

Nate had been in Sri-Lanka at the time and hadn't come home to witness the demise of his parents' marriage. 'I suppose it's normal these days,' he'd said in a terse little email. And since neither Arwel nor I had a new love-interest, it had been natural—pretty much—to maintain if not quite a friendship, then at least an amicable association.

The idea of dinner was posed as a moving to France celebration, but I knew Arwel was planning an assault. The restaurant—a new one, Italian with cautiously good reviews in spite of its clichéd menu- was crowded with Saturday night trade, but Arwel had reserved a table in a quiet corner.

'Nice place,' he said, glancing around at the exposed brickwork and vintage prints of the leaning tower of Pisa and the like. 'You used to love eating out...'

'Arwel, don't.'

I handed him his menu and a harassed-looking waiter in a smart black waistcoat arrived to take our drinks order.

'What say we push the boat out and have a bottle?' Arwel said, conveniently forgetting the fact that I rarely drink more than one glass of wine. He turned to the waiter. 'Anything you'd recommend?'

They settled on a bottle of Chianti and I nodded my assent. A burst of laughter erupted from a nearby table and we glanced over at the group of animated twenty-somethings.

'They're having fun,' Arwel said.

I guessed the subtext was that we ought to as well. I looked at him. It was clear he'd made an effort. His chin was newly bald and his pale blue shirt had been carefully ironed. I thought I detected a whiff of aftershave. *Oh, Arwel...*

His face contorted. He always read my mind, or thought he did. Our wine arrived and we had to sit there and watch the inept young waiter struggle with the corkscrew and then get flustered about a floating piece of cork in Arwel's glass.

'Its fine,' Arwel reassured him. 'My old dad always used to say it's good luck.'

We gave the waiter our order of pizza and salad and Arwel picked up his glass and—*god help us*—was about to propose a toast, when:

'Hold on,' I said. The smell of garlic bread was too delicious to ignore and I called the waiter back to order some along with a dish of olives to start.

'Okay,' I said once the waiter had scurried off. 'Continue.'

'Well,' said Arwel, raising his glass once more. 'I was about to say let's drink to the future, whatever it may hold.'

We clinked out glasses and I took a sip, wondering if we'd have to sit through an age of small-talk or whether he'd cut to the chase straight away. The small-talk lasted until our pizzas arrived, at which point he launched in with a faltering:

'Sian, are you sure moving to France is sensible? After all, you haven't been well…'

Seriously, that's his opening gambit? I started a tetchy reply but Arwel raised a hand.

'No listen, please,' he said. 'It's not long since you were seeing a psychiatrist. How can you consider moving abroad?'

I looked at him, fork poised over his salad bowl, brow furrowed, head tilted to the left. There were so many ways I could answer, but what would the truth be?

'I'm fine, Arwel,' I said. I put a piece of my pizza into my mouth and chewed slowly. 'You know damn well he's an Occupational Therapist, not a psychiatrist. And I wasn't seeing him because I was unwell. You know that as well.'

'But you were on medication!'

Effing hell, why do I tell him so much?

'Sleeping tablets, that's all.'

Alright, keep your voice down.' He flicked a look at our fellow pizza-eaters, none of whom seemed interested in me or my sleeping pills. Nonetheless Arwel changed tack. 'Well work then, money, how are you going to support yourself?'

I attempted to raise an eyebrow.

'Think about your son, what about him?'

I laughed out loud. 'Nate will be thousands of miles away whether I live in Cardiff or in France.'

What I wanted to say was *I'm an adult, I'll figure it all out.* But of course, I didn't. I suppose they were legitimate questions he was asking, anyone might have posed them, but the fact that it was *Arwel* doing the asking hacked me off. I looked around the restaurant at the other couples, mostly middle-aged. Do all wives feel like children or mothers, rather than simply women? *I'm not his wife.* Two women at a window table caught my eye and I watched them as they talked. One put a hand on the wrist of the other, leaving it there for a long moment…

'Sian, it's great that you're going to France, what an opportunity, Nate has his own life abroad, you're single, there's nothing stopping you, have a wonderful adventure.' Arwel could have said that—but he didn't. People don't like it when you do something for yourself, unless it involves making money. Even then, I'm not sure it applies to middle-aged women. What he said was:

'Come on Sian, please. Don't do your stone-faced thing, just talk to me for once.'

Stone-faced. I always hated it when he said that, it was as if he refused to see that any interaction has at least two participants. To be fair though, I never could talk to him. Not deeply. The answers were there in my head, but they rarely made it to my tongue. So, like countless times before, I sat there, mute, the buzz of the busy restaurant accentuating my silence as I ate pizza. Arwel, knowing that whining wouldn't help, wordlessly ate his.

'I'm going to rent the house out,' I said eventually. 'I've spoken to an agent and the rent I'll get will be enough to live on—just. I'll have to watch the pennies but my needs are pretty basic.'

Arwel raised an eyebrow. 'Well,' he grunted, 'I suppose that's one option. You'll be one of those dreadful ex-pats who take advantage of house-prices and do nothing for the country but prop up the wine industry.'

Bastard. How I'd support myself wasn't Arwel's business, but it was the easiest part of the move to talk about. I took a sip of wine and imagined him cursing my mam and dad for leaving enough of an inheritance to pay off my mortgage.

'And it's for a year, you say. Isn't that a bit…I don't know, self-indulgent? I mean, most people actually work for a living. You know, contribute.'

'Contribute what Arwel? I've spent my adult life working in call-centres. I'm not effing Mother Theresa.'

'No need to get vulgar, Sian.'

Always the same. When he doesn't like what I'm saying he criticises the way I say it.

'Look. I know I'm lucky to be able to do this and sure, most people aren't. But that's the point isn't it? I *do* have this opportunity. Constance and Jacques have said I can have their cottage for a year. After that they'll be selling the place. I might not have this chance again, so why not go for it?'

Arwel—no doubt now cursing my childless aunt and uncle —refilled his glass and I shook my head as he went to refill mine. He gulped down a long glug and took his frustration out on his pizza.

'And how will we keep in touch?' he said, spearing a tuna chunk with more force than was necessary. 'How will you keep in touch with Nate? Is there a phone? Internet? Will you at least give me your address, since it seems you're hell-bent on the idea?'

I hid a sigh and took a sip of my wine. 'It isn't outer space, Arwel, its France. There isn't a phone there or internet, but I have my mobile. And you can write to me, if you want. You know, with a pen and paper?'

Arwel snorted and went for a last shot. 'Sian, people our age just don't go off and start a new life all by themselves.'

Nearly thirty years I spent with this man. And he knows nothing about me.

Chapter Two

'I watched someone die once. To be honest, it was a bit of a let-down.'

My closet was pretty damn packed with skeletons but that wasn't one of them, and they weren't the reason I was seeing a shrink. There was no way those bony bastards were seeing the light of day. Technically, he wasn't a shrink; an 'Occupational Health appointment' it was called.

It was almost nine months before I moved to France, the day I told Doctor Jonathon Adebowale—BSc, MD, OTR/L about the dead woman. Sitting amid his expensive aftershave fug—I bet he'd slapped more on at lunch-time—all clean-shaven and pseudo-relaxed, in spite of his stupid Disney socks, the Good Doctor was swivelling in his oversized, fake-leather chair. Worse still, he was twiddling a posh pen, which would no doubt record the salient details of the hour's exchange—or perhaps only the salacious. It wouldn't, of course, be an exchange, I knew that much. It would be my life flowing from his ink. I glanced at his hands, still twirling the pen, not yet committing me to paper. *Did he manicure?* I frowned at his neat nails.

'I'd been sitting at home watching a film—something really long—*Gone with the Wind*, I think...' I tailed off hoping he didn't think I was a racist, but he simply nodded. 'Anyhow, old Mrs Next-Door came banging and shouting. Turns out her friend'd had a heart attack. She was still alive when I got there, her bloated stomach was quivering. I stared at her, wedged on the floor between the fridge and a cupboard, her skirt up around her thighs. I thought about mouth-to mouth, but one look at her dribbling mouth was enough to put paid to that idea. 'The ambulance is on its way,' Mrs Next-Door said. I don't know why she'd got me involved. I bent to pull the woman's skirt down. And then we both stood there staring at the thing on the floor till it stopped moving.'

I'd spoken the words slowly enough for the Good Doctor to write it down, but he didn't move his posh pen once.

'Why have you chosen to tell me this?'

What a question! Uttered in his low Good-Doctor voice. *Because it's your job to listen* I wanted to answer, but instead:

'It's okay, she wasn't a person.'

Dr Adebowale leant forward and I caught a whiff of his aftershave—not the cheap supermarket stuff that Arwel used to wear. He balanced his Good-Doctor elbows on his Good-Doctor knees, his hands propping up his chin, and repeated his last question more slowly.

'Okay. But. Why. Are. You. Telling. Me. This?'

Like I was a child. I breathed out hard and flicked a look towards the window where a puke-coloured blind made vague shadows of the view. I looked back at him, perched on the edge of his chair, pen poised in feigned anticipation. My heart wasn't in this.

'I don't know, you asked what I wanted to talk about today. Isn't death the kind of thing we're meant to discuss? You know, the trauma of it and all that?'

I swear he was trying not to smile. *Effing man,* wasn't that against some code of ethics? He wrote something down and, as he glanced up, I saw a big hairy mole on his neck. *He ought to get that checked out.* The clock was on the wall behind me, presumably so that he could surreptitiously check the time without seeming bored. I'd noticed that the first time I came. *He thinks that's clever,* I'd thought. He was checking it now. *Jesus, I've only been here five minutes!*

The first time I'd seen him, I'd been expecting more of a 'knit-your-own-chickens' type, all muesli-coloured jumpers, bits of brown bread stuck in his beard, that sort of thing. This guy looked like he would've been at home in a board-room and was wearing a tie-clip to prove it. Each of the three times I'd been, he'd worn a carefully ironed shirt and a coordinating tie, his suit jacket hanging with anal resolve on a hanger by the window. A wooden one. Looking around his office, I'd seen that there were no photographs on his desk, nor on the shelves, but now that I'd clocked the tie, I realised that every fibre of him screamed 'nuclear family', and I imagined a matching set of humans, two big, two little, in mirror-image genders, going on healthy ski-ing holidays to the Alps.

18

'You told me last week that you get days when you find it difficult to motivate yourself. That your work is suffering because of it?'

At least he'd stopped laughing at me, but I couldn't let Dr Adebowale, BSc, MD, OTR/L get away with that. Besides, there's only so much game-playing you can do if the Good Doctor won't do his bit, so I threw in the towel and decided to co-operate. The story about the dead woman was boring anyhow.

'Sort of,' I said, getting more comfortable in my seat. At least *I* had an armchair. 'I don't think my work *is* suffering. I'm a call-centre worker, it's not like people depend on me every day to do something vital, like if I were a teacher or a nurse or something. And I always meet my targets.' *Well, nearly always.* 'Okay, so I take the odd day off here and there. But I work hard. No one suffers because of it.'

Tap, tap, tap. I watched him playing with his pen and fought the urge to take it from him and put it on the desk.

'Tell me about your days off, Sian.'

I'm convinced people think your name is a key. Like it's a way in; that the door will swing open once they've used it and they can march right in. I stifled a sigh.

'I don't know what I can tell you, except that sometimes… I can't.'

'You can't…'

'Correct. I can't.'

'Why don't you tell me about that?'

Damn him. *Why don't you?* Such an odd turn of phrase. I could have listed some reasons: *Because I don't think you'd understand, because I don't trust you, because it's my private business…* Or made them up if necessary: *My cult leader won't let me.* 'Why don't you tell me about that?' In spite of the phrase, he obviously didn't want me to list reasons why I *don't* tell him. He wanted the exact opposite. In any case, I couldn't think of any good reason not to talk about my days off, it's not like I did anything weird, well not really. Plus, I knew he'd write down what he wanted anyhow and presumably give my HR department some kind of report. *My investigations conclude that there is nothing fundamentally wrong with Sian Evans. However, she is a highly sensitive person who would benefit greatly from being able to stay at home whenever she wants*. In any case, I decided to get on with it. After all, there are worst ways of spending an hour of work-time than talking about yourself.

'Okay, well on those days even the easiest tasks are too much,' I told him. 'I find myself dreading having to move… getting out of bed, getting dressed… And then I just stare at things, sort of…fixated by them. Like the moving patterns on the surface of my tea for example. Or I sit and stare at my bookshelf, not really seeing it, just sort of…being there with it…' Once again I tailed off, and once again he nodded. I warmed to the theme. 'I tell myself I need to move, I need to achieve something, anything, no matter how small. I might put the washing into the machine and after, I feel a kind of a reprieve as I know the cycle will last for an hour and as long as I hang up all the clothes when it's finished, I've accomplished something.'

Aha, now he writes.

'Do you feel tired on days like this?'

I considered the question. It was a reasonable thing to ask, but I wasn't sure I could answer adequately, it's so hard to describe a feeling. He noticed me pausing, and used it as a sneaky opportunity to write down something else.

'No, not physically tired,' I said. 'Well, maybe sometimes but I don't think that's it. It's like I need to…absorb.'

I was getting bored now. I flicked a glance around the room—why didn't he have pictures on those shelves, maybe a plant or two instead of just books and box-files?—and at the ugly window-blind, behind which I could hear rain starting. I wondered what the Good Doctor would do if I got up and opened it.

'You need to 'absorb' you say. How do you feel at these times?'

I looked back at him. *How do you feel?* It must be one of the hardest questions to answer. Dr Adebowale with his many degrees or whatever the BSc, MD, OTR/L stands for should have known that. I supposed I'd have to tell him.

'On the days when I can't go to work it's because I feel… soft.'

20

Chapter Three

I cheated on that internet quiz. France was the obvious choice, my Aunt's cottage was available and I spoke the language. I didn't tell Arwel of course. I was happy to move here to his disapproval after my meetings with the Good Doctor ended.

Breakdown. What a scoff-worthy word, what am I, an old car? It was Arwel who used the term not Dr Adebowale, and it *effing* pissed me off.

'Sian,' he whined, 'you can't quit your job! It's obvious things aren't right, you're…I don't know, depressed or something. A lot of people have breakdowns. Isn't that why you're seeing the shrink?'

He'd stopped short of using that catch-all weasel-phrase 'mid-life crisis', perhaps because he didn't fancy a slap.

Before I quit—quite a bit before—my manager, let's call her In-control Carol (though her name is Jill), was getting 'increasingly concerned about my absenteeism.' She'd called me into her cupboard—sorry, office—to whinge about it.

'Sian,' she smarmed, all shiny teeth and hushed concern. 'Sian, I really need to know what is *happening* with you.'

She clearly hadn't bought yesterday's plumbing-crisis excuse. What is *happening* with me? *Well, Carol,* I might have said, trying not to stare at her perky boobs doing battle with the buttons on her blouse. *Let me tell you. Breaths go in, breaths come out, two eyes see, two ears hear, a mouth speaks sometimes as it's doing now, and I suppose there's some organ action-going on, I'm hazy about the details.* I'd have loved to have said that. Instead, I mumbled something about a leaking washing machine.

'Sian, there must be something at the root of all this time off you're taking.'

Oh please, it wasn't that much time, it probably averaged, I don't know, three or four days a month, that's all. Carol, who had the precise number of days I'd missed that month (seven), was one of those spike-heel-skinny-and-efficient managers, expensively cut bottle-blonde hair, never late, never tired, never interesting. I imagined her dashing off to the gym for a quick tone-up of her perfect butt, before taking over from the nanny (of course there'd be a nanny), cooking something involving fish, (marble kitchen counters) while two blond kids coloured pictures at the kitchen table (oak), then greeting her clean-shaven husband, chit-chatting about asinine crap while eating fish and leaves, bathing the blond kids, reading to the blond kids, glass of wine while curled on a beige sofa with Mr Clean-Shaven (just one, it's a week-day), an episode of the same puerile American TV series the rest of the planet is watching, bed, (cream duvet), give Clean-Shaven a blow-job, (spit, not swallow), scrub teeth, sleep for a full eight hours, get up the next morning, do it all again.

Envy? Of course! Did I envy the countless In-control Carols and Commanding-Carls I'd worked for? Yes! But not because of their marble work-tops or the clean-shaven husband (over-rated) or the blond kids with their above average crayoning skills (Nate is blond). No. I envy them because their lives are so *effing* tidy.

I looked at her boobs pointing at me from across the desk (just messy enough to suggest industry), sipping herbal-tea and arranging her face into that *I'm here for you* expression.

'Sian, we can't help you if you won't help yourself.'

Yeah. I suppose the problem I was trying to avoid was the fact that I'd reached the two year point, almost to the day, in fact. Two years in a job seems to be my average, although I once worked for an oil company for three and a half, and for a pharmaceutical business for just over four. I speak French, you see, so I'm 'in-demand'—even in South Wales which you might not think of as a hub of Anglo-French commerce, I generally managed to find new jobs without too much stress. That four year stint was a record. And probably a fluke. I'm good at knowing when to jump before I'm pushed, and I sensed now, facing the wrath of Carol in her cupboard that the time was nigh. Shame really, I didn't hate the work.

Oh eff off, I wanted to say. Did she have any idea how patronising she sounded? As though she—or 'they' since she insisted on using the collective pronoun—had some kind of right to be supportive.

'You must be aware, Sian, that your absence record is beginning to cause concern. Is there anything you'd like to share with me?'

Yes. I don't know who I am. I'd have loved to answer like that, but instead I stifled a yawn.

Yesterday—the day of the 'plumbing-crisis' had begun in a pretty standard way. I'd woken up at the normal time, switched on the radio, listened to a bit of the news, got out of bed, showered, come back to my bedroom with a cup of tea, my hair in a towel-turban, and stood in front of the full-length mirror to dry it. Jim Naughtie was droning on—crooning on really, he has a lovely voice—about the usual impending economic doom, and I was only half-listening, thinking about what I had in the fridge that I could make for my lunch. Nothing amiss so far. I'd dropped the towel onto the bed and flicked on the hairdryer, blasting it at my upturned head, before tossing my hair over, and setting about drying the front, enjoying the scent of the apple shampoo. That's when it happened.

There was something in the mirror, a nude female homo-sapiens, but where was *I*? I switched off the hairdryer and dropped it to the floor where it landed with a muted thud. I don't know how long I stared, looking up and down the body, into the eyes. I couldn't work it out, it was like staring at that dead woman, nothing seemed to be in there. I put my hands to my mouth and amazingly, the thing in the mirror did the same.

Plonking myself on the bed, I glanced around. All seemed normal, the wardrobe there against the far wall, the chest-of-drawers with its jumble of potions laid out on top, the wicker-chair in the corner, all solid, real, resolutely *here*… but on the chair…*the clothes!* They were empty.

All the things I'd laid out last night, the grey pleated skirt, the pale-blue jumper and cardigan set, the matching knickers and bra, the tights, everything I'd intended to occupy today… empty. I couldn't move, I sat and stared. There was nothing in the mirror, and the clothes were all empty… Where was *I*?

Although today wasn't exactly the same as the other times —it rarely is—I knew from before, that if I could start, if I could only move my legs and arms, suddenly ridiculously heavy, if I could count the things that had to be done and if it was a manageable number—no more than sixteen—then I had a chance. There was no point in telling myself not to think—the problem was in my body as much as in my head, my body which wasn't my body, but which, if I could just start, I knew I could control...

...but this was when my heart started pounding and I felt the softness overwhelm me, when the air around me opened up with a viscous artistry, and *I knew, of course I knew what I should do*, but I just couldn't...

'Jill, I'm so sorry, I meant to tell you yesterday, I've got the plumber coming, could be any time, he said, so I'm going to have to stay home and wait for him.'

Somehow I'm able to hold on long enough to make the call. In-Control Carol's irritated voice at the end of the line betrays the fact that she isn't convinced. Again.

'Really, Sian, this is...'

'Sorry, Jill, better get off the phone, the plumber might be trying to call. I'll be in tomorrow, bye.'

And so, inevitably the following day, I was summoned to the cupboard where Carol's boobs pointed at me accusingly.

'Is there anything you'd like to share with me?' she'd asked.

'I'm sorry, Jill, I'm not sure it's anything I can discuss.'

I wasn't lying, there was no way she'd understand. What would I say? *My clothes were all empty and I had nothing to put in them?* Clearly, not a good idea. She nodded into my silence and took a sip of her non-tea.

'Of course, Sian,' she replied. 'I understand completely. But I think we're both agreed, there is an issue here that we need to address.'

Chapter Four

'What does it mean to you when you're 'soft', Sian?'

There hadn't been time at the last session for the Good Doctor to excavate my use of the term, so that's where we'd started today. A 'therapy hour' I'd discovered, is not an hour at all but forty five minutes. Isn't that against some trade-description law? It's just as well I wasn't the one forking out for these visits. On the other hand, it did mean that I was getting paid leave on ten Friday afternoons so, all in all, not the worst result.

'We value you, Sian, as an important part of the team,' In-Control Carol had said, leaning forward in her seat and sounding like a recruitment brochure. I knew what she really meant: *The European section is already struggling and you'd be hard to replace.* 'So we've booked you a series of sessions with an excellent Occupational Health specialist to get to the root of your…*issue.*'

A shrink, in other words. Important part of the team *my eye*, as my Aunt Constance used to say. Just because I dealt with customer issues in French didn't detract from the fact that I was a call-centre operator, not the *effing* Managing Director.

'What does it mean to you when you're 'soft', Sian?'

Despite my best intentions not to, I rather warmed to Dr Adebowale. His attempts not to laugh at my BS told me he knew what he was doing, even if today's socks did feature Tom and Jerry. Still, I still wasn't about to capitulate.

'I don't know what it means, sometimes I'm just soft,' I muttered. Not the most helpful reply in the world, but despite the fact that I liked him, I really didn't care. Or at least that's what I told myself. The Good Doctor seemed not to care either because he just sat there looking at me. I broke first.

'Okay. Well when I feel soft it's not…it's not like I'm sad as such. And I'm not emotional either. Well, there is emotion, but not one that I can name… it's just…being soft.' There, let him analyse that.

Last time I'd phoned in sick, it had nothing to do with my empty clothes or reflection. I just couldn't face the thought of having to talk to people. The day had started off like the last one, Jim Naughtie doom-mongering on the radio, cup of tea, shower. But in the shower-cubicle—this honestly happened—I couldn't move. I stood there for a good twenty minutes, the hot water washing over my reddening skin, and I couldn't bring myself to get out. When I eventually managed, I stood on the bathroom mat, steam rising off my body, feeling something close to panic at the thought of going into work. I'd rather volunteer to clean the office toilets if it meant being alone. So yeah, I left the usual message, this time fabricating a migraine as the reason I wouldn't be coming in.

There goes the eyebrow, the left one, jerked a full half an inch higher than the other. How do people do that? Actually, I wanted to know about being soft, myself, just for interest's sake. I mean yeah, I function, I manage my life, I cope. To all intents and purposes I'm a pretty normal kind of person. Aren't I?

'The thing is,' I told him, 'I can see how people might think it's just a way to get an extra day or two off work. After all, who wouldn't like a bit of time to themselves at home, to do whatever they liked with the day. But it isn't that. And the problem is, because it's so difficult to be honest about it, people assume you're sick or lazy if it happens too often.'

'Is being honest a problem, Sian?'

Using my name as a key again. Well it wouldn't work. A yawn caught me off-guard and I struggled to turn it into a cough. He must've known the answer to his own question—honesty is a problem because it has the power to break things. Arwel's face flashed into my mind...

No. Instead of honesty, we played the game, me stifling further yawns, Doctor Adebowale flicking sneaky looks at the clock. *What is this achieving?* My mind wandered to what I'd have for dinner that night—lasagne perhaps—and I wondered what the Good Doctor would have. Given his manicure and the hanging suit jacket, I guessed tuna.

'The thing is, our society isn't tolerant of inconsistency,' I said, throwing him a metaphorical fish. 'Especially if you're being paid to do a job. You're expected to perform regularly, come what may, and if you can't, it's seen as weakness.'

I remembered a guy at work years ago, his name escapes me. I'd overheard colleagues sniggering about him. He'd phoned to say he wouldn't be in that day. 'I'm calling from under the duvet,' he'd said, although he wasn't sick. He'd been mocked and ridiculed and eventually fired.

'You can't phone in and say *I won't be in today, I feel soft.*' You either have to force yourself to arrive as usual and do your best to hide your state of mind. Or else lie and pretend you have a more acceptable reason for not showing up. Like a bad back or food poisoning or something.'

There we are, reasonable, rational, logical. It was pretty much the most I'd said to the Good Doctor in one go and I thought I'd wrapped the problem up quite nicely. *You're right, Sian,* he should have said, *the problem isn't you at all. I'll talk to your HR department.* He didn't say that, although he did nod throughout my explanation and it seemed he was agreeing with me until:

'I notice you use a lot of words with negative overtones, Sian.' He picked up his notes—which were surely infused with his posh aftershave—and read from them: *'Society isn't tolerant,' 'can't perform regularly,' 'weakness,'* …

Effing Doctors! I cut him short before he could complete the character assassination.

'To be frank, Doctor Adebowale, and with respect—I don't think I am weak. It's true, sometimes I have no idea how I'll keep going until retirement. But I'm pretty damn sure I'm not the only one who feels that from time to time. And the fact that I do keep going surely makes me strong, not weak.'

'Are you sure you have to 'keep going' as you say?'

Right, because I'm a millionaire and can stop work whenever I like. What an entitled fool. I didn't dignify his question with an answer. That didn't deter him.

'Sian, you also used the words 'hide,' 'lie', 'pretend'. Is there something else you'd like to share with me?'

Chapter Five

The day we talked about my wedding, I'd gone home and dug out the old photograph album. All those guests with smiling faces I hadn't seen in years, decades in some cases. Some of them were dead now. I looked at Grandfather John, already in a wheelchair, cleanly shaven, which looked odd on him, suited and booted as he'd have said, but resolutely trilby-hatted as always. And there were my godparents, Dyffyd and Elin, chosen, so the family mythology goes, because they were the richest friends my parents had. My old mam denied that, of course. 'Good Christians,' she insisted. 'That's why we asked them.'

I turned the page and smiled at the meringue I was wearing, remembering the day I'd gone to choose it with Mam in *Bridal Creations* down the old high street.

'Takes your breath away, doesn't it?' the wedding-shop lady had said. 'Look at that tiny waist.'

My waist has never been tiny, the old bird was clearly doling out her well-rehearsed patter in the hope of a sale, but I liked the gown. I'd turned this way and that in the full-length mirror, trying the veil at different heights, wondering who on earth that shy-looking princess in the mirror was.

'What do you think, Mam?' I'd said.

My mam nodded. 'Beautiful,' she'd replied. I'd heard something else in her voice.

The weeks leading up to the big day had passed in a blur of florist visits, phone calls to the caterers, panic when they lost our booking, serious chats with the priest—in those days you had to convince him you were worthy of being married under his auspices—and indecision over the cake. 'Does anyone keep the top tier for a Christening these days?' I'd asked. 'They do if they're traditional,' Mam had replied. I kept mine, but I've no idea what happened to it.

It rained the morning of the wedding and, throwing back the curtains, up early and full of incredulity that the big day had finally arrived, I nearly cried with disappointment. But by eleven the sun had made a cautious appearance and at three it was sunny enough not to shiver through the photographs. I looked at them now, me grinning like a loon, looking more hysterical than happy, Dad looking stiff but proud, the trousers of his new suit too short for him by a good two inches. Walking down the aisle with him had felt strange. The forced intimacy of our linked arms, the painfully slow gait, not knowing where to look, the knowledge that both of us were squirming under the gaze of so many appraising eyes.

At the reception, I sought refuge in the buffet and managed to eat my way through most of the party, thereby avoiding too many conversations. I did dance—well, it was more like shuffling to the music, and I remember wondering whose idea it had been to book an Elvis look-a-like for the entertainment.

'Still, it went off well, the guests all seemed to have had a good time,' I told the Good Doctor. 'And the family seemed happy.'

Apart from my mam. She never said a negative word, but I saw her looking moody, like there was something she was fighting not to say. Dad was halfway down a bottle of Famous Grouse with Uncle Jacques by that time, both of them waving their hands around and bellowing at each other in French. I assumed that'd hacked Mam off big-time, it was the kind of thing that would. But at the end of the night she said something that I've never forgotten. I was exhausted and looking forward to the imminent departure of the last, die-hard guests—Dyffyd and Elin, who were deep in some inebriated debate with the purple-nosed priest.

'I'm so tired, Mam,' I'd said. 'I could sleep for a week.'

She narrowed her eyes and looked at me for a long, hard moment.

'You should have thought on that before you got married.'

It was more than a decade before I knew what she'd meant.

The Good Doctor had listened to all this without interruption. I couldn't remember how, much less why we'd got onto this track. What it had to do with my work record I had no idea and I made a mental note to be much more careful in future.

'Have you noticed something, Sian?' His voice was quiet and I wondered, with a wary glance at his rapidly-filling note book what gem of wisdom he was about to deliver.

I've noticed many things, Doctor. I've noticed you don't seem to mind not talking about my job, I've noticed it's raining out and I'm hacked off because I've got washing on the line. I've noticed that I'm really hungry, and I've also noticed that it's time for this effing *session to end.* I didn't say that. Instead, I sat there and listened as the notes were thumbed and the promised gem duly bestowed.

'Sian, in your description of your wedding you've talked about the weather, your dress, the cake, the guests, the priest, the photographs, the reception, the buffet, the music, your mother…something is missing, is it not? You've made no mention at all of the man you married.'

Chapter Six

That evening I met Arwel for a drink. It didn't happen often, but every now and then, particularly if we had something to discuss regarding Nate, we met at The Queen's Head which does an excellent cheese board.

'So, to what do I owe this pleasure?' I'd asked, thinking it uncanny that he'd phoned just as I was walking home from the wedding discussion with the Good Doctor. Arwel hadn't enlightened me on the purpose of this little soirée.

'Oh, no reason, I just thought it would be nice, that's all.' He took a gulp of his pint and glanced around the pub in what I thought was a shifty manner. I glanced around, taking in the regular after- work office-types.

'Since when did we do nice?' I said, turning back to him.

'I thought we did 'nice' quite a lot when we were married.'

'You know what I mean. Come on, why are we here? Nate okay is he?'

Ignoring the pain that even saying my son's name induced, I watched Arwel shift in his seat as a waitress appeared with a huge slate laden with cheeses, walnuts, grapes and rocket drizzled with olive oil, a pile of crackers in the middle. *Why can't they serve it with bread like they do in France?* As soon as she'd gone, I speared a hunk of stilton.

'Nate's fine,' he said, through a mouthful of cheese. 'Spoke to him just the other day. Says this yoga-teaching malarkey is going well. Damn funny job for a man if you ask me.' He swigged a gulp of beer as though demonstrating what real men do. I'd heard the jibe a thousand times and ignored it.

'He's still in India then? Did he say when he'd be home?'

'Sian…'

Arwel cast his gaze around the pub again. Was he looking for someone? *Imagine if Nate walked in now.* Of course, he didn't and I followed my ex-husband's gaze to the bar, which was mainly lined with suit-wearers of the male variety, and to the tables where there were plenty of women. A homely-looking thirty-something with big dark curls was checking her mobile at the window table; an arty woman sporting a purple scarf and shoes was sipping wine; a sexy cougar-type was preening herself at the table next to ours. The pub was full of single women. *Good grief he's going to tell me he's got a girlfriend.*

'Sian…' Arwel leaned in close and lowered his voice.

'Yes, Arwel?'

'Sian, the thing is…'

'Yes, Arwel.' *For goodness sake spit it out, I don't care if you have a woman.*

'Sian, are you seeing a psychiatrist?'

'Huh?' My mind was still with the girlfriend.

'A psychiatrist. Are you seeing one?'

Effing hell, that *is* what he said. I laughed out loud and the cougar glanced our way.

'That's none of your business, Arwel.'

'So you are then? I mean…are you okay, Sian? You can talk to me, you know.'

I stared at the cracker-crumbs in his beard and shook my head.

'First off, he isn't a psychiatrist, he's an Occupational Therapist. And secondly I'm seeing him because I've been absent from work more times than my boss likes. That's all.'

'Alright, keep you voice down. So you're okay then? I mean… you're not on any medication or anything like that?'

'Medication? I'm not on anti-depressants if that's what you mean. Sleeping pills I'm on, that's all. You know what I'm like, never could sleep much.'

Why on earth am I telling him?

'In any case, who the hell told you?'

Arwel looked sheepish and I thought he was going to avoid the question, but my accusing stare did the trick.

'Friend of Lynne's saw you in the waiting room. Apparently she's seeing him too—marriage problems, Lynne says.'

Arwel's sister Lynne—better known to me as Cruella—has a friend who saw me in the waiting room. You couldn't make it up.

'Could be a good thing, you know.'

'What, having my business spread all over Cardiff is a good thing? Doubt it.'

'No, not that. I mean talking to someone. You know. Opening up or whatever they call it. Lynne's friend swears by him.'

She does, does she? I watched Arwel plonk a corner of camembert and a dollop of Branston Pickle onto the last cracker before offering it to me.

'No thanks,' I said. 'Why? Why is it a good thing I'm seeing a shrink?'

He stuffed the cheese into his mouth, spraying me with bits of cracker as he spoke.

'Well, you never did talk much, did you?' he said, taking the napkin I was proffering and wiping a drip of pickle from his chin. 'Hard as rock, Lynne always said.'

'I'm going home, Arwel.'

I reached for my coat. My Friday afternoon character assassinations with the Good Doctor were more than enough without my ex-husband and his sister chiming in.

'Don't be like that, Sian, I didn't mean to criticise, believe me, I know exactly what you're like and I married you.' He gave my arm a playful shove in what I supposed was an attempt at levity. 'What I mean is, it can't be a bad thing to have someone to talk to. Might, you know, do you good.'

'I'll think about that,' I said, patting him on the shoulder and standing up. 'In the meantime—I'm going home.'

I left Arwel to finish his pint and winked at the cougar on the way out, wishing the reason for the rendezvous had in fact been a new girlfriend.

Chapter Seven

Nate Evans, twenty-eight years old, life-long teenager, world-traveller, and my son. 'He's got the travel-bug,' people said when they were being kind. 'Work-shy,' they'd mutter when they weren't. He's in India now, teaching yoga. I didn't even know he knew yoga. I spend evenings looking at pictures of him on his Facebook page, tanned, smiling, happy. It's the longest he's stayed anywhere.

Before India, Nate spent a couple of months as a farm hand in Tuscany. I've had post-cards from Buenos Aires where he was a waiter, from Albania, where he spent some months painting an orphanage, and from Kho Samui, where he worked in a cocktail bar. He's taught English in more countries than I can remember. Every now and then, I'd get an email: *make my bed up, Mam, I'll be home at the weekend.* 'The weekend' might mean any time over the coming month, but he'd arrive, bearded and brown, in need of a bath and a good night's sleep. He'd settle for a while, look up old friends, have his dad and me in fits of laughter with his stories. He'd get work on a building site, save some money and then be off again. I had no idea when I'd see him next. I'm used to that.

'How do you feel about your son's itinerant lifestyle?'

Bastard. The Good Doctor, I mean, not Nate. We're at it again, in his office, him swivelling, literally, me metaphorically. *I wish you'd sit still in your fake-leather chair,* I wanted to snap.

'I'm proud. He's seeing the world, not wasting his life.'

The Good Doctor wrote something in his notebook and I cursed myself. I knew by now that saying *'he's not wasting his life'* meant I thought he was.

'Do you miss him?'

I took a deep in-breath. *Every hour of every day.* But no, that's not true, not anymore. I suppose I say it as a reflex, but it used to be true. When Nate first went away, he ripped a planet-sized hole in me that's never really healed. But the pain has faded. Is motherhood always like this? Are mother's condemned to live in a perpetual state of dull anguish?

'Mam,' he'd said, that sunny springtime evening as I was washing up after dinner. 'I've got something to tell you.'

He'd been back from university for nearly a week, and I'd known something was up, he'd been quieter than usual, and spent far more time than he normally did in his room. I'd put it down to tiredness. Or maybe he'd broken up with a girlfriend, although he didn't seem upset. Whatever it was, I was sure he'd tell me about it sooner or later, in his jokey, off-hand way, either that or it would blow over. But here he was standing in the kitchen doorway, his face carefully calm. 'Mam, I've got something to tell you.'

Effing-hell, is he going to announce that he's gay?

'Should I sit down for this?' I asked. He raised an eyebrow and gave a sheepish half shrug.

Christ, maybe his girlfriend is pregnant? Of the two, I preferred the gay option.

'No, Mam, it's nothing serious. Well, I suppose it sort of is.'

He sat down at the table and I dried my hands on the tea-towel and sat opposite him. He had that look he used to have when he was little, when he felt compelled to own up. He'd always been able to tell me things. It wasn't as though he bared his soul to me, far from it, but he was never afraid of saying what needed to be said. Like the time he knocked over the crystal vase my Mam gave me the Christmas before she died. I admired his honesty. He picked up a tea-spoon from inside a mug and tapped it against his palm.

'What is it, Nate?' I asked. 'Come on, you're worrying me.'

He replaced the spoon and sat back in his seat.

'It's nothing bad, Mam, nothing to worry about. The thing is… I've decided to take a gap year. I'm going to travel.'

Ah, travel. He was looking at me with that expression he'd had since a boy when, having made me a birthday card or painted me a picture, he'd stand there hopping from one foot to the other. *Do you like it, Mam, do you?* I peered at him to see if there was anything more.

'So you're not gay then?' His bewildered frown made me smile.

'Gay? No, why?

'You're going travelling…'

'Yes. I've done all the research. I'm taking a TEFL course after the break so I can get work as I go, and I've been saving up for the flight and all that.'

Slow down there, Nate, I wanted to say. Work? Flight? To where, for how long? What about university? Instead I said:

'TEFL? What's that?'

'It stands for *Teach English as a Foreign Language*.' It's a certificate for teaching English to foreigners. There are hundreds of TEFL schools in all different countries and they're always looking for native English speakers. It's a really good way to work your way around the world.'

'Around the world...but...'

'I'm going to Thailand to start with. It's relatively cheap. Then Cambodia and Vietnam... I should be able to spend a good bit of time in all three countries, not just doing the tourist things, but working, meeting locals and you know... really *experiencing* it all.'

I didn't know what to say so I just sat staring at him. My son had always been an adventurous boy, but in a quiet way, not boisterous, simply fearless. It was never about excitement for its own sake. For him, it was about discovery. If there was a bird's nest in a high branch, he'd climb the tree to investigate. If he spotted something interesting on the opposite bank, he'd wade across the stream to get to it. And the odd sprained wrist or skinned knee never stopped him.

'Look Mam, I've given this a lot of thought. Everyone takes a gap-year these days. It's a great opportunity.' He gave me *that* look. 'I really hope you're okay with it.'

'But what about your degree? What about university?'

'Its fine, Mam, I've talked to them and they've agreed to let me pick up again the following year when I get back.'

'So it's just for a year?'

'Yeah, Mam, it's why they call it a gap-year.'

That was eight years ago.

Chapter Eight

Loss. It was at the heart of me. I didn't need some shrink to tell me that. Talking about Nate wasn't something I was used to and I shifted in my chair, avoiding eye-contact with Doctor Adebowale. 'Nate's a young man,' Arwel had said when he'd first gone. 'Of course he wants to cut the apron strings.' I knew he was hurting too, but we didn't share our pain.

'I miss him,' I said now. 'But I've learned to live with it.'

The Good Doctor nodded his sympathy, or what was meant to pass for it, eyebrows raised, lips pursed, leaning ever-so-slightly forward. I sighed and sat back. I wasn't in the mood to play games. I couldn't, not where Nate was concerned.

'Why don't you tell me about when your son first left?'

When Nate first left. What can I say about that? A work colleague once said to me, 'Ah, he's gone to university, that's it then, he won't be back.' It was bad enough then. 'Come on, Mam,' Nate had laughed, I'll be home at the weekends.' He wasn't. What with new friends, parties, university work, it soon became clear that I'd only see him in the holidays. I expected it and got used to it. But this travelling... now that he was on the other side of the world, his absence was so much more intense. At first, it was like he was leaving me every day. I don't think kids realise that. Why should they? They're so focused on their own life, their loves, their concerns, their adventures. It's natural. If there's one thing I've realised about being a mother, it's that it hurts.

'The house was so quiet,' I told the Good Doctor. 'I began to miss his loud music, him playing computer games with his friends, shouting at the screen. And the place was too tidy.'

I thought back to how I missed the things I used to curse —wet towels on the bathroom floor, smelly sports clothes and muddy trainers dumped in the hallway, used mugs and plates left all over the place. The lack of his clutter underlined his absence and made me restless.

'I think that was the start of the end of Arwel and me,' I said. 'We were good at being parents, thrived on it, I suppose.

But without Nate—well, there was only him and me. And that didn't work so well. We limped on for a couple of years but eventually divorced.'

The start of the end...That was a lie. I bit my tongue—literally—and stared at the Good Doctor. He stared back and I could tell he was storing something up for the future.

'Let's focus for now on when Nate left to go travelling.'

The Good Doctor's voice was quiet and he hadn't written anything down for a while. I appreciated that.

'Mam, you don't have to come if it'd be... you know, easier.'

Arwel and I had gone with Nate to the airport. He'd tried to protest, but feebly, and—I know my son—secretly not wanting me to concede. His backpack was half his size and stuffed to the brim. These days it's travel-worn, bearing its scuffs like badges of honour, and is never more than half full.

That first time, I'd watched him pack and re-pack. I brought him a cup of tea as he was setting everything out on his bed. I cleared his wicker-basket chair—a remnant from my childhood—and sat drinking my tea as he deliberated over each item. He'd produced a list weeks ago, which he'd circulated to family and friends, and which had yielded one pair of walking boots (Cousin Chris), a pair of sturdy sandals (his godfather Tim, who we hadn't heard from in years and probably felt guilty), water-purification tablets and a compass (an old Scout master), a travel wallet to wear around his waist (his best mate from school), two pairs of sand-coloured knee-zip trousers (Aunt Cruella—sorry Lynne). And, from his own savings, as well as his ticket, he'd bought a four-seasons jacket, a book called *Work your way around the World*, a set of maps of South East Asia and a camel-pack. ('It's a water bottle Mam, with a tube so that I don't have to keep getting it out of my backpack when I'm hiking.') Arwel and I bought the backpack, a substantial thing, full of pockets, belts and clips, which Nate had chosen after reading numerous reviews.

And now, brand-new backpack clipped and hoisted, hair newly shaven, limbs white and eager in his knee-zip trousers, new boots pinching his heels no doubt, he stood in the noise of Cardiff Airport scanning the departures board for his flight to London and on to Bangkok. I scanned his face. The face of my son, which I wouldn't see for another year. His mouth had a harder set to it than usual and his eyes were darting around. It was apprehension, but the kind that would soften once he was on his way for sure, and I supposed that was a good thing.

'Desk twelve,' Nate said, 'over there.'

We waited with him in the baggage-drop line, his Dad keeping up a comedic commentary between the security announcements. *Don't look, here come the Club Med crowd. Oops, hope grannie and grandpa over there splashed out on death insurance.* Nate kept diving into his hand-luggage to check he had something he might have forgotten. I said very little, but tried to maintain an encouraging grin, the result of which, I'm sure, was that I looked like the village idiot.

'Now then, son,' Arwel said, once Nate had checked in his backpack and we were standing at the point of no return, anxious-looking passengers rushing past us. 'You'll miss us, that's for sure, and we'll miss you, but it'll be the making of you.' He flicked a glance at me. 'Just keep in touch when you can, enjoy yourself and don't worry about us.' I nodded hard. 'You'll find more money than you expect in your bank-account. It isn't a fortune, but your mam and me… well, we've done what we could.'

The break in Arwel's voice was so subtle that only I'd be able to perceive it. They hugged hard, their eyes closed, each clapping the other on the back. I knew Arwel was fighting not to cry. He wasn't the only one.

'Come here, Nate,' I choked.

'…Mam…'

'We'll all be alright. Give me a hug and then off you go to discover the world.'

I held him. I held him like I might never see him again, like I could press him back into me, return him to his childhood self, when all he wanted, all he needed in the world was his mam. My neck and my jaw were aching from clenching back tears. I missed him already.

'You take good care, Nate.'

He looked back only once, and I wondered what he was thinking, what he was feeling, the two of us, his dad and me, standing there waving, me blowing kisses at him like he was a little girl. And then he was gone.

Oh God! I didn't tell him I love him! Come back, come back Nate...I love you, what if he thinks I don't, what if it's too late, I have to tell him. Nate!

Before I could make a show of myself, Arwel steered me through the crowd to the coffee shop, where he sat me down, handed me a wodge of serviettes and went to buy tea, while I tried to stem the flow of tears.

'...I saw you waving your son off...'

I jerked my head up. There was a woman standing by the table and I hastily wiped my face with the back of my hand. I nodded.

'He's gone to Thailand,' I said. 'For a year.'

The woman's face was puffy and red, as though she'd been crying too.

'I've just said goodbye to my daughter,' she said. 'She's going to Nepal with her boyfriend. May I?'

I nodded again and she pulled out a chair and sat down. Arwel, having returned with two mugs of tea, gave his to the woman and without sitting down, winked at me. 'Need to buy a newspaper, back soon,' he said, leaving the two of us.

'It's like you've lost them,' she said. 'When your kid goes so far away and for so long, it feels like you've lost them.'

My tears, my pain—they were all for Nate, but saying goodbye to him had stirred the ache of a deeper loss, one that had been there for years, hidden from everyone, even Arwel. An unfillable hole at the centre of me. Nate wasn't the cause of it, but his going made it deeper, the loss of my son becoming enmeshed with that other loss.

I never saw her again, the woman in the airport, never even learned her name, but for those moments, during the time it took the two of us to drink a cup of tea as we talked and cried together, that stranger was the closest I had to a friend.

Chapter Nine

'Is there something else you'd like to share with me?'

Doctor Adebowale had asked me that some weeks ago but even now, I didn't feel inclined to open up about any of the secrets that talking about Nate's leaving had riled up. One emotional shit-storm at a time was more than enough to focus on and besides, I found that I actually enjoyed talking about Nate, it was as though it brought my son that little bit closer to me. It's true, I'd often been sarcastic with him—at least in my head. 'You're the doctor, you tell me,' was one of the stock phrases I didn't utter out loud but thought often. Lately though I'd been less cynical. He was too damned good, the bastard. Today I was hesitating, on the brink of confiding the niggling suspicion I had about why Nate didn't come back from his travels. But the Good Doctor was ahead of me.

'You think Nate is deliberately putting distance between himself and you?'

I nodded and didn't respond. He hadn't used the word 'guilt' but it was there between us. Doctor Adebowale didn't break the silence.

I'd been over and over it, even tried without success to talk to Arwel about it. 'Get away with you,' he'd said, 'Nate's a young lad having some fun with his life, nothing deeper to it than that.' He changed his mind when Nate emailed towards the end of that first year to say he was extending his visa so he could see more of South-East Asia. At first he told us he'd sorted it out with the University and that they were holding his place. But the extra three months turned into six, and when he finally came back, it was to tell us he'd left his course, that he was saving up to go to South America, didn't know when he'd be back.

'Why else would Nate have gone so far for so long?' I said at last. 'He could've come back after the year, picked up where he left off, but he chose not to.'

I have to say, I did wonder what on earth all this had to do with the time I was taking off work but by this point I didn't care, it was just good to be talking about Nate. I even slipped off my shoes and curled my legs under me on the armchair.

'Arwel was furious,' I told the Good Doctor. 'They rowed about it day and night till I put a stop to it. It was obvious Nate's mind was made up and nothing Arwel or I could say was going to change it. And I didn't want Nate leaving on bad terms.'

Doctor Adebowale nodded. He had once more abandoned his notes and was leaning back in his chair, the ankle resting on his knee clearly displaying a Bugs Bunny sock. If he'd sneaked a look at the clock behind me, I hadn't noticed and I felt grateful.

'And how was your relationship with Nate at that time,' he asked?

'He'd changed,' I said. 'When we picked him up at the airport after that first trip, I could see it straight away. Not just his tan and his beard. I mean, he was quieter, more grown-up in a way. But that wasn't it exactly. He was more… more *solid*, if that makes sense. We didn't talk much. Don't get me wrong, he told us all about the places he'd seen, people he'd met. But I knew there was more going on in his head that he wasn't saying. In a way, I knew he had more to do in the world, if that doesn't sound too mystical.'

The Good Doctor continued his nodding and rather than being irritated by this, I had the feeling that he was really listening. 'And what about *you*, Sian?' he said. He still hadn't picked up his notes.

What *about* me? Here was my son, twenty years old, barely a man, on the brink of a life I couldn't understand.

'I just wish he'd get in touch more,' I said. And yeah, my voice caught. 'I don't blame him for the life he's chosen, god knows, I might have done it myself if I could, but he never gets in touch. I'm lucky if I see him once a year. Fair enough, but there must be a reason he doesn't even Skype…'

Silence from Dr Adebowale. At least he hadn't handed me an effing box of tissues.

'…I mean, other people's children get it out of their system, don't they? They go travelling, then they come home, they finish their studies, get a job, get married, have children...'

Even as I spoke, I knew how petulant I sounded. Like I resented not being able to write Nate into some cheesy sit-com. Seriously, when you compare married suburban, family life in a red-brick new-build, an office job and a two-week holiday a year, to painting an orphanage in Albania before flying off to Brazil to teach English, then boating down the Amazon, well...

The Good Doctor finally picked his note-book up from his lap, but instead of writing in it, he turned and placed it along with his posh pen on the desk. Facing me, he leant forward. *This should be interesting.* Finally, he used the 'G' word —guilt. But not in the way I'd been expecting.

'Sian,' he said, his chin resting on his clasped hands. 'I wonder whether it's not guilt you're feeling about Nate going away, but envy?'

Chapter Ten

It was around that time that I did the internet quiz. I wasn't thinking about moving abroad at that point, but Doctor Adebowale's pronouncement about my adventure-envy had got me thinking and I'd begun to consider a holiday.

'A holiday?' Arwel looked at me as though I'd suggested I join a cult. 'What, on your own?' God knows why I'd told him.

'Yes, Arwel. On my own. I'm not a child, I don't need a baby sitter. I thought I might go to France.'

The internet having informed me that France was my natural home, I'd decided to visit my aunt and uncle's cottage. Why not, I hadn't had a break in years, not since an ill-fated trip to Malta when we were still married, Arwel attempting to re-kindle our romance, me desperate for a divorce. A summer break in rural France sounded exactly what I needed. I'd hire a car, take my time driving through the countryside and spend two blissful weeks in the sunshine, reading, relaxing and indulging in all that cheese and wine the quiz told me I enjoy. I spent a contented Sunday afternoon researching hire car and channel-crossing options before I contacted my aunt and uncle. My plans were to come to nothing though.

'I'm sorry, Sian, I can't allow you any annual leave before November.' In-Control Carol smirked. 'Time off has to be booked well in advance, you know that, Sian. We can't have people popping off at a moment's notice.'

Effing woman! My insistence that I hadn't booked a holiday in over a year was no doubt overshadowed by the fact that I regularly popped off at a moment's notice—a fact that In-Control Carol took great satisfaction in reminding me. November in rural France held less appeal and besides, I wasn't about to have anyone dictate when I could have my holiday. I began to think of what kind of illness I could feign for two weeks. The whole thing had put me in a foul mood and when I arrived for my next session with the Good Doctor, I was ready for a fight.

'I thought these sessions were supposed to be about exploring my feelings, not you telling me what's wrong with me.'

I could tell by the angle of Doctor Adebowale's raised eyebrow that he was unfazed.

'Is that what you think I'm doing, Sian?'

Always a question, never an answer.

'Sian, I'd like us to talk about your relationship with people in authority.'

I should have seen that coming. It's obvious, isn't it, employee flouts her bosses by taking time off whenever she wants, clearly has a problem accepting authority. He could lump my divorce in there as well at a stretch. Hell, why not blame Nate living abroad on my refusal to accept his adult autonomy.

The Good Doctor glanced at the clock and I wanted to say to him 'in a hurry are you?' but I knew he'd write it down as an example of my anarchism.

'The reasons I take time off work,' I said, 'have nothing to do with my relationship with my boss, nor with my ex-husband and certainly not my son.' There, let him write that down in his silly little notebook. He didn't. Instead he posed another question.

'Okay, Sian. Would you like to tell me what you think *is* causing your absenteeism?'

What I *'think'* is causing it. Code, of course for *'tell me your opinion and I'll decide whether or not it's valid'*.

'Why,' I asked, 'are we focusing on me? Why don't we look at my job for the reason for my *absenteeism* as you put it?'

'Go on.'

Damn it, I will go on!

'Well, it's unnatural, isn't it?' I retorted. 'I mean to expect people to turn up day after day, sit in an impersonal room with relative strangers, and have the same conversation over and over again with people I don't know and don't care about.'

The irony of that. The Good Doctor raised his eyes to mine and smiled.

'I suppose some people can do it,' I muttered. 'But me...I just can't. At least not every day. Over and over again for hours, the same chair, the same people, the same conversations, the same *effing*—pardon my French—noise. It's as simple as that.'

But of course when it came to the Good Doctor and our rehabilitation sessions, very little was ever simple. Walking home, I decided to take the long route, and looking around me as I made my way through the crowds in the wide, paved city centre, stopping now and then to look at the displays in the shop-windows, I marvelled that all these people hurrying home from work or gathering in the chic city-bars were able to show up day after day, week after week, at jobs that they probably hated.

'It's not that I dislike my job,' I'd told the Good Doctor. 'I mean there are aspects of it that I like—when I can fix a problem for a client for example. That can be satisfying. The thing is the… it's the *relentlessness* of it.'

Outside the cinema, I paused to look at the posters. I hadn't been to see a film in months. I didn't mind going alone. I enjoyed sitting in the dark, drinking tea out of a paper cup, eaves-dropping on the conversations around me before the adverts began. Today the posters were all of muscle-bound men doing heroic things. I walked on.

The early evening sun was shining warmly in a clear blue sky and I decided to make the most of it and take the long route back along the riverside. I walked down the steps and along the bank before sitting on one of the benches that dotted the path. Three little boys on the other side were feeding ducks. 'Not like that, like *this*,' I heard one of them say. A future Commanding Carl. I was gratified to see the smaller lad ignoring him. My mind turned to the session I'd just left. I was still in a bad mood about my holiday and now I was fed up with the Good Doctor as well.

'Sian,' he had said, 'if the fault lies with your employment, then how do you explain the fact that lots of people don't take excessive time off work?'

He'd got it all wrong of course. I was beginning to doubt Dr Adebowale, BSc, MD, OTR/L's credentials, but then, I supposed his job was to change people's behaviour, not to reinforce it. 'I don't know,' I'd felt like saying, 'because the others lack imagination?'

Two young women in business suits walked down the steps and along the riverside towards me. 'I'm going to impress the hell out of him by working on that spreadsheet all weekend,' I heard one of them say. *Seriously?* I didn't remember ever feeling anything like as motivated about work. But then, I was a call-centre operator and those Ambitious Amys were obviously career-women. I wondered as I stared after the Amys, their rears wiggling prettily in their tight skirts, whether she'd count that weekend-spreadsheet as one of her life's successes.

The trouble is I thought, standing, stretching and starting off towards home, I can't make myself feel something that I don't. I'm simply not an Ambitious Amy, pay-rises and promotions don't do it for me. Perhaps the Good Doctor was right after all, maybe the problem was me. I set my thoughts once more on how I could manage this holiday in France.

Chapter Eleven

The two-week holiday didn't happen, but I was off to France all the same. I woke up on the boat an hour before we docked and was pleased I'd spent the extra money on a cabin. 'I've got no interest in watching the sea go past,' I'd told Arwel. 'I'd rather sleep through the crossing.' It meant I could step onto French soil fresh from a comfortable bed, showered and ready for the next stage of my adventure. That was the theory, anyhow. Even after carefully avoiding eating anything that could add to my queasiness, I woke sweating and restless in the starched white duvet, but it was preferable to heaving into a toilet for hours, like the last time I'd braved the seas.

After a long scrub in the surprisingly forceful shower and, having downed a bottle of water, I made my way to the deck, clutching the handrail to steady my swaying gait. The French have 'giboulées de mars' rather than 'April showers', but still there was fine rain coming down in over the yellow-blue sea, and I pulled my jacket around me against the spring wind. At the prow I took my place beside a family whose immaculately dressed children were arguing loudly in French over whose turn it was to ride in the front of the car—*c'est pas juste, c'est moi maintentant!* As France loomed, I breathed in the salty sea air and boat fuel. Five seagulls flew past in a line, one lagging behind and I followed them to the shoreline in the distance, rugged and white in the early morning sunshine. It was perfect rainbow weather, but I could see none.

The vibration of my mobile phone in my jacket pocket interrupted my excitement at having arrived, and pulling it out I wasn't surprised to see Arwel's name on the screen. I could imagine the conversation:

'How was the crossing?'

'Fine thanks'

'Still determined to go through with it then?'

'Yes I'm still determined.'

'Because you can always change your mind blah blah blah… there'd be no shame in coming back blah blah blah…

why don't you treat it as that holiday you wanted blah blah, *effing* blah.'

Before I could change my mind, I glanced left and right to make sure no one was watching and dropped the phone into the sea. I didn't hurl it or fling it, I simply dropped it. *Plop.* It was still ringing when it hit the water.

I'm plunging headfirst into the unknown, I thought, creating the drama that the disposal of my phone lacked. Looking around at the gathering passengers eagerly surveying the rocky coast, I saw that they were mainly families with small children, young couples, grand-parents. 'Are we on holiday yet?' I heard a little girl ask in English and I felt a jolt of pleasure—in fact, superiority—at being alone, and not on holiday.

It had been a strange time in my life planning to leave for France. My new tenants—a young couple with a baby on the way—had signed a six-month lease and the letting-agent had told me to pack away everything but my furniture. 'I doubt they'll give you any problems, you'll probably be wanting to extend the lease in due course,' the agent said as I sat signing papers in the stark white office. At least one person had confidence in my decision.

In addition to liaising with my aunt and uncle on an almost daily basis, I'd spent the weeks between the decision and actually leaving in a state of restless excitement. I assessed everything I owned. Regardless of the fact that I only had the cottage for a year, I'd made the decision to sell anything that held no special value to me and that wouldn't be used by the tenants. Ornaments, paintings, clothes, books, kitchen equipment, an old tent, CDs, Christmas decorations—everything that anyone was prepared to pay for was sold, the rest taken to charity shops or to the dump.

'Christ, Sian what about when you come back, you'll have to start all over again!'

Arwel, whose lifetime ambition had been to collect as much junk as possible, had come to take my DVD collection. He looked horrified as he gazed around my sparse lounge.

'It's only stuff, Arwel,' I'd answered.

And to my surprise, I realised I was right. Things I'd lived happily alongside for more years than I could remember became just that—things—not part of me, and no longer part of the fabric of my life. I'd expected to feel a combination of grief, panic and freedom at having got rid of so much, but what I felt was detachment.

There were some things I did keep. Five big boxes full of memories were stowed in Arwel's loft: Photograph albums, Nate's school reports, his childhood books and toys, drawings and gifts he'd given me over the years.

'Don't have a fire,' I'd told Arwel. '*This* is the important stuff.'

The boat docked surprisingly quickly, sliding in beside an even bigger ferry, and I took a last look at the flashes of liquid fire that the sun was casting on the restless water, before stretching my back and joining the queue for the car-deck. After a short wait, we were back in the coach, out of the port and winding our way through the little town, grey in the spring drizzle. Before long we'd left behind the uninspiring suburbs with their big, bland mega-stores and were speeding along the open road. I'd greedily taken in all that we passed, trying to cram the country into a mental box called 'home.' Sure, I'd been to France many times as a child, but it seemed so unfamiliar. *This is where I live,* I told myself, as fields of colza and artichokes gave way to vineyards and budding sunflowers. Listening to the French chatter of the pony-tailed teenagers behind me, I had the sense that while I wanted to call this country 'home', I nonetheless savoured my foreignness.

Three hours later we arrived at a provincial town. The rain had stopped and the pretty cream buildings with their balconies full of red and pink geraniums were glowing in the sunshine as we shuddered to a stop at the coach station. Emerging from the sharply air-conditioned coach, I blinked in the light which had a Mediterranean warmth to it despite our distance from the sea, and waited with the backpack-toting teenagers and olive-skinned men, as the driver heaved our cases out of the hold and onto the pavement. '*Maman!*' A woman cried, and ran to an elderly woman who I hadn't noticed on the coach. The teenage boys received kisses on each cheek by a stern-looking man. I smiled as a young couple, clad in skinny jeans and t-shirts greeted one another with the deepest of kisses.

Turning away, I was relieved to see a taxi rank nearby. *'Merci beaucoup Monsieur, c'était un très bon voyage,'* I said to the driver, the French words tasting so much sweeter in their homeland than in a call-centre. I dragged my two enormous cases towards the gaggle of people waiting for cabs and it wasn't long before I reached the front of the queue. *'Bonjour Monsieur,'* I greeted the smiling young man who jumped out of his car, and watched as he hoisted my suitcases into the boot with practiced ease.

'Est ce que c'est loin?' I asked, having handed him a piece of paper bearing the address.

'Pas trop loin,' he replied, still smiling. Not too far.

At my request we stopped at a Carrefour super-market on the edge of town—much too big and inevitably confusing, but necessary if I was to start my new life with the basic essentials. The driver waited by his car and chain smoked Camels with the meter running while I jostled past chic young parents with well-dressed babies, competed with formidable matrons for the best vegetables and deliberated over the delightfully bewildering cheese counter, stocking up on as many groceries as my trolley could hold. Forty minutes later, the back seat loaded with four cardboard boxes and two enormous bags full of supplies, which my admirably helpful driver rushed to carry, we finally headed out of town.

It didn't take long for the main road to give way to sweeping, vine-bordered lanes dotted with sleepy creamy-stoned villages. 'I am transfixed,' I said in English to the driver, who simply smiled as I stared through the window at the series of winding roads, which got progressively smaller and narrower as we headed deeper into the countryside. The road finally dwindled to single track, the last and narrowest of which lead to the cottage.

'C'est la maison?' the taxi-driver asked as we slowed to a halt beside a little stone house hiding behind two enormous red gates. I supposed this *was* the house. I climbed out of the passenger seat and breathed deeply. That smell. You don't get it in the city. The scent of freshly-cut grass and the

honeysuckle which was tumbling over the stone wall. But it was more—it was fresh, moist, living earth.

The driver got out and began heaving my suit-cases and shopping as I gazed at the building. The gates obscured much of the cottage but I could see the upstairs windows, their closed wooden shutters lending the place a greater sense of mystery. As the driver hauled the last of my boxes out of the car, I scanned my distant memories of summers and Christmases here with my aunt and uncle but I didn't recognise the place. The driver came to stand beside me and followed my gaze up to the house.

'Voulez-vous que je vous aide?' he asked.

Thanking him for his offer of help, I tried the gate and together we managed to shove it open, a great screeching of hinges sending a shower of startled birds into the air. The two of us went back and forth four times through the wild little garden with my boxes, bags and cases.

'Merci beaucoup Monsieur, vous êtes très sympa,' I said once all my things were piled by the front door, and I dug into my bag for the fair, adding a healthy tip. The driver smiled his thanks and I walked with him up the overgrown path to the gate.

'Bonnes vacances, Madame,' he said as he climbed back into his car and started the engine.

'Ce n'sont pas des vacances, j'habite ici,' I replied, smiling.

I live here. My words didn't ring true, but I knew they would eventually. I stared after the car as it sped off into the early evening sunshine, the driver giving a little wave of his hand before leaving the lane deserted as he rounded a bend. The only sounds now were the chip-chip-chipping of birds and the rustling leaves of a cherry tree in full blossom. I looked up the lane and down. I could see two other houses and thought I remembered passing a third. Certain that my neighbours must have heard me arrive, I imagined the twitching of voile curtains and curious locals peering at me from behind them. I turned to my cottage. *My cottage!* For a while at least. I heaved shut the squealing red gates, located the key in the flowerpot Uncle Jacques had described and, after turning it in the lock, managed to push open the stiff wooden door.

Chapter Twelve

How best to fish a mouse out of the toilet? (Don't. Flush it and hope it can't swim). How to open a window that's stuck fast? (A combination of cursing and violence can work—if not, zap it with the modern miracle that is WD40). How to replace the cylinder of a bottled gas cooker without blowing yourself to high heaven? (Really easy actually, but scary). Such domestic challenges became the stuff of my new life and I rose to each, if not valiantly, at least with a naïve optimism.

My uncle had sent me—in a hand-written letter—a list of instructions—how to turn on the electricity and the water, for a start. The day I arrived, my suitcases and boxes by the door, I'd stood blinking at the gloomy kitchen, the unfamiliar shapes becoming distinct as my eyes got used to the dark. The room smelt musty but I was keen to see my new home. My uncle had told me that the electricity cupboard was easy to locate in the far left corner of the room and I navigated my way in the gloom around a big table. The cupboard was obvious enough and on opening the door I sneezed twice in quick succession with the dust and strings of cobwebs that stretched across the opening. Once composed, I stared at the arcane gubbins inside. There were three things that could conceivably be the master switch and none of them looked like my 'on' switch in Cardiff. I chose one at random and flicked it, fully expecting to be blown to kingdom come...*light*.

A damn good start. I stared around at the orderly little kitchen. It was like something out of a kid's storybook. A big fireplace dominated the room, its grey stones blackened by two centuries of fire. I took in the big farmhouse table and chairs and a jumble of wooden furniture. Two closed doors, one at either end of the room piqued my interest but—*first things first*—I resisted the urge to start exploring and went outside to find the water tap. The round stone cover was right where Uncle Jacques had described, inside the front gate, though hidden in a scrubby stand of tall weeds. It was a heavy bugger but I managed to heave it aside, cleared away the accumulated gunk and, after a couple of turns of the stiff metal stop-cock, turned it full-on. Alright, I wasn't exactly scaling the heights of female achievement, but it felt great to do something Arwel would have taken charge of had he been here. The sink was in a corner of the kitchen and back inside I turned the tap. After a few sputtering coughs—*water*.

That first evening, I did little more than turn on the fridge and unpack the food. I'd wandered around the house through trails of cobwebs, peeking into each of the rooms, hoping to recognise something from my childhood visits. I didn't feel any sense of familiarity, taking in not much more than large furniture and the smell of disuse. *Petit à petit*, I said out loud in a little bedroom with faded wallpaper, containing only an enormous bed, a wooden wardrobe and a chest of drawers. Had I slept here as a child? I had no recollection of the room but decided that this was where I'd sleep. I resolved not to rush my re-acquaintance with the cottage but to let it reveal itself to me at its own pace, and with that in mind I closed the door and went downstairs.

Back in the kitchen, I rummaged in drawers and cupboards and found a knife, a plate and a glass and set about preparing a light supper of hunks of fresh baguette, fat green olives and Camembert cheese. After wrestling with the old-fashioned corkscrew I'd found on a shelf, I popped the cork of a bottle of local red wine, poured myself a good glug and took my French feast into the garden.

The sun had already set and dusk was giving way to darkness. Sitting amid the weeds at a rickety table at the foot of a big cheery tree, its blossoms fluffy and pink, I pulled my cardigan around me against the chill spring air. I sipped my wine and watched the stars emerge one by one, feeling a thousand things. *I'm here*. I could barely believe I'd arrived and, looking up at the little cottage, its stone glowing yellow in the twilight, the wooden shutters still closed, I knew it would be everything I'd hoped. *Santé*, I said and raised my glass to the house.

I wondered, as I sipped my wine, about the field beyond the gate and I considered going to look. But it was dark and, although I was tempted to linger in the star-lit garden, the two-day journey from Cardiff to Saint Vey had exhausted me. I decided it would be wise to go to bed before my state of fatigued euphoria turned to melancholy. I finished the last of my bread and cheese, drained my glass and got up to take my supper things inside.

Although wary of being in a strange house at night, the combination of exhaustion and excitement conspired to ensure that on that first night I didn't feel scared in the unfamiliar cottage. After making sure I'd locked the door securely, I climbed the stairs with only the faintest sense of unease. *Don't bother tonight, ghosts, I'm too tired to care.* I hadn't unpacked my clothes, my suitcases still downstairs by the kitchen door, and after opening the shutters and taking a final look out of the window at the shadowy garden, I closed the curtains, stripped to my underwear and, shivering with cold, climbed into the big old bed. The bedsheets must have smelt dank, but I hardly noticed and, tiredness outweighing the strangeness of the unfamiliar room, I fell into a deep and dreamless sleep, not waking till the next morning with the sound of the dawn chorus.

Chapter Thirteen

When I woke I knew exactly where I was and sat up immediately. Very little light was creeping past the thick curtains—just enough to confirm, along with the fulsome birdsong, that day had broken. I saw that opposite my bed there was a big oval mirror framed in dark wood, but I studiously avoided looking into it, afraid that I wouldn't find myself there. Instead, I flung back the quilt, threw on my clothes and opened the curtains.

The idea that the countryside is a haven of peace and tranquillity is, frankly, nonsense. I leaned out of the window and, sure, there was no traffic noise coming from the little lane beyond the red gates, no people could be heard in nearby houses or gardens, no evidence of human life made itself known at all. I was glad. But the place was alive with noise and activity. To my right a line of twittery garden birds sat chattering on an electricity wire; somewhere to the left, a crow was laughing from a burst of pink cherry blossom; overhead swallows eeeshed and sheeeshed, while flappy pigeons in bushes called 'por poor.. pooooooor, por poor'. It was a wonder I hadn't woken hours ago.

Downstairs, I located the kettle and a cafetière, made coffee from my Carrefour supplies and stood in the kitchen. My two outsized red suitcases were in front of the oak dresser, where I'd heaved them last night. I was keen to discover my new home so, rather than unpacking, I decided to leave the cases where they were and go exploring. There were two things I did want though so, in spite of my excitement, I unzipped both cases and rummaged around in first one and then the other. My hands finally located what I was looking for: a pale blue porcelain mug with the Welsh inscription *'Mam Gorau yn y Byd'*—World's Best Mum—in cream lettering—a present from Nate before he went travelling that first time; and a little onyx egg—a birthday gift, not from Nate nor Arwel, but someone else…it was very precious to me. Feeling the familiar tug of pain, muted now after so many years but nonetheless profound, I kissed the cool stone of the egg and placed it on the dresser where I'd see it every day.

It had taken me an age to decide what to bring. Considering I'd be in France for a full year, I needed clothes for all seasons, and back home in Cardiff I'd laid out everything I had in my bedroom. 'Capsule wardrobe' is a buzz phrase and I'd decided that's what I needed. Not knowing what facilities were available at the cottage (Aunt Constance had told me there was a washing machine, but she didn't know whether it would still work) I'd decided to bring enough to have a set to wear, a set in the wash and a set drying for each season. I'd made a pile of everything I thought would be impractical or unnecessary—high heeled shoes, work skirts and blouses, cocktail dresses. What if I were invited to a party though? After a rummage, a simple blue party-dress was retrieved from the 'no' pile. And the weather? Certainly hot in the summer, but I was sure I remembered freezing cold French Christmases. Layers, I told myself. I ended up mainly with jeans, cotton blouses, tee-shirts and jumpers, plus a jacket or coat for each season. And a pair each of winter boots, sandals and deck-shoes. One pair of smart shoes just in case, to go with the blue dress. I nodded to myself as I surveyed what I'd chosen. My small leather back pack would double as a handbag. Everything else—seven bin-bags—was sold if it was worth anything (two leather handbags, a pair of boots, a ball-gown (never worn) three work-suits and a winter coat), or given to charity shops.

Now, standing in the cottage kitchen, I wondered as I stared at the neatly packed clothes whether I'd been over-zealous. I closed the lids and spent the next hour wandering around the house and garden.

I'd been here many times as a child and as I walked around I tried to recall the summer holidays and Christmases I'd spent with my aunt and uncle. That was more than forty years ago and I could only retrieve the haziest of memories. Standing on a chair to help my aunt bake cakes—*'Oui ma chérie, comme ça, très bien…'* and the smell of baking… Hadn't there been a big spider once behind my bed? *'Awww elle est mignonne, elle est votre amie.'* And outside, wasn't there a swing? *'Allez ma puce, c'est très bien...*' Peering beyond the back gate into an overgrown field, I couldn't see one. What are the real memories and what are the dreams, I wondered?

Opening creaking doors to dusty rooms, the remnants of other lives still here, I felt sad for my uncle and aunt, as though something of their life had died here without them to nourish it. Upstairs, I thought about how excited they must have been when choosing the now mottled wall-paper and faded furniture, the piles of heavy linens my Aunt must have washed countless times. Downstairs in the kitchen, the huge fireplace seemed to long for flames, while the big wooden dresser, stacked full of chipped jugs, mugs and bowls, was proud to once more show off its striped and flowered crockery. Each cupboard, each drawer revealed a fragment of paused history, and I imagined my aunt and uncle happy here.

They'd been surprised to hear from me. I'd started a letter, but changed my mind, thinking that because it had been so long since we'd been in contact, it would be better to talk. Luckily, I still had Mam's old phone book and, after poking around in a drawer, managed to find it.

'Sian!' Aunt Constance exclaimed, *'Ma petite! Ma puce! Comment allez-vous?'*

Her unusual way of speaking stirred distant memories of hot chocolate for breakfast, which we drank out of bowls... *'Voulez-vous plus, ma petite?'* Constance and Jacques had always used the formal 'vous' form of address whoever they were talking to, which I hadn't realised was strange until I studied French at school. 'You will now learn ze correct forms of address, Miss Evans,' Madame Cambraque had blared, furious that I already spoke French. It was a gamble asking my aunt and uncle about the cottage. For all I knew, they could have sold it years ago.

'Aunt Constance,' I'd begun after we'd exchanged news of Uncle Jacques, Nate and Arwel -*'Aw, vous avez divorcé, c'est triste.'*—'I have something to ask you. The thing is, now that I'm no longer with Arwel and Nate lives abroad, I've reached a point in my life where I want to make a change. A real change I mean. I've thought this over a lot and I want to come to France. I'd love to stay in your country-house, for whatever period of time you would allow. I'd be prepared to pay rent, of course.'

I held my breath. I was sure I'd be able to detect in her voice whether she could entertain the idea or not.

'Ah, Sian, je ne sais pas si c'est possible,' she said. I don't know if it's possible.

She told me that she and Jacques never used the house any more, that they were too old to make the journey from Paris, much less to maintain it and the garden. They'd rented it out to holiday makers for a few years but had decided not to do that anymore after the last couple who'd stayed had stolen their television and left the house in a shocking state. *'C'était terrible,'* my Aunt sighed. After a final visit to clean the mess, they'd closed the house and not returned. *'C'est dommage,'* she said. *'J'aime beaucoup la maison.'* The sadness in her voice was evident. The house had been on the market for years, she told me, and even though interested people sometimes went to view it, no one had made an offer. *J'imagine que c'est trop de travail.*

I'd come off the phone despondent, but Aunt Constance had called back the next day after discussing it with my uncle. They'd be pleased to have a caretaker who would ready the house for a sale, she told me. If I undertook to thoroughly clean it and tame the garden, making it attractive for a prospective buyer, I could stay rent free for a year, at which point they'd put the house back on the market. Just pay the utility bills, she said.

'Mais, êtes vous sûre? La maison est belle mais très basique. Et c'est beaucoup de travail,' my Aunt had cautioned when I'd jumped at the arrangement. I'd reassured her that basic facilities and hard work would be no problem for me.

Now, staring around at the farmhouse kitchen, with its huge ceiling-beams, flag-stone floor and oak furniture, I could barely believe what had happened. *I live here!* I said out loud. I couldn't see that anything was lacking. The house was fully furnished, it had beautiful fireplaces, a cooker, fridge, shower, a lovely garden. What more did I need? I picked up my blue mug and my onyx egg and kissed each in turn. *Chez nous…*I whispered.

Chapter Fourteen

'Bonjour Madame Clairjo, ça va?'

Clairjo I was and Clairjo I am, despite the fact that my late husband—god rest his soul—was a Chiverny. This baker will wear my name out with her twittering. Madame Volt, bagging my croissants motioned with her head, up the lane.

'*Alors,* apparently, there's a foreigner in the Duchamp house,' she said. 'English I shouldn't wonder.' She raised a knowing eyebrow as she handed over the brown paper bag. 'Your daughter visiting with the grandsons is she, Madame Clairjo?'

I shook my head and ground a stray weed into the road with the toe of my shoe. Thinks her business is to know more than she ought, does Volt.

'*Bah non.* Fancy a change, is all, I like a croissant every now and then. I'll take a baguette as well.'

Volt's bread, in spite of it's tempting smell is never more than mediocre but we villagers, with nearly an hour's walk to the nearest bakery, have no choice and each Tuesday, Thursday and Saturday, on hearing the tooting of her horn, we shuffle out of our cottages and congregate around the van for baguettes and the day's news.

'No Monsieur Delariche today?' I knew she was trying to sound casual. Why Volt thought a stick-legged widow like her stood a chance with the likes of Delariche was beyond me, but then all the village knew she'd toss her hair at anyone who owned his own place.

'He's in Paris,' I said, glancing down the lane to the Delariche place, its wooden shutters resolutely closed. I know all his comings and goings, in spite of his tight-lipped ways. 'Expect he'll be back at the weekend.'

Madame Volt clucked a non-committal response. '*Zut alors,* this sun!' She said, taking off her bakers-cap and fanning herself with it. She flicked a look up the lane again. 'Good to have someone in the Duchamp place, wasn't nice seeing it empty.' Then, blinking her eyes in quick succession as she does when she's thinking: 'The Duchamps, they must be past eighty by now. Shame they stopped using the place.'

'Parisians,' I replied, with a roll of my eyes and we nodded in mutual distrust.

'Name's Sian, the foreigner. I can't remember her nom de famille. Postman told me.'

Volt and I whirled round. It isn't often old Monsieur Ripaille gets ahead of us on the news. I glared at him as he savoured his triumph.

'Sian? What kind of a name is that?' Volt asked.

'Foreign,' I replied.

We all nodded.

'Does she know about the bread-run?' Volt handed me my paper-wrapped baguette and turned to Monsieur Ripaille who, as usual, was deliberating over the bread.

'She'll have heard the horn,' he declared, as though horn-blowing bakery vans were a fact of everyone's life.

Ripaille, his back more bent than it needed to be (I know his game), his face gnarly, screwed up his eyes against the afternoon sun. He lets on he's older than me, but we both know the truth. Why Volt is taken in by him I don't know, she might as easily stop her van by my cottage. Ripaille tapped the rubber end of his walking stick against the van's front tyre.

'Wants air, that,' he said.

Madame Volt ignored him and turned to pick up a long, thin *baguette traditionnelle*, wrapping it in paper.

'Add a tartelette aux fraises to that would you, fancy something sweet I do. Make it two.' Same as every week, it's a wonder he's any teeth left. Ripaille pointed a misshapen finger at the tray of cakes then, nodding and wiping his brow with a grubby handkerchief: 'On her own, apparently, the Englisher. No man with her.'

I pecked him a sharp look but he ignored me.

'What's she doing here, anyway?' He rummaged in his pocket for change as Madame Volt proffered a paper bag containing his cakes. On retrieving a handful of coins, he peered at us, his obvious suspicion of a woman choosing to live alone forcing his brows to the bridge of his nose. 'Odd, if you ask me. Got to be a story there.'

Madame Volt and I eyed one another. 'You leave her be, Monsieur,' Volt scolded, dropping the coins into her leather satchel. 'If she wants her hedges cutting or her grass mowing, let her ask.'

'But she'll have to be told *who* to ask,' Ripaille grumbled. 'I don't want Delariche getting there first, muscles in he does, and then only does a half-decent job. Besides, the Duchamps always used to ask *me*.'

All three of us gazed down the lane to where we could just see the Duchamp cottage before the road curved to the left. The place looked as abandoned and unkempt as it had for years, un-cut grass and straggly bindweed reaching in clumps under the big iron gates, the stones of the boundary wall crumbling at the base. Madame Volt heaved shut the side-door of the van with a practiced yank and two jittery sparrows flew out of the hedge in a burst of chirruping. She walked to the driver's door.

'I'll have Macarons on Saturday,' she said climbing inside. 'You got your shopping list, Madame Clairjo?'

I handed her my list and Monsieur Ripaille and I stood back as Volt started up the engine, scaring a pigeon which flapped out of a cherry tree towards my place. *You watch it, or Fripouille will make a meal of you,* I thought, catching a glimpse of my scraggy old grey lurking under the hedge. Leaning out of the van-window, Madame Volt wagged a bony finger at us and proffered a parting caution before heading down the lane.

'Leave the newcomer be,' she warned. 'It's obvious she wants her peace.'

Ripaille nodded a good-day at me and clutching our bread, we turned to go back to our cottages but not without a final glance at the Duchamp house. I knew the old man was thinking the same as me: What *was* this foreign woman doing here?

Chapter Fifteen

The buzzing of flies has to be amongst the most annoying sounds in the world, right up there with barking dogs and burping. Have so many beasts of all sizes and levels of scariness existed anywhere, ever? No, Saint Vey is the fly-capital of the world. Every night the window in the lounge re-purposes itself as an insect graveyard and even after I sweep them away, the next morning it's full once more of predatory spiders standing guard over mummified corpses, while the flies that are still alive buzz manically and hurl themselves against the glass. Some are as big as wasps.

The first time I witnessed this ghastly display, I stood there, horror-struck. *Effing hell.* The window looked as though no one had opened it in years and I couldn't budge it. 'Arwel, can you come and open this window for me?' I barked out a laugh at the thought of making him come all the way from Cardiff, then screamed as a fly flew into my hair.

On my first morning in the cottage the new day brought with it an inevitable truth. The evening I'd arrived, I'd managed, in my excitement, to look beyond the soiled layers of empty years, seeing in the wooden beams and the fireplaces and the ancient furniture, only the cottage's bucolic charm. Now, in the light of day, it was impossible to retain the idea that the place simply needed sprucing up. The grime of years had laid claim to every surface and as I wandered from room to room, I breathed in the fetid smell of accumulated neglect.

The wafer-thin carpets were encrusted with damp and dust, dank curtains hung limply at each window, so faded it was impossible to guess their true colours, while cobweb-strewn ceilings and walls harboured all manner of insect life. Downstairs, smoke-blackened walls, piles of wood and stacks of yellowed newspapers, surely home to the mice whose droppings were evident, graced the lounge and the kitchen, while upstairs, the bedrooms, revealed soiled rugs, cobwebs replete with their insect catch, hideously engorged spiders, stained wallpaper, wooden cupboards, chests of drawers and wardrobes full of ancient, mildewed linens and moth-eaten clothes. No wonder the Duchamps couldn't sell the place.

I hadn't washed since arriving and decided that I'd investigate the possibility of taking a long, hot shower before getting stuck in. Aunt Constance had assured me that the plumbing worked well enough so, armed with a towel, my toiletry bag in hand, I padded barefooted along the corridor, pleasantly surprised by the morning warmth. I was thinking about what I'd do today, certainly unpack my suitcases and find homes for everything. My first job—after a coffee of course—ought to be to make a plan, otherwise I could end up running round in... *effing hell!*

The bathroom was teaming with flies. They were in every corner, clinging in clusters to the ceiling, crawling about on the floor, falling into the bath... I closed the door again, fast. How could I not have noticed them before? I fled downstairs and plopped myself into an armchair, sneezing repeatedly as a cloud of musty dust rose around me. Staring around the lounge, the fug of abandonment obscured any charm the cottage had held last night.

It's been a few years since we were there, Aunt Constance had said. I picked up a newspaper from the top of a pile—it was nine years old.

I got up, walked into the kitchen, slipped on my shoes and opened the door to the garden. Outside, the fresh morning air already held the promise of heat. I faced the jungle of weeds before me—a far cry from the pretty garden I'd thought I'd entered last night. A row of swallows was sitting on the electricity line making zizzing noises and they flew off in a shower of noise as some large vehicle stopped in the lane. The sound of the commotion and French voices beyond the gates told me it was bin-day. At least I knew that. I sat down at the little table where I'd sat the night before when I'd looked up at the stars feeling only delight and anticipation for the new life I'd begun, and stared up at the house. It was a picture postcard cottage. But the roof was sagging and the pretty casement windows were eaten away with age. And they belied the horrors that laid in wait inside. I could well imagine what

Arwel would say: 'Come home, love, you know it was a silly idea to begin with.'

Is feeling overwhelmed a choice? I told myself that in this case, yes, it was. *Come on Sian, it's only dirt and flies.* Deciding that coffee would be a good start, I went back into the kitchen and started banging around with the kettle, a cafètiere I found in a cupboard and my Mam Gorau yn y Byd mug. I'm not sure if it was the familiarity of something precious to me or the fact of performing this small domestic act—one I'd carried out hundreds—no doubt thousands of times before—but making the coffee, holding the steaming cup between my hands, sipping the hot, bitter liquid—created in me a feeling of calm. I forced myself to look beyond the grime and the cobwebs, to see the cottage how it had been when my aunt and uncle were here, how it could be again, homely and pretty in the sunshine, clean and spruce with the windows flung open, sunlight streaming in. I took my coffee into the salon, sat once more in the old armchair and imagined myself here in the winter, cosy and warm by a crackling fire, sitting in its glow, drinking hot chocolate and reading. *Sian, you have a year if you want it*, I told myself. *You can make this your home.*

Home. Yes, I needed to make it that. It's odd that the French have no word for 'home'. Not in the way that the British use it. Well, this sadly neglected cottage was 'chez moi' now and, back in the kitchen, I flung open the window and resolved amid strings of cobwebs translucent in the sunshine, to treat it as such.

Chapter Sixteen

'Operation fly' was clearly the priority. Having finished my coffee, I garnered my nerve and marched upstairs. Outside the bathroom, I gingerly pushed open the door at arm's length and peered inside, wondering what on earth could have attracted such an infestation. Some animal, a mouse or a bird I supposed, must have died in the roof space. I noted a ventilation cover above the sink, through which the flies must have come. Swarmed, more like. Armed with the two cans of what looked to be industrial-strength fly-spray I'd found under the kitchen sink, and wearing one headscarf tied over my mouth and nose and another on my head, my hair painstakingly tucked away, I held my breath as I sprayed not once, not twice, but three times, every cranny in that room that harboured or could conceivably harbour flies, screaming as some fell on my head, or landed near my feet but forcing myself to stay until the job was done. The hiss of hundreds of dying insects is a sound I'll never forget and watching their pathetic bodies writhing in the bath, the sink and on the floor as they buzzed out their last, intermittent sounds, I felt something akin to guilt. But it had been them or me and, still holding my breath against the chemical tang of the spray, I backed out of the room and closed the door behind me.

Surveying the ceiling in the corridor and the upstairs rooms, I considered the challenge of getting into the roof-space to locate the dead thing. I didn't relish the thought and was almost relieved not to find a loft hatch. I just had to hope that the fly-spray would finish the job—I wouldn't be showering any time soon unless it did.

I didn't bother making a plan, deciding after a second cup of coffee and a tartine—*so French*—to simply get stuck in. Having committed fly-genocide, I decided that I wasn't quite ready to dispose of the corpses yet, and elected to tackle the bedroom I'd chosen as my own. Luckily, the one bottle of all-purpose cleaner I'd naïvely bought at the Carrefour was supplemented by a cupboard-full of plentiful, if ancient cleaning supplies so, armed with a bucket of hot, soapy water, cloths, sponges, feather duster, a surprisingly modern vacuum cleaner I'd found in a tall closet and cleaning products of every conceivable kind, I headed upstairs to make a start.

The room wasn't infested like the bathroom but, nonetheless, there was more wildlife in there than I was prepared to live with. *Sorry spiders. Sorry flies. This is my domain now.* Out with all the bedding, out with the rugs, down with the curtains. I threw the window wide open and stood facing the room. Cleaning it would be easy enough. But that smell— the fetid stench of deeply ingrained filth—I doubted washing the curtains and the bedding would get rid of it. I looked down at the carpet, thin and dank with age. *It's got to go.* Having heaved the bulky chest of drawers as best as I could into the hallway, I started in the far corner and began to rip up the carpet. It was stuck to the floor but I was pleased to see once I prised it up, fairly decent wooden floorboards underneath. I finally managed to get the thing up from under the bed and and heaved it out of the window—a combination of brute strength, ingenuity and invective. It took effing ages.

After a well-deserved lunch of cherry tomatoes, a crusty baguette, a few olives and a cup of coffee—I didn't want to lose momentum by stopping to cook—I went back upstairs and began again, collecting the curtains and the linen, including what had been stacked in the wardrobe, and systematically washed the lot. I'm sure that little machine had never worked so hard in its life. I took the liberty of tossing all the old clothes into a wheelie bin I found in the garden by the gate, feeling certain that Aunt Constance and Uncle Jacques weren't going to miss anything they'd left here nine years ago.

Next, I brushed and swept the ceiling, walls and scrubbed the new wooden floor, which wasn't exactly a beautiful parquet vision but was better than a mouldy carpet. I tried to upend the bed, but that being beyond even my newfound superwoman strength, I settled for heaving it to one side to clean underneath. Then I went over everything again with the vacuum cleaner in case of any lingering hard-core spiders that thought they might be my match. The mattress got turned and vacuumed and the insides of the furniture received a thorough

67

sweep and sponging. And the rugs—which weren't too bad as it turns out—were taken outside and given a thwacking on the washing line, using a plank of wood I found in the garden shed. It was the first (but not the last) time I'd ever thwacked anything in my life and the amount of dust it yielded was a sight to behold.

Eventually (at least until they sneaked back in) there wasn't a single spider, fly—mummified or otherwise—or speck of dust to be seen in that bedroom. Once I'd replaced the rugs and freshly laundered linen, bedspread and curtains—line-dried in the afternoon sun—it was even pretty. I stood in the early evening light rubbing my aching back and surveying my work, feeling pleased with my efforts. With the aid of a fresh cup of coffee, I spent a contented half hour finding homes in the cupboards and drawers for my clothes.

Once more, I ate a meal of bread and cheese, with the addition of a bowl of tossed chicory leaves, a lemon soaked avocado, and a banana. I couldn't remember ever having felt this tired and I was impressed I had the energy to prepare even that modest repast. The stars had no witness in me that night, and I fell into my newly-fresh bed long before the sun had set, with the honest exhaustion of a baby.

Chapter Seventeen

The next room I tackled was the kitchen. Other than the fresh food which I'd put into the fridge, I hadn't yet found permanent homes for the bottled, tinned and packet food, knowing that I'd want to give the place a thorough clean first. Having woken early in my fresh bedroom, I decided that I'd spend the day making the kitchen the heart of the house. I breakfasted in the jungly garden on coffee, yogurt and strawberries, vowing to make fresh bread once I had a spic and span room in which to make it. With that thought, I set about doing battle with the cobwebs and spiders that had colonised the room.

I peered at the dresser. There was no way I'd move that by myself. Probably not the other cupboards either. Any spiders or dust behind them would get a reprieve for now. I began emptying the contents of all the cupboards, shelves and drawers, stacking piles of ancient crockery, cutlery and various assorted cooking implements on the huge farmhouse table. I was impressed at what my aunt and uncle had left behind but I supposed they had everything they needed in Paris. The big oak dresser was home to more crockery than I'd ever need, a lot of it chipped but pretty. I was delighted to discover, in another cupboard baking tins, moulds and trays of all shapes and sizes as well as an ancient but working food processor. Aunt Constance must have liked cooking—I could recollect helping her in the kitchen—*voulez vous lécher le bol, ma petite?*— but the memories I had were fragmented and episodic and, looking around, the kitchen didn't feel familiar. Yet. I had the oddest sensation of being at a point between—*I will stitch the past and future together.*

Stacks of aged table clothes, napkins and tea-towels took their place on the table along with candles, matches (too damp to be of use) table mats, empty jars and old cleaning materials. Surprisingly, I found a pet dish bearing the word *chat* in the dresser. I didn't remember there being a cat here. Or did I? In one of the drawers—the 'might be useful one day' drawer—I

69

found a list of ingredients written on a brittle, yellowing sheet of paper. I sat down to read it—4 oeufs, 100g de farine tamisée, 1g levure, 30g de beurre, 100g de sucre en poudre, 100g de noisettes grilles, 60g chocolats... What had my aunt being making? It was clearly a cake of some kind. I turned the sheet. Ah—a Bûche de Noël—a Christmas log. Here were the instructions. Had I helped her make it? *Oui ma puce, saupoudre la neige comme ça.* I vowed to make it at Christmas.

I stared at the table piled high with bric-a-brac. It resembled a church jumble sale. The cupboards and drawers were all open and, rubbing my already aching back, I was sorely tempted to leave it all and find a good book to read. But instead I filled the sink with warm soapy water and began the task of sweeping, wiping and scrubbing the dresser, drawers, cupboards and shelves. My next job was to decide what I'd keep, which ended up being almost everything—only the useless or broken was turfed into the wheely-bin—an old hand blender with a broken blade, a few cracked cups, the grubbiest of the tea-towels, some useless knives, an array of rusty bottles containing dubious cleaning products. I looked at the pet dish. I couldn't imagine ever needing such a thing but it wasn't broken so I put it in the sink. Then, fortified by more coffee, I set about washing everything—including my *Mam Gorau yn y Byd* mug and the onyx egg which I gave a little kiss first—and began putting it all away. It took an efffing age.

Now that I'd organised the kitchen hardware I began to find homes for the food. Tinned tomatoes, chickpeas and coconut milk where housed in the cupboard next to mustard, flour, sugar, olive oil, vinegar and all the other tins, jars and packets, while pasta, rice, lentils, beans and other dried stuff was tipped into newly gleaming canning jars and set out on the shelves. With the table empty once more, I set about emptying the contents of the fridge onto it and gave that a proper clean. Then came the turn of the cooker—a modern enough thing but fuelled by Calor gas. I'd need to experiment with it so I could get baking. Not today though. Today the thing was treated to a comprehensive scrub and my lunch was once again cold—a tin of tuna with mayonnaise and sweetcorn, the last of the cherry tomatoes; some lettuce and a hunk of crusty baguette. Plus, of course, more coffee. I ate at the table, surveying my newly-organised kitchen with pleasure.

The afternoon began with hoovering. Any spiders that had been stubborn enough not to flee in the morning were unceremoniously vacuumed. I even hoovered the ceiling. Having started a wash-load of curtains, table-cloths and other kitchen linens, I stretched, and rubbed my back, then got on with sweeping, vacuuming and scrubbing the floor.

I didn't get everything done that I wanted. By six o'clock I was so tired, I decided to call it a day. The lampshades and windows could wait until tomorrow, as could taking out the bags of rubbish I'd filled. I hoped the bin men weren't 'jobsworths.' All I wanted to do was crash out in bed and watch a cheesy romcom. But there was no TV and no internet either. I hadn't even brought with me a laptop so I could watch DVDs. Had that been a mistake?

After a quick but welcome shower, I made up a little cheeseboard, poured myself a glass of wine and went out into the garden. The evening was warm and still and the swallows were high in the sky over the field beyond the little gate. I decided to go and investigate. The field, I knew, belonged to the house and Uncle Jacques had told me that it was usually let to a local farmer—this year though, it was fallow. I tried the gate. It was stiff but it opened once I'd cleared its path of weeds. Outside, the field opened out in a long, narrow stretch, bordered on one side by vines and on the other by huge trees —walnut, I'd later learn. There was a house beyond the trees. I glanced up at it but all was quiet, the windows closed and shuttered. Walking out into the high grass I discovered an old wooden bench. *How lovely.* I cleared the tallest of the grasses from around it as best as I could and went to fetch my cheese and wine.

I remember that evening so well. It was the first time I sat in the field and, in spite of my tiredness, I watched the day turn to night, stars appearing one by one with the bats. I sipped my wine and thought about a thousand things and nothing. I remember watching a hoard of low-flying brown bugs hovering busily over the grass and wondering whether they might be scarab beetles. A rustling noise made me sit stock still. I stared. The trees had turned black in the moonless night, the field a mass of shadows and at first I couldn't make out what was making the noise. *There it was.* A dark shape had emerged from the little copse and was making its way across the meadow. I peered into the darkness. A hare. Its ears were evident now, cocked and alert as it loped from one bush to another. Suddenly the animal stopped, froze for a moment, then darted off into the vines. I smiled. Surely this was a good omen. I realised, as I picked up my things to go inside, that I'd completely forgotten about watching a film.

Chapter Eighteen

I'll say it again, Clairjo I was and Clairjo I am.

Alors, a quiet one this foreigner, this Sian. Too quiet, if you ask me. Aside from her name no one knows anything about her. Wants her peace, Madame Volt had said. I wonder. After her arrival, we saw nothing of her for nigh on two weeks. When he got back from Paris, Ripaille wasted no time filling in Monsieur Delariche on the mystery of the foreign woman.

'Came in the middle of night she did, all alone,' he said, with that lick of triumph in his voice he gets when he's embellishing the news. 'Saw her arrive with a man. Dumped all her bags and boxes by her door and left her standing there. Crying, she was—no doubt begged him not to go.'

'Arrête, get away with you!' I'll bet my turnips it was only half the truth, but it was too hot to argue so I let it go.

'Best to steer clear, in any case,' Volt said, flicking a look at Delariche. 'Obviously something going on if you ask me. Her man'll be back. Don't doubt they'll be off home soon enough.'

Ripaille turned and glared at Monsieur Delariche.

'Well if 'ee doesn't come back, it's me who's to clear her weeds if she wants it,' he muttered, pulling a dirty rag out of his pocket and wiping his brow.

Like a couple of old hens, Ripaille and Volt, pecking around what they think is theirs. Delariche, holding his tongue as usual, glanced at the Duchamp cottage before bidding us a curt *au-revoir* and taking himself and his baguette off home.

Each time Madame Volt arrived, tooting her horn and coming to a halt outside Ripaille's place, we'd compare notes on the mysterious foreigner.

'Mais oui, someone ought to tell her about the bread-run,' Volt said one Thursday, swatting away a fat bee with her cap. 'And about the meat-van. Don't know what she's doing in there, she's got no car to get into town.'

It's not like Volt to give a fig; thinking about her purse no doubt. I rolled my eyes at her and batted the same bee, which had taken a liking to my bread. We looked towards the

Duchamp cottage as a row of swallows on a wire took off with more screeching than necessary. The house looked as abandoned as ever, except for that the shutters were open.

'*C'est terrible,* look at her grass. Wants cutting.' Ripaille pointed his stick at the tufty weeds poking under the gate and over the top of the wall. I glared at him. He and I both know the only reason he carries a stick is to get Volt to park her van outside his place. 'Spoil the lane, them weeds do, what does she do in there all day?' He hitched up his trousers, which, I noticed with a frown, were held up with a length of rope.

'Avoiding the likes of you, I wouldn't wonder.'

We all turned at the sound of Monsieur Delariche's voice. Now there's a man who wears a proper belt. Volt turned a suspicious shade of pink under her cap, which she snatched off her head and fanned herself with vigorously, in a barely-disguised attempt at coquetry.

'Ah, Monsieur Delariche,' she fawned, squinting into the sunlight. 'I've got your favourite *pain au chocolat* today.'

Don't know why she bothers. Delariche merely nodded like he always does.

'Make it two would you. And I'll take a baguette as well.'

'…two is it…?'

Volt peered at him but I knew he wouldn't rise to it.

Ripaille, still frowning at Delariche's jibe, mumbled into his whiskers. A whisker-free Delariche handed Madame Volt the exact change, took his bread and turned to leave without commenting further. Volt though, wasn't giving up so easily.

'Your daughter well? Visiting from Paris is she?'

A sudden movement at the Duchamp house made us all turn. At an upstairs window, there she was and gone in a twinkle but it was her all right. The foreigner. Delariche narrowed his eyes.

Someone once told me the English have a saying for the likes of him: a man of few words. Always was tight-lipped, Paul Delariche, even as a child. Remarked on it once to his old ma. 'Let him be, Clairjo,' she'd retorted, 'shouldn't children be seen and not heard?' Fifty five years old now and he's just the same. Shifty I call it. I threw him a look but Delariche didn't notice. He was staring up at the Duchamp cottage.

Chapter Nineteen

Here we go. The time had come, as I knew it would, to address the topic shrinks consider second only in significance to how you got on with your parents: Sex. He'd started with a sly sidewise nudge:

'You mentioned that you'd had only one relationship since your marriage ended?'

I was damn sure I hadn't used the word 'relationship'. God. What the hell to tell him? That particular skeleton had been well and truly shoved to the back, but it seemed the bastard felt emboldened to rattle away at a locked door. I stared at the window and leant back in my chair while the Good Doctor swivelled on his perch. *Come on, you're a big girl.* The episode with Creepy Roger loomed large and the prospect of talking about it wasn't appealing. I'd chalked it up to bad luck and given speed-dating a miss, certain I didn't have any baggage about it. None that I wanted to unburden myself to Dr Adebowale anyhow.

'It used to be that weirdos were serially attracted to me,' I said, throwing the Good Doctor a half-hearted line. 'But my husband was reassuringly normal.'

Granted, before I married Arwel, there had been a short but memorable string of suspect boyfriends—highlights included: Charles, who wanted me to join his cult, Ewan, who told his mother everything—and I do mean *everything*—and Meurigg, who'd seemed promising, but began arriving at my halls of residence in the early hours, sobbing and threatening to kill himself unless I married him. But we were young, who isn't slightly un-hinged at that age?

I had to give the Good Doctor something to write about or he'd have nothing to tell to his wife to prove to her how clever he is. I was too tired to play games. What could laughingly be referred to as my 'dating life' has been depressingly pedestrian and fictionalising something worthy of the growing tome beneath the Good Doctor's pen was too much for a late Friday afternoon. *I ought to move these sessions to a*

Tuesday morning, I could make up so much more rubbish then. I looked at the Good Doctor. He looked back… Should I tell him…? I'd hadn't told a living soul about Creepy Roger. I wasn't sure I had the words… and in any case, it was so far from the issue of my job—wasn't *that* why I was here?

'I met him at a speed-dating evening,' I said, deciding I could choose how much or how little to reveal. The Good Doctor's eyebrows shot up. 'I know, I know, I sound like a sad, middle-aged divorcee–but it wasn't like that. It seemed like a good idea at the time and it's not like I was expecting to meet… I don't know, George Clooney or whatever. I wasn't… you know, desperate for a man.'

'Desperate…' I swear the Good Doctor mouthed the word as he wrote. Bastard. He looked up at me. 'So you were looking for a relationship?'

'Not really…well, yes and no.' I was squirming and I knew he could tell. If I told him the real reason I'd gone to speed-dating, what would he make of it? *Get a grip, Sian.* 'Okay, no, I hadn't been intent on finding a man, but a colleague suggested I go and I thought, well, why not? I wanted to… to test myself.'

'Test yourself? In what way.'

Oh no you don't. I certainly wasn't prepared to open the door to *that* one. The Roger affair suddenly seemed the least dangerous of the two.

'I thought I might meet someone nice,' I lied. *Tell me about that,'* I said silently in time with the Good Doctor.

It had been my first and only attempt at meeting a man since my divorce, much prompted by my colleague, Janet, who had met her husband at a speed dating event.

'Honestly, Sian,' she'd said, jabbing a finger at the advert, which promised 'a fast, fun and, if you don't meet someone you'd like to see again, FREE evening' 'It's the way you meet a man these days, what have you got to lose?'

My dignity, I thought? I was quite sure I didn't want to meet a man but saw that this could be a way to be certain so I decided to go.

The advert said the venue would be lively but discreet. It turned out to be upstairs at the Pig and Whistle, where, on stepping inside, it seemed I'd entered some kind of punk dystopia complete with scantily-clad green-hair girls and their mohawked young suitors. Resisting the urge to turn tail and flee to the comfort of Saturday night TV—or perhaps because of that—I straightened my floral blouse and sidled through the crowd. At the bar, I wedged myself between a six-foot tattooed Adonis and two bald girls, and attempted to catch the attention of the bizarrely-bearded barman—bar-boy really, he wasn't much more than a teenager. The Adonis raised an eyebrow at me. I've never learned to do that and I was impressed. Apparently visibly so, because he leaned back, ran his gaze up and down my body and said:

'Drink?'

'Excuse me...?' Not fully cognisant of what he wanted, I doubly reinforced my sensible middle-aged mum identity, which apparently appealed to the Adonis because he said:

'Buy you a drink?' He plonked a tattooed arm on the bar and flexed a not-inconsiderable muscle.

Effing hell. I don't know what shocked me more, that I was being hit on by someone younger than my son, or that it was someone with his taste in body-art. I stifled a laugh and went back to waving at the bar-boy who, I was sorry to have noticed, was wearing trousers so tight, we could see his religion. The Adonis snapped his fingers at him and pointed down at my head. The boy loped over. I leaned in as far as I dared across the sticky bar and mumbled: 'Where's the speed-dating?' The Adonis raised his other eyebrow.

'What?' The bar-boy turned a multiply-pierced ear in my direction.

'The speed-dating,' I whisper-shouted, desperate not to be heard by the leather-and-chain-clad bald girls.

'Oy, Spider,' the bar-boy yelled. 'This lady wants to know where's the speed-dating.'

I swear the place went silent and everyone in the entire pub turned to look at me, but that might only have happened in my head. In any case, Spider, her perky, twenty-year-old breasts barely contained beneath a black vest bearing the certain prediction 'You're Fucked', yelled back from the far end of the bar: 'Speed-dating? Through the red door, top of the stairs.'

Glances flicked my way and I was sure I heard a snigger. *Christ, what am I doing here?* I didn't know what would be worse, making a run for it amid hordes of laughing punks, or holding my head high and marching through the red door. The fact that I was the only one there not wearing a punk-uniform gave me a nudge of confidence and I tossed my hair back in what I hoped was a combination of casual ease and unheeding indifference and plunged ahead. 'Good luck,' the Adonis said, giving me the sexiest wink.

'Come in, come in,' said a kindly-looking woman of about my age who was guarding the threshold at the top of a beer-sticky flight of stairs. She was dressed in reassuringly normal jeans and her teeshirt bore no ominous prophecies, so I smiled and followed her through the door.

In contrast to the pub, the room was brightly lit and surprisingly quiet, with only the faint rhythmic thump of the music downstairs for accompaniment. A long row of tables was set out in an 'L' shape towards the end of the room and there was a gaggle of women seated at discreet distances from one another, playing with their mobile phones. The advert, which specified people between 35 and 55 years old, had clearly been interpreted liberally as they were a motley bunch ranging from fifty to sixtyish—with distinct emphasis on the 'ish.' Two of the woman, both with heaving décolletage, were chatting and laughing together. None looked crazy or scared and this gave me hope.

'Come on in and sit down,' the organiser said, leading the way. 'I'm Debz. With a zed. This your first time?'

I wondered why she felt the need to tell me about the z but I simply nodded.

'Sian,' I said. 'Without a zed.'

Debz flicked me a confused look but ploughed ahead.

'Well we're all very friendly here, Sian.' She laughed hoarsely. 'We don't bite and most of our ladies come back.'

Was that a good thing? I followed Debz-with-a-zed to one of the one seats—orange plastic like we had at school—

where, once I was installed, she handed me a pile of square sheets of paper and a Bic biro.

'There, you can put your coat on the back of the seat. Now, how it works is, the ladies stay sitting, while the men file round to each one.' I flicked my eyes around the room once more—there were no men. Debz-with-a-zed seemed unconcerned. 'You'll have a few minutes to ask your questions and answer his. At the end, you write down either 'yes' 'no' or 'friends' on one of the cards and hand it to the gent.' She laughed again, making me jump. 'You pay on the way out, but only if you have at least one 'yes'. You wait, I'll be a millionaire this time next year.'

Fat chance of that, I thought, noticing a man entering the room, surveying us women furtively. He had to be seventy, if he was a day.

'What's the difference between 'yes' and 'friends'?' I asked.

Debz-with-a-zed looked at me as though I'd asked her to conjugate a French verb.

'The 'yesses' are for the ones you want to go on a date with, dear. Here you go, write your name on this sticker and put it on your blouse.'

It wasn't long before more men arrived, some looking sheepish and more nervous than the women, others, seasoned speed-daters, openly appraising what was on offer. It was obvious in some cases they'd been storing up their Dutch courage in liquid form. More women had arrived as well, some clearly having had the same idea.

'Okay ladies and gents,' Debz-with-a-zed called. My mouth went dry and I swallowed. I was there under false pretences, it wasn't fair to these hopefuls and I sorely wished I'd left the pub when I'd had the chance. 'If each man would sit opposite a lady, we'll make a start.'

A man sporting a grey goatee-beard and slimy-looking pony-tail winked at me and mouthed something that looked suspiciously like 'cupcake' and I decided that rather than endure any further assaults on my dignity, I'd sneak out before we got going. I was just reaching for my coat when—damn her—eagle-eyed Debz-with-a-zed noticed.

'There you go, Sian,' she said, flashing a glance at my name-badge, here is your first gent.' Then, under her breath, 'Everyone's nervous at first, dear, just go for it.'

I smiled weakly at the man standing behind her, who smiled back thinly as he sat down.

At first sight, Creepy Roger was distinctly uncreepy. His beige chinos and green checked shirt spoke of quiet interests and a recent divorce. He didn't seem like a speed-dating habitué, nor did he seem drunk, so I decided it couldn't hurt to talk to him.

'Creepy Roger, good to meet you.' A hairy-backed hand shot across to me. 'Attorney at law. Retired.'

Obviously that's not actually what he said. He introduced himself as Roger Bond, and I wondered at the time whether that was his real name, but I let it slide.

'Sian Evans,' I replied, giving the hand the briefest of shakes. 'Call-centre worker. Sadly, not retired.'

I guessed Not-Yet-Creepy Roger must be in his mid-sixties, (so much for the 55 upper age limit) probably once handsome, his salt-and-pepper hair neatly cut and only just balding. But I forgave him his lack of dash on the grounds that my own looks were more clapped-out model than super-model these days, although the Adonis downstairs hadn't had a problem with that.

'Well, let's see,' Roger said. 'I'm widowed, two grown up boys, no grand-children yet. I like weekends away, pub-lunches and going for walks with my dog, Pete.'

Yawn. I'd been wrong about the divorce then. I glanced around the room. Cupcake was talking animatedly to a woman's breasts and Debz-with-a-zed was ushering in a frail latecomer on a zimmer-frame. Roger seemed suddenly promising.

'Your dog is called Pete?' I asked with enthusiasm. 'Like Aidan's dog in *Sex and the City*?'

'…err…sex and…'

His look of bewilderment—rather fetching I had to concede—made me warm to him, and less than a minute later, not knowing what the heck I was doing, I handed him a 'yes' card. Then, armed with his mobile number and a dinner invitation for the following Friday, I made a dash for it, shoving some coins at a concerned-looking Debz-with-a-zed as I left.

'So you took the first offer of a date you received?'

The Good Doctor seemed unimpressed with my bravery at attempting the speed dating dignity-stripping ordeal and as usual decided to focus on what he clearly saw as my faults. Not for the first time, I wondered what on earth this had to do with my work attendance record.

'He seemed nice,' I told him. 'And I didn't see the point in trying to get more dates after that.'

I still didn't reveal the truth behind the whole facade. In fact, I'd done a pretty good job of hiding it from myself at that point—after all, I'd handed Roger a 'yes' card.

'And did Roger stay to complete the evening?'

Good question. He hadn't left with me, that's for certain.

Chapter Twenty

'Are you familiar with the term 'projection', Sian?'

I wasn't, not in the psychological sense anyhow, but I didn't doubt that the Good Doctor would enlighten me. At this point, one could be forgiven for wondering why I went through with it. The speed-dating I mean. But that and the subsequent dates with Roger make perfect sense if you consider that I was trying to work out whether I should be going on this type of date at all. At least that's what I told myself.

The day arrived and unsurprisingly I felt more trepidation than anticipation. Nonetheless, in fairness to Roger, I decided to make an effort to look effortlessly attractive. Out came a floral-print dress I used to wear for Sunday lunches with Arwel. I held it up in front of me. Dressy but understated. Out came a pair of fawn-coloured wedge heels and a matching handbag—I'd forgotten I had that. On went the lipstick—I settled on deep rose rather than aging-hooker-red or mutton-dressed-as-lamb-pink. Navy jacket? Too formal. Cream jacket? Perfect. I surveyed the result in the full-length mirror. God, I thought. I look like my mother.

'Let's meet at Dylan's, that new wine-bar in the centre,' Roger had said. 'I've been meaning to try it.'

Setting off early into the breezy but warm autumn evening, I took my time—along with half of Cardiff it seemed—wandering through the pedestrianised city centre so that I could arrive relaxed and unflustered. I spotted Roger sitting at an outdoor table just as he spotted me and, after waving, had to go through the agony of walking over to him while he watched. I'm never sure where to look in those situations, maintaining eye-contact seems too intense but looking around seems contrived, and all the while I'm so conscious of my body being scrutinised. I feigned a phone call on my mobile, deciding, as I fished it out of my bag, that this would have the added effect of making me seem popular. 'Bye then, I'll call you soon,' I said into the silent phone as I reached the table, nearly dropping the thing when it actually did ring. *Effing Arwel!*

'Sorry about that, good to see you.' I composed myself and simpered at him in my best woman-of-the-world voice.

Roger stood up and, as I thrust my hand out for a shake, he leaned in to kiss my cheek, the result of which was a somewhat botched cheek-graze. The start notwithstanding, the evening passed well enough, the place was lively and Roger turned out to be pleasant company. We shared a carafe of Californian white and Roger regaled me with amusing tales of a road-trip he'd made in America with a friend when they were young. 'Those where the days,' he said, draining his glass and helping himself to another. I stuck subtly to my traditional one glass. 'Oh, let your hair down once in a while,' Arwel used to say, but I'm one of those boring types who doesn't need alcohol to have a good time. But in spite of myself, I can't say I didn't enjoy the evening. The same was true the next weekend when we arranged to meet for a light lunch, followed by an early screening of a film. 'How about grabbing a glass of wine at Dylans?' Roger said after. I hadn't objected.

'Retired solicitor, eh? Not bad.' I could tell from his tone that Arwel had misgivings, but since he couldn't possibly have known how creepy he would get, I put these down to jealousy. I'd hesitated at first to tell him about Roger, it wasn't his business. But there was no reason not to tell him.

'I don't know if it'll go anywhere,' I said. 'But he's a nice chap. If it goes well, I'm thinking of taking him to my office Christmas-do.'

I'm sure I have not the faintest idea why I said that. It certainly hadn't crossed my mind to invite Roger to the company Christmas party and I can only conclude that it must have been to send a clear message to Arwel. My dear ex-husband hadn't replied. A nice chap, I'd said. And after not very long, a most communicative chap, with his daily emails, texts and phone-calls. I noticed that the emails were often sent in the middle of the night. Is that strange? And had they started to carry the slightest trace of paranoia?

The Good Doctor was interested in this.

'Paranoia?' he said, writing something down. 'What exactly made you think Roger was paranoid?'

Sian, one of the emails had said, I called you last night. I found it strange that you weren't in, you didn't mention you had plans. I missed our evening chat.

'I wasn't sure whether it was romantic or—I don't know… unsettling,' I told the Good Doctor.

'Unsettling?' His pen went crazy. 'Tell me what you mean.'

I'd decided to opt for romantic, mainly because our meetings were always pleasant. But another email, sent at three in the morning, made me wonder again:

I've been thinking about something you said tonight and I feel I have to correct you. The fact that I haven't been to Rome is entirely my own choice and although it might well be nice to visit there one day, perhaps with you, I want to reiterate that the fact that I haven't been should be in no way taken to my detriment.

Huh? I read the email three times, trying to work out what it meant. The conversation he was referring to had simply been about which cities we'd enjoyed visiting. 'I'm surprised you've never been to Rome,' I'd said. 'I fell in love with it the first time I went.' Maybe I thought, examining the email for the fourth time, he didn't like me talking about places I'd enjoyed with Arwel? Or perhaps it's his way of saying he wants to go to Rome with me?

'I didn't like the way he wanted to "correct" me.' I told the Good Doctor. He wrote it down.

I'd feigned 'family commitments' for a couple of weekends after that and by the time I'd decided to give him a second chance, the unseasonably warm autumn had turned to a wet winter, putting paid to our drinks on the terrace at Dylan's. I was glad. Roger had begun to refer to it as 'our wine-bar' which made me cringe.

'You didn't like Roger using the word "our"?' the Good Doctor noted, scribbling away. I rolled my eyes.

'In any case,' I told him, 'There were no more odd emails —not at that point anyhow—and I decided I'd been wrong about him being paranoid. We had a few more pleasant dates and everything was going fine. I eventually decided to invite him to my house for dinner.'

The Good Doctor raised his eyebrows. And well he might. I did enjoy Roger's company, but the fun conversations over glasses of wine weren't getting me any closer to what I wanted to know. After a great deal of thought and vacillating, I had, in spite of my misgivings, finally decided that I needed to conduct the 'ultimate test'. That's not, of course how I put it to the Good Doctor.

'I'm not particularly old-fashioned about sex before marriage,' I told him, 'I mean I'd thought about if and when that particular development would happen. Roger wasn't pushy, which I'll admit I found pleasantly surprising. I hinted to him that he might like to bring an overnight bag. I thought Saturday might be—you know—*the* night.'

'So would you say that you were asking him for sex?'

'Well, no, not asking—more like implying that I wouldn't be against the idea if it happened.'

But in any case, I didn't get to conduct my test—Saturday wasn't *the* night. The morning after Roger had received my text, he'd sent another early-hours missive, which both perturbed and confused me. The Good Doctor's pen danced furiously across the page as I told him about it.

My dear Sian, on consideration, I've decided to decline your invitation. Coming to your home, ostensibly for dinner, is not a good idea. I'll be frank with you, it seems clear that you are hoping I will stay the night and, although I am flattered, I would rather you weren't so forward. I'm a somewhat traditional man and I'd prefer to take you out for dinner on Saturday, where I'd be more than happy to discuss how we move our relationship to the next level.

Effing hell, did he think I was some sex-starved harpy? I wanted to ask Arwel what he thought about it, but that clearly wasn't an option. Perhaps Roger wanted to be the one to make the first move? But then, why hadn't he? Maybe he simply didn't like me in that way. I accepted his dinner invitation out of stark curiosity and, despite some trepidation on my part, we had a surprisingly enjoyable evening.

'Sian,' Roger said, raising his glass for a clink, 'you and I seem really very compatible.' Neither of us mentioned the issue of the email, or "moving our relationship to the next level", which, I have to admit, disappointed me in spite of the good time we'd had.

'I see,' said the Good Doctor. 'So you didn't actually tell him you wanted sex. But you were disappointed when it wasn't made available.'

Seriously? I tried to formulate a balanced response before I yelled at him, but before I could speak, the Good Doctor put down his pen and peered at me. Oh god, I thought, something significant must be coming. It was then that he'd mentioned 'projection'.

'It's when someone unconsciously transfers her own feelings onto another person instead of owning them herself.'

'Okay...'

'Sian, we've reached a point in our therapeutic relationship where I feel you are confident enough in the process for me to offer something for your consideration.'

'Okay...' I repeated. I raised both eyebrows.

'I'm not asking for a response at this stage. You are of course free to reject anything I say, but all I want for now is that you think about what I'm going to suggest. Alright? And we can discuss it more at our next session.'

The Good Doctor was clearly doing his best to sound reassuring. I nodded, intrigued in spite of myself, wondering what fresh insights about my character flaws I was about to be treated to. He outdid himself.

'I wonder, Sian, whether it is possible that your failed marriage has made you wary of men, but that your loneliness and the need for sex spurred you into taking the initiative. Do you think you may have looked for and found reasons to push Roger away in order to justify your view that solitude is preferable to intimacy?'

Bastard. The skeleton was grinning at me, daring me to let it out of the damned closet. Should I? I stared at Doctor Adebowale, my heart thumping in my chest, my mouth dry—all the clichéd signs—and the words *staring down the barrel of a gun* popped into my mind—another effing cliché. I realised I was digging my fingernails into my palms and I felt a sudden urge to pee. I had two options. I could either ignore the Good Doctor's misinterpretation, or I could tell him the truth.

Chapter Twenty-one

No, absolutely not. Opening up about Nate was one thing, but this? I was supposed to be there to talk about my job, not confess my darkest secrets. After he suggested that Roger's problems were my fault, I'd decided that the effing Doctor was undeserving of the truth and I vowed not to go back. The truth. Ha! Where do we start with that? Two secrets were jostling to get out. One was the truth of what happened that night with Roger. The other was the truth of what I was doing with Roger in the first place. Neither were what the Good Doctor thought they were and I wasn't about to enlighten him. The following week, instead of going to his office at 3.30 as I usually did, I left my job and went home where I spent a contented afternoon baking a vanilla sponge cake.

I thought I'd got away with it having, after a quiet weekend, passed a busy but uneventful Monday in the office. I was wrong. In-Control Carol had found out by the power of some cunning administrative conspiracy and on Tuesday morning I was hauled in front of her. The walk to her cupboard felt like the walk of shame and, glancing around at my colleagues, I wondered how many of them knew why I left early each Friday.

'Sian,' Carol smarmed as I put my head round her door, 'Come on in, do take a seat.' I sat, unconvinced either by her perky breasts or her plastic smile. 'Now then, after all the trouble I went to, arranging your OT, you didn't attend your session on Friday, did you?'

Naughty Sian. In-Control Carol's toddler-scolding voice didn't quite hide her edge of threat. It's always like that with these rescuer-types, they entice you in with the appearance of caring and then *bang!* They whack you over the head with how much you've let them down. I opened my mouth to make up a story about a plumbing disaster but remembered that I'd already used that one. I decided instead that since she was playing the rescuer, I'd go with victim, and I nodded, looked at my hands folded in my lap in a manner I hoped indicated contrition and said in a voice as timid as I could make it:

'I'm so sorry, Car...' *(Jill, Jill, her name is Jill!)* 'I'm so sorry *Jill*, it's just that the sessions are hard on me sometimes. I'm sure you understand.'

I swear her condescending fake-smile was exactly that one you see on daytime-TV bullies. It's designed to convey 'I'm going to pretend that I feel your pain and then I'm going to *effing* crucify you.'

'Of course, I appreciate the sessions must be challenging, but that *is* the point of them, Sian. And Sian..?' *Uh oh...* 'I feel bound to remind you that your employment here *is* dependent on seeing the Occupational Therapist for the *full* series of appointments.'

Okay so not so much of the rescuing then, but she had managed to say my name three times within the space of five minutes—her psychology teacher would be proud of her. I muttered something about doing better in future and, maintaining my look of humbled contrition until I was out of her cupboard, went to waste some time at the coffee machine.

I could just quit, I thought, punching in the numbers for a vanilla latte, which I knew would taste like nothing of the sort. To be honest though, until that last session, talking to the Good Doctor on Friday afternoons instead of answering phones to French people who can't operate their software wasn't the worst of the two options. I stood by the machine, eking out my faux-latte for as long as I could as revenge for In-Control Carol's smugness, before taking flight as Nigel from Accounts rounded a corner and homed in on me.

Back at my desk, I put my headphones on and tried to look as though I was working. The console lit up in front of me and I groaned inwardly as the name of a particularly awkward client flashed onto my screen. I felt sorely tempted to get up and go home but instead I clicked a key and put *Monsieur I-haven't-a-Clue* on hold. *Let him listen to music-to-die-to for a while.* I nodded to Janet as she passed my desk.

'All right?' she said with what seemed to me to be a suspicious level of enthusiasm.

'Fine thanks,' I breezed.

She looked set to dig in for a conversation, so I busied myself with my keyboard, pointed at the headset and mouthed, *catch you later*.

Effing place. But as patronised as I felt by Carol and her breasts, I knew my boss was right. With all my attempts at leading him a merry dance, it was Doctor Adebowale's job to challenge me. Besides, I didn't relish losing my job and having to find another one, which certainly wouldn't be any better than this, awkward clients, annoying colleagues and all. I clicked a key and said in my best *'how can I help you'* voice:

'Bonjour Monsieur, je m'appelle Sian Evens, comment puis-je vous aider aujourd'hui?'

The following Friday afternoon saw me dutifully packing up my things, waving to In-Control Carol, who gave me an encouraging nod back, and walking the fifteen minutes to Doctor Adebowale's office, preparing to be shown the error of my ways. By the time I got there, in spite of my best intentions to simply get on with it, I'd decided to show the Good Doctor the error of his.

'Look,' I told him, once I'd got myself settled in the armchair. 'Last time I saw you, you talked about me being wary of men, being lonely. You wanted me to think about whether I invented reasons to push Roger away so that I could avoid intimacy...' I paused, and the Good Doctor nodded, seeming to sense that I might be wavering, and I ploughed on before I could change my mind. 'The point is, I understand why you formed that opinion, I really do. If the shoe were on the other foot, I'd might have reached the same conclusion myself, given what I've told you.'

The Doctor nodded once more. 'Go on,' he said. I got the impression that he liked it when I challenged him back. Something about the set of his mouth or the creases around his eyes perhaps. In any case, he tapped a foot, perhaps in anticipation. I did a double take at his Little Mermaid socks.

'The thing is...' I hesitated at the edge of no return. '...the thing is last time I was here, when we talked about Roger... I didn't tell you the full story.'

Chapter Twenty-two

Dripping wet and naked in front of my wardrobe mirror, I stood drying myself roughly with the towel, four different outfits flung across the bed. I turned this way and that, regarding myself from different angles. If I sucked my stomach in tight I could get away with being called slim, but frankly I didn't see why I should have to.

My hesitation at inviting Roger to the staff Christmas party was easily explainable. I hated the effing things. It's the same whoever you work for, people you're forced to spend your days with exchange inane chit-chat over cheap wine, while drunk middle-managers in paper hats slobber over anyone who will listen to them. I'd rather be home watching a good film. And yet, as the date drew nearer, I'd given myself a good talking to. Roger was fun to be with, generous and caring, so why not invite him? At least it would keep Nigel from Accounts at bay. I don't doubt that a part of me was hoping he'd refuse but: 'I'd love to come, Sian,' he'd said. I scanned the dresses on the bed, wondering which to choose. 'All men notice is how low the neckline is,' Arwel once told me. He was probably right. I grabbed the one nearest to me.

On the night of the party, Roger arrived in a taxi to pick me up.

'You look lovely,' he said, eyeing me appreciatively, and I'd been pleased in spite of my indifference that I'd gone with the deep blue sparkly dress.

'You don't look so bad yourself,' I replied.

Walking into the function room at the hotel was excruciating. Christ, I thought, I'm a middle-aged woman, not a would-be prom queen. I forced myself to hold my head high and walked through the door, which Roger had opened for me. Inside, the lights were dim and thirty or so people were standing in groups or sitting at tables sipping sparkling wine (I doubted it was Champagne), which an attractive young waitress was handing round on a tray. A few of my colleagues looked at us curiously, smiling and nodding as Roger and I made our way to a table and took off our coats.

'Why don't I get us a drink?' he said.

Janet—of speed-dating introduction fame—arrived with a man who looked much older than her. She spotted me, waved and came hurrying over, the man trailing behind her. She arrived just as Roger did, carrying two full glasses, which he placed on the table.

'Lovely that you could come,' Janet said, putting her coat over the back of a chair. *Effing hell*, I thought, as her husband did likewise.

'Well, let's get the introductions out of the way and grab a drink, then we'll join you, if that's okay. This is my husband Greg. Greg, this is my good friend, Sian, and…'

She looked expectantly at Roger. Despite her incessant hints, I had never given her the lowdown on the speed-dating outcome. Her curiosity was palpable.

'Roger Bond, attorney at Law, retired. Pleased to meet you.' Roger thrust out a hand, first at Janet, then at Greg. I was too confused by the fact that she'd called me her good friend to respond.

Most surprisingly, my awkwardness soon vanished. Roger was the ideal companion, laughing and chatting easily with Janet and my other colleagues, topping up their glasses—it actually *was* Champagne—for all the world seeming genuinely happy to be there. Even In-Control Carole was charmed. In fact, she actually seemed to be flirting with him. 'He's a keeper, that one,' Janet whispered, as Carole laughed loudly at a joke Roger made, and I'd not known what to feel. In any case, I decided that for once I *would* let my hair down, accepting a second glass of Champagne, which made my arms feel heavy in a pleasant sort of way. After the third glass, Roger and I danced—for me, the first time in I don't know how many years—self-consciously at first, but laughing and bopping to the music anyhow. My fourth—or was it my fifth?—glass of Champagne met an untimely end when I knocked it over the table as I told some animated story about why the French don't use the gerund, and I remember laughing loudly before throwing back what remained in the glass. The next thing I remember is slow-dancing to some romantic end-of-the-evening music, Roger's body pressed tight against mine as I swayed against him.

A sudden wave of nausea rose to my throat and I don't remember how I got back to my seat. I think I remember Roger telling Janet, 'she's fine, just a little tipsy.' I think I recall being sick in the bathroom. I'd like to say I feel certain that I asked to be taken home, but truthfully, I don't know.

We went to his home. I half-remember saying goodbye to my colleagues—I think Janet gave me a hug—and I have a vague impression of leaving the hotel clutching Roger's arm and getting into a waiting cab—did I stumble on the kerb? I don't recall much of the journey. My impressions are of a short drive and I think I remember feeling surprised that we stopped at an apartment building rather than my house.

Getting out of the cab, going inside, whether we walked upstairs or took a lift, it's all a blank. I do remember sitting on a big sofa no longer wearing my coat or shoes. I must have protested at the Cognac Roger poured into two glasses because I recall him saying, 'Come on Sian, we're having such a good night, just a little night-cap.' And I must have drunk it because I remember the hot, sharp taste.

It's vague and episodic after that. Him leaning over me, his wet mouth tasting of stale food and Cognac, stubble scratching my face, hands pawing at me, the sound of his belt buckle opening, the smell of male sweat, *Come on Sian, come on...*

The next morning I woke sweating and queasy in his bed, head thumping, mouth acid, my blue sparkly dress around my waist, tights torn, knickers around one leg, and an unmistakable stickiness between my legs. I'm sure I said no, I'm certain...

He'd fucked me anyhow.

Chapter Twenty-three

'Chalked it up to bad luck and given speed-dating a miss.' That's what I'd initially told Doctor Adebowale. The reality, he learned now, was somewhat different.

Cardiff was cold and wet and Christmas was just around the corner. Nate wasn't coming home until New Year. 'You don't mind, do you, Mam?' he'd said in a poor-quality Skype call. 'The fights are half-price in January.' I'd been disappointed but also relieved. I didn't want my son seeing me in the state I was in. I was also glad that Arwel was spending Christmas with his sister and her husband—a pleasure I would happily have declined in the unlikely event of an invitation. And since I would never, ever willingly see Roger again, that solitary Christmas afforded me plenty of time to think.

'What did you think about, Sian?'

Doctor Adebowale had set aside his notes and was speaking quietly. I—curled up in the armchair—was not unaware that my body language was that of a foetus. I'd seen it coming, of course. Having told the Good Doctor what had really happened with Roger, there would follow the inevitable post-mortem. I told myself I was prepared. There was nothing he could ask or say that I hadn't thought about, so I figured I might as well get it over with.

I'd spent that Christmas baking unnecessary cakes—seven to be precise—and doing battle with my wallpaper. That came about one evening as I was flicking aimlessly though the TV channels hoping to find a suitably distracting film. I'd discovered that the fashionable new floral wall-paper that adorned the feature wall behind my television was permeable. Yeah, permeable. It suddenly seemed obvious that all manner of dubiously-motivated creatures could escape through the tunnels that ended at the big pink roses that looked innocent enough until you realised they were portals. How could I not have noticed this before? I flicked off the TV and stared, not knowing what I'd do if the creatures escaped. I left my watch only to get one of the cakes, which I presented as an offering.

That seemed to work but I remained vigilant. Eventually, sometime in the early hours, the portals closed, although this was only a temporary reprieve, I knew. Despite my decision to tell the Good Doctor the truth about Roger, I chose not to tell him any of this.

'I thought about what happened,' I said. I suppose in a way it was true.

I told the Good Doctor that I didn't know whether Roger had called or emailed after that night, that I'd deleted and blocked every trace of him from my life before he had the chance. He knew where I lived, of course, but I didn't think he'd show up at my door. Even so, I made sure I locked and bolted the door during the day as well as the night and I took to sleeping with an old cricket bat of Nate's by the bed.

'I tried to work out what had happened,' I said. 'I mean, I'm not a kid, I'm a middle-aged woman, I should know by now how to look after myself.' The Good Doctor didn't respond to this, which I knew by now was a sign to continue. 'I know I'd made it clear to him before that I wanted to spend the night with him, but...'

Now come the questions...

'Did you indicate that you wanted to have sex with him that night?'

'No—well not explicitly. I can see how he might have thought so because, after all, I'd been slow dancing with him at the party, drinking Champagne... If those aren't come-on signs, I don't know what are. Plus I'd agreed to go back to his flat.'

'Had you agreed to that?'

'Well, not as such. But I was drunk, I honestly don't remember what I said. I'm pretty sure I just got into the car and that's where we ended up.'

The Good Doctor paused and looked at me for a long moment. This time he broke the silence.

'Sian, why did you delete Roger's phone number and block his calls after that night?'

That wasn't one of the questions I'd been expecting. I'd braced myself for the clichés—*why had I drank so much, why did I go back to his flat, was my dress revealing, had I been behaving*

95

provocatively, was I wearing sexy underwear? I'd thought about all of that myself that dreadful Christmas, as I fought as hard as I could not to be dragged into the tunnels in the wall-paper, questioned myself until there were no questions left about each and every decision I'd made that god-awful night that might, had I behaved differently, have stopped that man going beyond that point of no return. I looked at the Doctor, the faux leather chair was still, his hands folded in his lap, his face showing no sign of emotion, and I suddenly had the strangest feeling that all there was in the world was this moment, the Doctor's eyes on mine, our breath, the space between us shrinking…

He repeated his question: Why had I deleted Roger's phone number and blocked his calls?

'I don't know,' I answered. 'There were so many emotions behind the reason, it's hard to name them. I suppose… I suppose it was because I felt ashamed. I mean, I'd pretty much led him on, hadn't I? It sounds so clichéd, I know. And stupid. I think above all I felt just so stupid.'

'Why stupid, Sian?'

'Well it's obvious isn't it? I should have known better.'

I looked at the window, its blind characteristically closed, the shadows of clouds casting vague shapes on the fabric. Was any of this helping? What is done can't be undone, my Mam used to say, and she was right.

'It sounds to me, Sian, like you are taking on all the responsibility for what happened to you.'

Neither of us spoke for a long moment and the only word in my head was *no*.

'It doesn't matter whose responsibility it is, does it?' I said, despising myself even as I spoke, for trying to make light of it. 'There's no changing things now.'

The Good Doctor wasn't fooled. His voice was quieter still. 'I think it does matter, Sian. Do you realise what you've described to me?'

… *the wall-paper, creatures in the tunnels, portals, opening…*

'…Sian?…'

…*close them, there's still time…*

'Sian, what you have described to me is rape.'

96

Chapter Twenty-four

When Nate was born and we looked for the first time into one another's eyes I felt a bliss so complete that there were no words. Nothing I've felt before or since has ever come close to that feeling. Here though, alone in my French home, I'd begun to feel sudden bursts of intense joy.

The first time it happened I was sitting in the field one evening, drinking my one glass of wine, watching the stars come up and wondering whether I'd be lucky enough to see a hare. I wasn't. But I was joined by another of the residents. A dark shape had emerged from a clump of weeds and was making its ungainly way towards the garden gate. What was it? Certainly not a cat and too big to be a mouse. *Effing hell, surely not a rat?* I lifted my feet instinctively and peered into the shadows. A hedgehog! Its quills were evident now, framing its fat little body in a perfect ball. I smiled. The hedgehog scuttled off at a surprisingly swift trot and disappeared under the gate. And there it was. A feeling—more a realisation—that absolutely nothing was missing. It was more than simple happiness. It was as though I'd cleared my internal decks of all the rubbish and found the bliss that was waiting to be felt.

My new life wasn't all wildlife playmates and joyful epiphanies, though. The rhythm of those early days and nights flowed from solitary hours cleaning and organising, into restless nights spent conquering my nocturnal fears. Oddly—although perhaps understandably—the first week saw me so fatigued by the days' exhaustions that I fell asleep almost immediately with little time for thought. Eventually though, I began to adjust to my new regime and consequently had begun to imagine all sorts of grim nocturnal goings-on.

My fears were encouraged by the cottage's night-time settlings and shiftings. Anyone who has lived in an old building will tell you that houses made of stone and wood have a life of their own. Not only is all manner of wildlife harboured in the crevices, cracks and crannies, but the house itself breaths. Wood expands and contracts, wind rattles through ill-fitting windows, roof slates slip... Science notwithstanding, my explanation for the sporadic creakings, bumps and rustlings was related neither to the house's abundant animal life nor to changes in the weather. Neither did I assign sudden nocturnal noises to human intruders. No. After one particularly resonant *thump* which came one night from the roof-space, it became clear to me what was going on. The nightly disturbances were obviously of the supernatural kind. Some disgruntled house-ghost was not at all happy with my arrival and consequently had begun to plot my demise.

After a week of avoiding going to the loo at night and jumping at every creak and thud, I decided that something would have to be done. I gave myself a stern talking to—in fact several—but to no avail. Daytimes were fine. I went about my chores with little or no thought of the ghoul I was sharing my new home with, but it was quite a different matter once darkness fell. There was nothing for it, the ghost and I would have to get acquainted. So one night, a fortifying glass of wine in one hand, a lighted candle in the other—everyone knows ghosts are all about the drama—I forced myself to walk slowly around the dark house.

'Hello there, I'm Sian. You might remember me from about fifty years ago,' I said out loud into a shadowy and silent lounge.

Fifty years ago—it sounded so long. I gazed around. I hadn't spent much time in the salon, having decided to leave this room's makeover until last. Paintings of seascapes and mountain vistas graced the walls, while rows of musty old paperbacks lined the shelves. I picked up a book at random— *The Storyteller* by Patricia Highsmith—in translation, of course. Plopping myself down on the sofa, I imagined myself reading it by a roaring fire. It all seemed cosy rather than spooky. Two paintings caught my eye. One of a woman and one of a man, both gazing steadily out at me from their wooden frames— Aunt Constance and Uncle Jacques in their younger years, probably done by some seaside artist. I peered up at them but the flickering of the shadows on their faces made them look kindly rather than scary.

'See ghost, they're pleased I'm here.' I took a sip of wine. 'Well,' I continued, 'I'm not casting aspersions on your age, but I'm guessing that you've been here for a long time. So I don't blame you for feeling put out.'

Still nothing. *The ghoul obviously isn't in the lounge.* I stood, picked up my candle and walked through the door into the kitchen, taking care not to set fire to the door curtain as I went. Feeling my way around the table—*eff-it*—I stubbed a toe on a chair.

'Was that you, ghost?'

The ghost didn't answer. I downed a large gulp of wine and sat on a chair.

'I'll wait.'

Sitting, sipping, I glanced around the cosy little kitchen, chilly in the night-dark. With candle-light glinting in the canning jars and the big old furniture reassuringly solid, rather than scary, this room too, was quite lovely. I tried again.

'Okay, well the thing is, I used to come here when I was a child. I don't remember much to be honest but what I do remember is good. Anyhow, I'm back now...'

But it was clear the ghost wasn't here. *Probably legged it upstairs.* I don't know why but the upstairs of old houses always seems creepier than down. Even during the daytime, I'd sometimes felt spooked up there. Nonetheless, I was prepared to face the ghoul if I had to and I got up and opened the door to the stairs.

What the *Effing hell* was that?

My heart raced. It's a cliché, but honestly, there isn't a better way to describe it, my heart literally began to thump. I held the candle out in front of me and edged up the stairs. In the corridor I glanced up and down. Nothing seemed amiss, the blanket box and cane chair hadn't been up-ended by some ghoulish force... I stared at the spare-room door.

'Okay then...'

Giving it a shove at arm's length, I stepped back and thrust the candle in front of me... nothing seemed out of place. The window was closed and shuttered, the old bed and wardrobe were solid shadowy shapes in the flickering light.

'I know you want me to put the light on ghost and to be frank, so do I, but we're going to do it this way...'

There it is again!

'Okay, here I am... and I'm not leaving...'

I knocked back another gulp of wine and moved along the corridor to the bathroom. I was sure the noise had come from there. The thought of some ghostly revenge for my fly genocide nearly had me hightail it back downstairs but instead, I gave the door a push and stepped back.

'Did you do that, ghost?'

The window was open, the shutter unfastened from its hook, swaying in the night breeze. I placed my wine glass and the candle in its holder on the shelf, fastened the shutters and closed the window.

'Okay then, now we're getting somewhere. I have no problem with you as long as you have no problem with me. How about we be friends?'

Picking up my ghost-hunting equipment, I chucked back the final glug of wine, made my way along the dark hallway and finally reached my bedroom, where I flicked on the light and banged the door shut behind me.

'Well then, ghost, can we say we're friends now?'

He didn't answer, but I felt we were.

Chapter Twenty-five

Silence. That was one of the things that characterised my new life. Or rather lack of talk, since the profusion of living things I was sharing my country life with ensured that it was rarely silent. People who live alone and who don't go out to work—especially those without a TV or internet—don't exercise their throat muscles much. For me, this state of mute non-communication was interrupted by the sudden arrival of my new friend. Oddly, or perhaps not so oddly, my ghost-befriending strategy worked and he turned out to be surprisingly chatty. *Scared of me, are you?* He'd laugh as I'd go upstairs to my room at night, still just a touch wary. *Behave yourself, ghost,* I'd say, rolling my eyes. I wondered what the Good Doctor would make of it all. *Projection, Sian,* I imagined him saying, probably with a swivel of his chair. *You convinced yourself of the problem and created a solution that matched.* Fair enough. Perhaps though, there was more than one way of explaining things. I had no problem with the house-ghost explanation and felt it was entirely possible that the disgruntled spirit had simply re-gruntled himself.

A thought struck me as I prepared to go to bed one night. As I turned the lights off and headed up the stairs, *The Storyteller* in one hand, a steaming mug of hot chocolate in the other, it occurred to me that we tend to assume that ghosts are the spirits of people long dead. Visitors from the past. But what if some are visitors from the future? What if I was catching glimpses through time of someone who would live here in years to come, long after I'd passed on? And was it also possible that others were catching glimpses of me? Perhaps my own comings and goings in the cottage permeate the fabric of time and make people from the past and the future jump in fright at knocks and bumps and shadows they can't explain? I slapped my book down on the bedside-table with a satisfying thump. Were we—the past, present and future inhabitants of this cottage—locked into some mutual time-transcending bond? Were we all haunting each other?

Although the ghost chose not get involved in my conjectures, the thought was strangely comforting.

The cottage makeover continued room by room, interspersed by reading my way through Constance and Jacque's paperback collection. I hadn't read in French in years and it was good to exercise my language muscles for something more pleasant than call-centre work. Despite not talking to—indeed not even seeing—any actual French people, other than the ghost, of course, I felt, with each turn of a page, more and more connected with my host country.

Finally, exhausted but immensely proud of myself, I could honestly say that stage one of project cottage was complete: The house was fit to live in. Each room was fresh and clean and I breathed deeply the scent, not of mildew and damp but of honeysuckle and roses. The shed was bursting at the seams —already home to the huge stacks of wood which I hoped would see me through the winter—it was now also stacked with the old rolled-up carpets. At least the bin-men had agreed to take the bags of rubbish I put out with the wheely-bin each week. A healthy tip encouraged them in their efforts. I realised that the work I'd done, though, was purely cosmetic and that the place needed more serious attention. The stains on the wallpaper might simply be age or might be some underlying damp. The windows and their frames were pretty, but the wood was ancient and they'd need replacing at some point.

The sun had real force in it as the days lengthened and one Tuesday afternoon, sporting an enormous pair of Wellington boots I'd found in the shed, I went outside to the garden to consider stage two of my mission—the outside. Squinting up at the roof, I could see that it was beginning to sag and that a number of slates had slipped. There would certainly be leaks in the winter-time. *Well I'm sorry, ghost, there's not a lot I can do about that.* I looked at the windows. Painting or oiling the frames might extend their life, I supposed, but I doubted my aunt and uncle would to pay for a workman, and I didn't relish the thought of paying out of what little savings I had.

What's that, ghost? Do it myself? To be frank, I preferred my ghostly friend when he was chucking things around the attic rather than giving DIY advice, but I supposed he was right. I'd noticed a ladder in the shed. I'd be able to clear out the guttering as well, which I could see was full of dead leaves. I'd never cleared a gutter in my life, but there was no reason I shouldn't start with this one.

Having bobbed indoors to make a coffee, I came out to turn my attention to the garden, where I was greeted by the delightful sound of a cuckoo. Instantly transported back to my childhood visits to the cottage, I could almost hear my aunt singing; *coucou-hibou, coucou-hibou, coucou-hibou, coucou!* I smiled and looked around. The scene before me was somewhat less evocative. As well as the jungly path leading from the gate to the kitchen door, the whole area was a wild tangle of dense vegetation, covered in fallen cherry blossom. During the time I'd been here the weeds had claimed even more territory. Trailing honeysuckle was competing for dominance with tendrils of sticky green bindweed which clung to my jeans as I passed, gangly grasses had tufted up everywhere, ivy, thistles and nettles were devouring all in their way, while deceptively delicate yellow flowers had all but strangled the roses.

A few tulips had dared to open their bright orange petals amid the fecund mass and they made me think of Uncle Jacques patiently planting, weeding and watering the beds. I took a sip of coffee and hoped he had something equally rewarding to do in his Paris dotage. The thought of all his love and labour amounting to *this* made me sad and, vowing to get the garden into a state he would approve of, I grabbed a handful of long grass and pulled. *It'll take much more to get to grips with that lot.* The ghost planted the word 'trepidation' in my mind. I nodded. *True, ghost, it will certainly be a challenge.* I picked a bunch of pretty purple blossoms whose name I didn't know and took them inside to brighten up the kitchen.

For now, a more pressing challenge than the garden was looming. I'd pretty much exhausted my supply of fresh fruit and vegetables and the bread and cheese were long gone. My food stocks were getting low and the matter of how to get to the town to replenish them was a problem I couldn't solve alone.

'The nearest place to do your shopping is Etienne-Saint-Cloud,' my aunt had written. As well as the shops, there is a bank and a post-office, a pharmacy plus a few cafés and restaurants. The best one is Auberge Saint-Cloud, which is run by an old family friend. Best of all, there's a Saturday farmers market. Get there early and go to Michel's stall, the last one on the right opposite the café.

She'd explained that there were busses from the cross roads at the end of the lane, quite a walk she said, and she didn't know the times. I didn't care about the cafés or old family friends but I was tempted by the market and its stands, surely full of farm-fresh asparagus, courgettes, artichokes, melons, cheeses… I wondered whether old Michel would still be there.

The fact that I'd eaten all the salad and most of the fruit was testimony not just to the glorious early summer but also to the fact that I hadn't at first trusted the Calor-gas cooker. When the salad and cheese ran out, I'd had no other option but to attempt to cook something. I'm not a bad cook and I've always loved baking but I'm used to civilised cookers that threaten their owners with neither gas poisoning nor explosion. I'd stood in front of the thing regarding it with suspicion. It looked modern enough. I'd used a gas cooker, but this thing was hooked up to a canister via a rubber tube that went through a hole in the wall, and it hadn't been used in years.

I went into the store-room where the washing-machine was housed and looked at the gas canister. It was attached to the other end of the rubber tube with a big metal cap. I gave it a waggle. It seemed tight enough. I located the valve and turned on the gas flow as per Uncle Jacques instructions. He'd told me there was a full bottle of gas which should last around six months. I'd been impressed that he remembered. I sniffed. I couldn't smell gas. And listening hard, I couldn't hear any sounds of leakage either. Going back into the kitchen, I gingerly lit the stove and ran out of the room into the garden, in case it blew me and the ghost to kingdom come. To my amazement, the cooker was both safe and efficient. Especially the oven, I discovered, and I happily began experimenting with my favourite cake, biscuit and tart recipes.

Now though, I'd cooked almost everything fresh I'd brought and was pretty much down to dried pasta and rice. And I'd certainly soon need to replenish the basics like loo-paper and washing-up liquid. I thought about walking into town. It would make a lovely early morning walk, the weather was certainly good for it and I'd spotted a moth-eaten backpack in the shed that I could brush off and take with me. But I had no idea how long that would take, at least an hour one way—perhaps considerably longer—and the idea of wandering along winding, pavement-less country roads laden with vegetables going soft in the heat didn't fill me with eagerness. Since my mobile phone was somewhere under the English Channel, I couldn't call a taxi and, besides, that would be the most expensive option. *There's nothing for it, ghost. I'll have to get the bus.*

The ghost agreed and I'd pretty much resigned myself to knocking at a neighbour's house to get the necessary information, but decided first to bake some olive bread, which would last me a day or two. The oven was already hot from a batch of ginger snaps I'd popped in a while ago and I set out all that I needed for the bread, pleased that I'd thought to buy dried yeast and plenty of flour at my first super-market stop. I was wrist deep in dough and considering which of the neighbours' houses I'd go to when, as though I'd conjured one of them up, the bell at my gate clanged.

Chapter Twenty-six

Clairjo I was. Clairjo I am. And I don't care who questions it.

Donc, I changed my mind about leaving the foreigner be. Been here for weeks she had, and we still didn't know the first thing about her, in spite of Ripaille quizzing the postman. *'Not my business to say,'* he'd said. *'But she doesn't get much post.'* Now, I'm not one of those who goes nosing into other people's affairs but the baker was right, this Sian needed to be told about the van-runs at least. So the next time Volt arrived I bought an extra baguette and took myself along the lane to the Duchamp cottage.

'Go with you, shall I?' Ripaille had said, mopping his brow with a rag.

'Va-t'en' I'd replied, 'get away with you, I'll tell you if she wants her hedges trimming.'

'What if she doesn't speak French?'

'And how would *you* help with that?'

Ripaille shrugged and shuffled off to his cottage, stooping to pull up a weed which had dared take root by his gate.

I stood listening outside the Duchamp cottage and was surprised to hear a woman's voice talking—thought she was here alone—but although it sounded French, I couldn't make out the words. The old bell was rusty and stiff and it took a few tugs of the chain to get it to sound, but eventually it clanged loudly, bringing the girl to the big, iron gates which she dragged open with an unpractised lurch.

'Bonjour Madame, je m'appelle Madame Clairjo,' I said, pronouncing the words carefully. *'Ça va?'*

The woman was covered in flour and, by the look on her face, seemed flustered, a squinty kind of frown shoving her eyelids down so I couldn't tell what colour her eyes were.

'We're neighbours,' I said once she'd composed herself. 'I hope I haven't disturbed you. Were you on the phone?'

The foreigner stood there like a rabbit caught in headlights and I looked her up and down, taking in her unruly curls tumbling from a badly tied head-scarf, the grubby jeans and t-shirt, the rubber boots at least five sizes too big for her. I wondered whether the girl had understood me, but she dusted off her hand, took mine and gave it a quick shake.

'Bonjour Madame, ça va bien merci, it's nice to meet you,' she said, in surprisingly passable French. 'I'm Sian Evans.'

'Time for a coffee, Madame Evans?'

She didn't object and I was already through the gate, so she led the way along what passed for a path. I glanced from side to side as I went. Ripaille was right, it wasn't just her hedges that wanted cutting. The place was a veritable wilderness and I shoved the bread under my arm and picked my way cautiously through waist-high grasses, *chèvre-feuille* gone mad and nettles that stung my ankles through my tights. Shocking.

'Used to be a nice garden this,' I tutted. The foreigner didn't respond. The back gate lay open, and I peered through it to the field beyond, taking in the combined assault of wild roses and ivy that were threatening to bring down the boundary wall. Other than some screeching swallows swooping overhead, there wasn't much more I could make out over the top of the grass.

'Lovely weather,' I said, swatting away a wasp.

Madame Evans didn't reply other than to nod and I followed her through the door into the kitchen where we both stood blinking for a moment as our eyes adjusted to the dim light inside. I was surprised to breathe in the smell of baking.

'Stayed here once when I was a girl, I did, when my old Mum was sick,' I said, once I could focus. 'That was before the Duchamps of course. Bit different, the place is now.'

Actually, I thought, glancing around, the room wasn't that different. The big oak table still stood in the centre of the room with its six lath-backed chairs—the girl had stuck a few weeds in a jar which I suppose she thought passed as a centre-piece. The open shelves were lined with mason jars same as in the Duchamp days except today they were mostly empty. There was the huge carved dresser, its rows of china plates chipped but neatly stacked. And of course the inglenook which I noted with approval had been recently swept. Only the addition of a fridge and a gas cooker marked the passage of time. And the electric kettle, which Madame Evans set to boil while she busied herself spooning coffee into a cafetière. I put the baguette on the table and took a furtive swipe along the mantle-piece—not bad—before lowering myself into one of the chairs by the empty grate, grasping the wooden arms tightly. Why do they make seats so low?

'Glad you're keeping the place well,' I said. The girl looked startled but didn't respond. I eyed an old broom propped against a wall and a bucket-full of cleaning products by the door, a pair of pink rubber gloves hanging over its edge. A clean tea-towel neatly graced the oven door. I wouldn't say the place was spotless—she clearly didn't like drying dishes—but it was clean enough. I watched her pour water from the kettle into the waiting cafetière which she brought over with two mugs on a wooden tray. One of them sported some foreign words.

'I'm out of sugar,' the girl said, placing the tray on the hearth. 'I used the last to bake biscuits.'

'No matter,' I replied. 'I don't need it. I've brought you some bread.'

I indicated the baguette on the table and the girl took it with a nod and placed it inside an old wooden *huche à pain*. I hoped she'd given it a good clean.

'How much do I owe you?' she asked.

I shook my head. 'Return the favour one day.'

I watched her fold a tea-towel in half and place it over some waiting dough and use another to take a tray of biscuits out of the oven, their buttery smell wafting through the kitchen. Likes to bake then. She shook the biscuits onto a plate and brought them over.

'These will soon crisp up,' she said. 'Ginger snaps.'

I nodded as she sat down on the other chair and pressed the waiting coffee, pouring it into the two mugs. A sign of her age, I supposed, I knew there were proper cups and saucers in the dresser. She took the one with the foreign writing. I peered at her. How old was she? Her hair wasn't showing signs of grey but that's no indicator these days. The backs of her hands were bony though and displayed raised blue veins as she sipped her coffee. No spring-chicken then, but still young—forty something? Fifty? She didn't like being called English.

'I'm not English, I'm Welsh,' she said, when I asked. I thought it was all the same.

'How long are you planning to stay?'

She looked surprised. Not used to straight talking. Too bad, at my age, anything else is a waste of time.

'Oh, long enough,' the girl replied, gazing into the non-existent fire.

I raised my eyebrows. I wasn't letting her get away with that. 'Long enough for what?'

She turned to me with an odd look in her eye—like she was weighing me up.

'Constance and Jacques have said I can have the place for a year. They don't use the house anymore, as I'm sure you know.'

A year, eh? Bet old Ripaille doesn't know that. I eyed her carefully. Constance and Jacques? So, she's on first name terms with the Duchamps.

'How do you know the Duchamps?' I asked, picking up a biscuit.

'They're my aunt and Uncle,' she replied, swatting away a fly. 'Well, my great-Aunt and uncle, on my father's side. We're not close,' she added as if an afterthought.

'Your aunt and uncle are they?' I took a cautious peck at my biscuit and was surprised to find it edible.

'Yes, I used to visit them here when I was young. I don't really remember it anymore.'

I peered at her closely.

'Been lots of babies here over the years. Can't say I'd know you from any of the others.'

'No, of course not...'

She trailed off and stared into her coffee. Not much of a talker.

'Husband be joining you, will he?' I took another bite of the biscuit.

She gave me a defiant look, like she was going to say something, but she seemed to think the better of it. Pity.

'Never mind,' I said, 'you'll be pleased to know there's a bread-van stops by Tuesdays, Thursdays and Saturdays. Madame Volt is the baker. And every other Monday there's a charcuterie van. It's run by Jean-Luc and Jean-Paul. They're on holiday—the Bourgogne—go there every year, so you'll have to wait for your meat.

The girl nodded and I eyed the shelves with their half-empty jars. She'd probably been living on dry beans for the past week. 'How do you plan on doing your shopping?' She brightened up immediately.

'I'm hoping there's a bus that will take me into town,' she said. 'Would you happen to…'

I cut her off. 'There's a bus if you like, once a day 'cept on Sunday's and Wednesdays. Don't bother with it myself, takes an age and the return is always full of noisy children.'

'Hold on, I'll write down the details.'

She darted off to the salon and came back with a note-pad and pen. Got herself well organised, she has.

'Like I say, I don't bother with it, but you'll find the bus stop a good walk yonder,' I pointed towards the lane. 10.30 sharp it goes but not Sundays or Wednesdays.' She scribbled it down on her pad.

'Oh,' she said, 'isn't there an earlier bus on Saturdays? I was hoping to go to the farmers market.'

'Best stuff will be gone by the time the bus gets there.'

The girl looked disappointed.

'Madame Volt brings my shopping Saturday afternoons. Gets the fruit and veg fresh first thing from the market.' *Got an eye for the best veg has Volt, I'll give her that.* 'Does it for a price of course.'

The Englisher put down her pen. 'Oh?' she said.

'Then there's Monsieur Ripaille who orders his on the internet. I don't hold with that myself, never know what you're getting. You got internet here?' I looked around the room, not exactly sure what I was looking for. The girl shook her head. 'Well then you can ask Madame Volt if she'll do your shopping. She won't mind, she's always on the look-out for extra cash.' *Until she snares a husband.*

Madame Evans gave a half-nod and sipped her coffee. Is she quite right in the head, I wondered? She seemed so… vague. Still, I thought, taking a final biscuit—they weren't bad at all—and, preparing to stand, regardless of her French relatives, and her French speaking, she *is* foreign.

Chapter Twenty-seven

So that was Madame Clairjo. After she left, I considered the idea that she was another ghost—after all, the first one had proved that they don't only come out at night. But in the end —perhaps because she left the delicious-smelling baguette that begged me to smear it with goat's cheese—I concluded that she wasn't a phantom of the future or the past but a flesh and blood woman of the neighbourly persuasion; one of those country types, all prickly suspicions and narrowed eyes, fishing for information to show off to her cronies.

'Where you from, then?' she'd asked.

'I'm from the UK.'

'English, eh?'

'I'm not English, I'm Welsh.'

It was clear from her raised eyebrow that England and Wales were all the same to her and, much as it irked me, I hadn't felt inclined to explain the history of the four nations to the old bird. She hadn't gotten much more out of me than my nationality and that suited me just fine. At least I now knew the bus times.

There was one local who had caught my attention. I'd just taken in a line-full of clean washing, tutting audibly at whichever bird had chosen to drop its calling card on a t-shirt. Since it was after seven, I'd decided to console myself with my evening tipple and was sitting in the field amid the witterings and twitterings of the birds. I'd come to love this little lull between finishing the day's chores and preparing my evening meal, and I'd made my single glass of wine on the bench a nightly habit. That particular evening, I was mulling over the problem of how to get to the market. I wasn't overly keen on the idea of the baker doing my shopping but at least I'd be able to buy fresh bread. As I considered my options, a swirl of sweet-scented incense smoke kept the army of annoying little midges at bay.

That day, sorting through a big old chest of drawers in the salon, I'd found, amid the half–full boxes of matches, old postcards—I resolved to read them all one day—ancient rusting keys, rubber bands, a box of incense sticks. Pondering the unlikely possibility that my aunt and uncle were hippies, I had, out of simple curiosity, lit one. It smelt good—rich and exotic. I remembered Nate sneakily flirting with cannabis one summer when he was fifteen, trying and failing to cover the smell in his room with such sticks. *What the blazes is that stench?'* Arwel had barked. Thankfully the phase hadn't lasted. I smiled, imagining Jacques and Constance sporting kaftans, gazing at the stars and saying *'wow man'* and *'far out'* amid swirls of incense.

On casting around for something in which to stand it, I made a discovery. These smoking sticks deter flies. I experimented. Taking the incense to the window where, inevitably, a few choice specimens were flinging themselves with enthusiasm against the glass, I wafted the smoke at them. They flew away. I pursued. The flies fled. Until now a combination of fly-spray and violence had been the only way to keep the insect hoards to manageable numbers. I took the stick, along with my glass of wine, to the field and stuck it between two slats in the bench. *Voilà*—a fly-free zone.

I sat revelling in my discovery, sipping wine and enjoying the warmth of the pre-setting sun. A group of swallows was chasing one another over the field, their *shreeeeep shreeeep* mingling with the cooing of pigeons and the elaborate warbling of chaffinches—the truth birds whose final flourish reminded me that *it's reeeal!*—while various rustlings and scratchings suggested suspiciously abundant terrestrial life. I kicked a tuft of grass and an army of Gendarmes beetles scurried under the bench. I was feeling hungry and the meagre offerings that remained in the kitchen had me fantasising about the market and Michel's stall, laden with a rainbow of succulent fruit, vegetables and fresh herbs... I was wondering whether my tightly-guarded budget would stretch to a bicycle and chuckling at the idea of wobbling along the lanes with a full backpack of shopping, when a sudden movement interrupted my reverie. I looked up.

From my place in the field I could see one of my neighbours' cottages. Madame Clairjo's place? Most of the house was hidden by a clump of trees which I was pleased about, but I could tell that the place was bigger than mine and, from what I could see of its roof and gable end, in a better state of repair. One corner of the house jutted out, revealing a large casement window which had always been closed and shuttered. Today though, the shutters had been flung open. *I wouldn't put it past the old bat to spy on me.* Curious in spite of myself, I peered up at the window, but could make nothing out through the glass. I sipped my wine and kept my eye on it.

Until the arrival of Madame Clairjo, I'd not been curious about my neighbours. I didn't doubt that they were interested in me and I supposed I ought to do the proper thing and introduce myself. But I hadn't come here to do the 'proper thing' and, in spite of the old woman's visit, I hoped that country reserve would enable me to live in seclusion. *'Sian's a loner, you won't tempt her out of her own head,'* my Mam used to say. Why is that seen as a bad thing? My Mam was only half-right. I can enjoy company, but it's true that I don't need it. The Good Doctor had been interested in that and tried to make a case for social isolation being the cause of my so-called 'problems'.

'Would you say, Sian, that it's possible your difficulties in connecting with people are making you feel lonely?'

Where to start with that? 'I don't have difficulties connecting,' I'd retorted, aware of the defensiveness in my voice. 'It's a choice not a handicap. And I'm not lonely. I'm just quiet. Big difference.'

I pondered the arrival of Madam Clairjo as I sipped my wine and listened to the *shir-shirring* of the elusive grass-hoppers, which I'd concluded were like the opposite of good children, heard but not seen. I suppose I'd expected a visit from one or other of the neighbours sooner or later. How old was Madam Clairjo? In her late seventies? Was there a Monsieur Clairjo, Clairjo juniors scattered round and about? Had my aunt called to warn her about my arrival? I glanced again at the window, but could see nothing.

Other than to let the old woman in when she'd called, I'd had very little reason to open the front gate, checking the post and putting out the rubbish being the only exceptions.

Cocooned, the ghost said. I supposed I was. Now, I set my wine down on the bench, walked back through the weedy-wild tangle of garden and heaved open the big red gates, making a mental note, as they screeched in protest, to look for some oil for the hinges. Stepping outside, I peered up and down the lane. All was quiet save the quarrelling sparrows. The two houses I could see were similar to my own, their big limestone blocks glowing warm yellow in the evening sun. One of them could be Madame Clairjo's. She had mentioned a Monsieur Riponte or Ripaille or some such name. The other cottage could be his. I imagined him to be a male version of her, old, prickly and nosey. I hadn't once heard the sounds of children playing or of general domestic bustle, which suggested elderly neighbours. That suited me, as long as their interest in the new foreign neighbour didn't get the better of them. I wondered who the third cottage belonged to, jumping as a big grey cat leapt from a wall, regarded me with a haughty sneer and slinked off down the lane.

Back in the field, the air around the bench was once more fizzing with insect life and I made another mental note—this time to save the house from being razed to the ground by never again leaving burning incense alone beside dry grass. I sat on the bench and fished a soggy moth out of my glass. The sun was casting long shadows over the field but it was still hot enough to prickle my skin. I stroked my arms and thought about what I might rustle up for dinner, the prospect of more lentil soup not filling me with enthusiasm.

I was watching two white butterflies chase each other round a purple flowered bush as some farm machine started up in the distance, when something made me look up. *Was that...?* Yes, there again in the window, movement. Old Madame Clairjo watching my every move? I fixed my gaze on it, screwing my eyes against the sunset shadows. There it was again, a shift in the light on the glass...someone moving around inside. All was still for a long moment until... a figure appeared at the window—definitely watching me. It wasn't Madame Clairjo, but it was a woman. A naked woman.

Chapter Twenty-eight

What are you doing here?

The ghost's question came out of nowhere one night as I was reading in bed. I'd finished *The Story Teller* and moved onto George Sand's *Winter in Majorca*, which I'd concluded wasn't as good as her other books.

What?

What exactly are you doing here?

What sort of a question is that? I dog-eared my page, put the book down and thought about it. The cottage had begun to feel like home. I was completely familiar with the house, occupying it intimately, the suitcases long since packed away, my clothes neatly stowed in drawers and cupboards, the treasures I'd brought with me part of the place—the *Mam Gorau yn y Byd* mug hanging on its hook under one of the shelves, the onyx egg on the kitchen dresser.

I live here, I told the ghost, *hadn't you noticed?*

I know that, but what are you doing here?

Sod off and haunt someone else, I retorted turning out the light.

The next day, I decided to tackle something I'd been putting off for days and, by mid morning, there I stood, sweating and aching, a bucket of murky water in one hand, a filthy wet cloth in the other, assessing my handiwork. Cleaning windows was a chore I'd always hated. When I'd been married it had been Arwel's job. After divorcing, in spite of his insistence that he'd still do them, I'd found a window cleaner, a weasel-faced thing called Nobby who leered at me through the suds and thought it was part of his job to comment on everything I wore. Even he was preferable to washing the windows myself. Here, I had no choice and, with nine years of grime in the bucket, I felt like I'd paid for my previous window-related indolence. As the ghost pointed out, I hadn't done a bad job.

I'd decided to have my coffee break on the bench in the field before tackling the upstairs windows. I sat amid the insecty fizz—an army of bees had joined the flies and were buzzing loudly in a honeysuckle bush. I was enjoying its sweet scent and gazing into the distance to a field resplendent with sunflowers, when a dog started an incessant barking. I'd already checked the naked-woman window and she was noticeable by her absence. By the volume of barking, I knew this dog wasn't too far away. And, by its tone, I could tell it was big. I peered once more at the naked-house. Was she the owner of the canine culprit?

Back in the garden, I continued washing windows, balancing precariously on the ladder as I sloshed the rag over the filthy glass. *Dog, you're not helping!* As I toiled away, I tried ignoring it, I tried focusing on everything else, even the insects that were dive-bombing me as I worked. Every time I thought it had exhausted itself, the wretched thing started again.

The barking brought my mood down. I hadn't slept well the night before, probably because of the ghost's stupid question and, feeling tired and tetchy, I climbed down the ladder, washed my hands and went, with my third cup of coffee of the day, *that won't help me sleep!* to ponder in the buzzy, barky field.

It's a question the Good Doctor might have posed: *'Sian, what you are doing all alone in this isolated cottage in France?'* I expect we'd get a swivel or two of the leatherette chair and a tap of his posh pen. The problem was, I realised, that the question posed was a diversion from the real question.

The question is actually an existential one, I told the ghost. *I mean, wouldn't the issue of what I'm doing here apply just as well in a Cardiff call-centre as in a cottage in Saint Vey?*

The ghost would have rolled its eyes if it had any, but I'd warmed to the theme. I mean, we find things to do to fill our time, what we find to do expands to fit the time we have and *voila*—we are busy. Busy making money, keeping house, looking after people. Yeah, some of those things are necessary to keep body and soul together, and for that reason we don't question the whys and the wherefores. Fair enough. But all the same, isn't the question of what we are doing here always there, biting at our heels, messing with our certainties?

As I explained all this to the ghost, I remembered that I'd suggested as much to the Good Doctor—not about living in France obviously—but about why I was seeing him.

'The point is,' I'd said, 'I don't see why filling up our time, being busy all the time is seen as functional. Surely we all get days when we need to stop, just to *be*. Doesn't everyone feel like that sometimes? In which case how come when I feel like that it's seen as a problem that needs to be addressed?'

'So you feel that talking about your feelings won't help you?'

It's not about feelings, I'd wanted to say—*it's deeper than that.* I hadn't bothered.

In the field, I sipped my coffee and stretched my back, enjoying the heat of the sun against my bear arms. I thought about Nate. What was his globe-trotting about? People were quick to judge that too. 'Oh he'll settle down one day, when he meets a nice girl.' Or, 'Oh, Nate's *discovering* himself, is he?' with that smugness of tone that really means 'Oh, Nate's too immature to find a *proper* job, is he?' I've heard it said that people travel to find themselves. I've never asked Nate what it was about for him. Was that why I was here? To find myself?

Well Ghost, I said, *it seems to me that 'finding yourself' is simply working out how to fill your time in such a way that doesn't make you want to scream.*

I watched the little white butterflies flitting around the purple bush. The dog was still barking, and I realised that, for a time, I *had* managed to zone him out. An enormous fly buzzed past my ear, no doubt on its way to hurl itself against the lounge window. *Ghost—kill it!* I could hear the distant sound of some farm machine at work. It's odd that in spite of its constant drone, *that* sound wasn't at all annoying. The sky was that milky-blue you never see in paintings and I let my gaze follow it to the horizon, where a clump of trees rose behind the vines to the east, and the sunflower field blazed yellow. Whatever I was doing here, whether I was finding myself or not, there were worse places to look.

Chapter Twenty-nine

So my tasks expanded to fit my days and the days flew by. If anyone had asked, I'd not be sure what to say about what I did all day other than housework, cooking, reading and thinking, but I was never bored and the days had turned to weeks.

And the dog was still barking. After another long afternoon of trying to ignore the effing thing I decided tolerance be damned! I slammed down the saucepan I was about to fill with rice. *Ghost, that's it.* I shoved my feet into Uncle Duchamp's wellies and went in search of the owner.

Heaving open the big red gates—*I must get round to oiling them*—I peered up and down the lane as I had the other day. Unsurprisingly, no one was about and the dog, as though it was onto my mission, was silent. *Come on dog, where are you?* Confounded, I headed up the lane towards what I hoped was Madame Clairjo's house. I doubted the dog belonged to her— if anything, I imagined her with some miniature rodent-dog-thing—but she would certainly know who the wretched beast belonged to. Before I'd gone more than five steps, the barking started once more. It was coming from the naked-woman cottage. So, determined to be polite but firm, even if faced with bare breasts, I braced myself and marched down the lane.

As I'd seen from the field, the house was a different style to mine, taller and grander. A wooden gate stood open in the high stone wall and I peered inside at the tidy, gravelled grounds. There were very few flowers, only a couple of potted shrubs gracing the front of the house. The window where I'd seen the woman was at the side of the house and wasn't visible from this angle and I could make out nothing through the other windows. I stood staring up the short path at a big green front door. A chain hung by the gate, presumably attached to a bell somewhere inside, much the same as the one at my own cottage. I gave it a tug and was immediately rewarded by the sound of the clanging bell and the dog barking more frantically than usual. Marching up the path and rehearsing how I'd begin, I was startled when the front door was yanked open and I was faced neither with Madame Clairjo nor a naked woman, but with a man about my age, wearing shirt-sleeves and faded calico trousers. He didn't look happy to have a visitor.

There was no dog to be seen and all was quiet once more. The man stood frowning at me and I realised that I must look a complete sketch in Uncle Jacques enormous Wellingtons, a dirty t-shirt and hair that hadn't seen shampoo in over a week. My personal hygiene had really suffered these past weeks. Well I wasn't here to impress anyone.

'*Bonjour Monsieur, je m'appelle Sian Evans,*' I began, determined not to let him faze me. 'I'm your new neighbour.'

The man stared at me. A shy Frenchman is an oxymoron so, when he didn't reply, I put his silence down to rudeness.

'I've come about your dog.'

'...my dog?'

His bulk, not fat but hefty, barred the door and I could see nothing inside. It was clear he wasn't about to invite me in so I resigned myself to having the conversation on the doorstep.

'Yes your dog,' I said. 'It barks.'

Deafening silence from the animal as well as its owner.

'Your dog barks,' I repeated, raising my voice.

'Well yes, she *is* a dog!'

Oh, a joker, is he?

'What I mean is, your dog barks rather a lot—sometimes all day. It must be when you're out—perhaps it gets lonely.'

'Lonely? She's a dog, not a maiden aunt.'

I suppose it's conceivable that's not what he actually said, it was in colloquial French. But I was sure it was nothing friendly. And why had the mutt decided to desist now?

'Well I'm telling you,' I said, straightening myself up to my full five feet three and holding his stare—blue eyes—cold. 'There are days when your dog doesn't stop barking and I simply can't stand it anymore. You're going to have to do something about it.'

'That all?'

'Yes, that's all.'

'Then I'll say good day to you, Madame.'

The door slammed shut and I was left standing there open mouthed and fuming. Well! What a horrible man! A horrible man with a horrible dog. I had half a mind to ring the bell again and demand to know exactly what he was going to do about it, but instead I turned and trudged off home.

Chapter Thirty

'*Bonjour*, Madame Evans, passable weather.' It was Thursday, bread-run day and the weather was blazing hot.

Having suffered yet another morning trying to ignore Mr Hostile's dog, I'd decided to see whether the neighbours had the same problem—perhaps a combined assault would persuade the man to do something. Much against my better judgement, I'd also made up my mind to ask this Madame Volt about doing my shopping. *Needs must*, the ghost had said after watching me eat a bowl of plain rice for dinner. So, as I slopped soapy water around the kitchen floor with an old-fashioned mop that made me feel like I was in a period drama, I'd been listening out for the baker's van. At precisely one o clock the dog, as if on cue, paused its racket long enough for me to hear the tooting of the horn.

Having dumped the mop into the grey bucket-water, grabbed some money from the dresser drawer and stuffed my feet into Uncle Jacque's wellies, I sprinted across the garden, screeched open the gates and rushed outside, where I was relieved to see the van still there, parked by one of the cottages along the lane. I flumped along in the giant boots, the hedge fragrant with the scent of honeysuckle and wild roses, noting the assembled company. Two Madames plus an old man were gathered around the van. The man was leaning on a stick and regarded me as I made my way towards them with a look of open-mouthed curiosity. He lifted his chin in my direction and said something I didn't catch, the result of which was six beady eyes fixed on my progress. As I reached the group I nodded my hellos, relieved to note that Mr Hostile wasn't among their number.

Madame Clairjo, her ample girth entombed in a voluminous black cardigan in spite of the heat, bellowed her greeting at me cordially but without the customary kiss on each cheek. Madame Volt the baker, all sharp elbows and pointy cheekbones, bid me the briefest of '*bonjour*' before walking round the van to yank open the side door. The sight and smell of baskets stacked high with freshly baked baguettes, pastries and tarts made me feel ravenous.

'I don't believe you've met Monsieur Ripaille,' Madame Clairjo said, indicating the old man with a be-jewelled hand. Monsieur Ripaille proffered a gnarled hand of his own, which I shook.

'*Bonjour Monsieur,*' I said.

'You speak French ...' he began, but the baker cut in.

'So *here* you are,' she snapped, as though she'd been waiting for me.

The woman looked me up and down, visibly unimpressed by my sweat-stained t-shirt—the same one I'd worn to Mr Hostile's. I returned the stare, taking in the immaculately starched baker's jacket and cap, her bony face pulled taut by her scraped-back hair. Our eyes met.

'We wondered when you'd venture out of that burrow of yours.' Madame Volt's high pitched laugh suggested no mirth.

As she bagged pastries for old-man Ripaille, I glanced towards Mr Hostile's house. All was quiet and I couldn't see much but a sudden burst of sparrows from the tree in the courtyard suggested that something—the stupid dog, no doubt—had startled them. I turned back to the van where Madame Clairjo was prodding suspiciously at a baguette with a knobbly finger. Volt was watching me. I decided to get the matter of shopping out of the way before mentioning the dog. Would it be rude, I wondered, to get straight to the point? As it happened, I didn't have to.

'Madame Evans could use your shopping-run,' Clairjo said, turning to face the baker. 'No car you see, and you know what the busses are like.'

'I do my shopping on the internet,' Monsieur Ripaille said, puffing out his weedy chest. The two women ignored him.

'I can do that,' Madame Volt said in a no-nonsense manner. 'Do the shopping for all the old folk round about.'

I noted her use of the word 'old' which she uttered with far too much relish for a woman no younger than me, but decided it didn't matter as long as she brought my groceries.

'I go to the market and to Carrefour, Saturday's,' she said. 'You got a list?'

I nodded and pulled a folded sheet of paper out of my jeans pocket, the old Monsieur peering at it with interest.

'Money up front, since you're new,' Volt snapped, handing Madame Clairjo a paper-wrapped croissant before taking my list. 'Plus my fee. Twenty five per-cent.'

Clairjo pecked her a sharp look but said nothing. It was steep, I thought, but less than half what a taxi would cost. The baker scanned the list and nodded. My requirements were apparently to her satisfaction and she folded the sheet and put it into the leather satchel that hung from her shoulder. I handed over the money.

'No receipt?' I asked when none was forthcoming.

'What's that girl, speak up.' Madame Clairjo shouted.

Volt smirked and turned to tidy her bread.

'Do I get a receipt?' I repeated, raising my voice in the general direction of both Madames.

'We don't do things like that here.' Madame Volt flashed me a frown.

She'd clearly decided that our transaction was over and slammed shut the van door. The group looked ready to disband and, not wanting them to leave before getting to the other reason I'd ventured out, I spoke quickly, addressing my question to the group at large:

'That house around the corner, do you know the man who lives there?'

Stupid question, of course they did. Nonetheless, the group turned its collective gaze to where my finger pointed, to where the only sound that broke the peaceful afternoon calm was the *shree-shree-ing* of swallows perched in a long row on the electricity line. Madame Volt gave me a look that I couldn't interpret. No one responded.

'I met the man the other day…it's their dog, you see…'

Sharp eyes turned to me and I trailed off, realising that a stranger criticising one of their number wasn't to be tolerated.

'That's Monsieur Delariche,' Ripaille answered with a frown. 'But if it's about your hedges, I've got all the tools.'

Damn that dog, it barks all the time except when I'm complaining about it. And why is this old man talking about hedges?

'It's just,' I persevered, deciding that I may as well dive in. 'It's just that the dog barks a lot. You must all have heard it. Do they leave it on its own? Perhaps they work all day?'

The two Madame's exchanged a glance.

'Can't say I've heard it,' said Madame Clairjo. I didn't believe her, though it was conceivable the old girl was deaf as a post.

'Can't stop a dog from barking,' Monsieur Ripaille said, taking off his hat and scratching his bald head as though he'd been confronted with some manner of imbecile. 'In its nature, it is.'

Madame Volt said nothing, but regarded me through narrowed eyes.

I gave up. It was clear these people were not about to help with the dog situation. I'd have to confront Monsieur Delariche again.

Chapter Thirty-one

My body aches, I'm on the verge of crying, I can't concentrate, don't know what to do or what I should be doing, can't sleep, can barely move, the simplest task seems insurmountable. Nothing is wrong… but nothing is right. The only way I can describe my state is that I feel 'soft'.

I don't know why but I'd been thinking about a conversation I'd had with Doctor Adebowale, even dreaming about it. I was pondering it in bed, my hot chocolate going cold on the bedside table, my book abandoned. The Good Doctor had frequently returned to the matter of me being 'soft', which I suppose was unsurprising as it had caused my days off work. Having faced one of the skeletons in my closet, I'd somehow come to trust him more. Maybe I'd felt he wouldn't judge me. In any case, talking about being 'soft' was nothing compared with what I'd already told him about Creepy Roger.

'Get up, dress up, show up,' Arwel used to say. He actually put me in the shower once. Seriously, he pulled me from the bed, steered me into the bathroom, dragged my nightdress over my head and turned the water on while I sat there curled up in the shower tray. 'Don't give in to it, Sian,' he said. He told me I was being self-indulgent.

It wasn't that my husband was cruel, far from it, I told the Doctor as he bent to hike up a Huckleberry Hound sock—but Arwel didn't understand. He was the kind of man who was good at routine and who thought that sticking to one, no matter what, was good for everyone. And yes, there was a sense in which his approach worked, or at least appeared to. I'd get myself out of bed, showered, dressed and out of the house, show up at work, get through the day. Get up, dress up, show up. 'You see, Sian,' he'd say when we got home in the evening. 'Routine and discipline. It works.'

'The thing is,' I said, 'he thought that when I followed his advice, when I got myself to work no matter how I felt, he thought that meant I was *dealing* with it, that I was overcoming my so-called 'problem', whereas I knew I was simply being…

I don't know, false. It only *appeared* as though things were better because I was functioning in the way that was expected. In the end, because I couldn't be who I really am, I no longer felt close to him. I'm not saying that's why we divorced, but it didn't help.'

The Doctor nodded, wrote something down and looked at me, not at the clock behind me, but at me. He did that a lot. Not saying anything, sitting there, pen poised, waiting. And every time, I'd feel so *effing* uncomfortable, that I'd babble something to break the silence. Which was, of course, his plan. At least we were finally talking about my job.

'As long as you don't say how you feel, as long as you don't act on your feelings, then you're okay,' I continued. 'As long as you get up, dress up and show up, people don't question how you really are. I honestly don't think they want to know, as long as you function.'

'You've used the word 'function' more than once today, Sian. What does the word mean for you?'

That's another of the Good Doctor's strategies. He'll take an ordinary word in a perfectly understandable sentence and ask what it means to me, as though meanings are like sweets and we can choose the flavour we like best. I peered at him. Is *he* ever soft? Is he simply going through the motions, sitting there on his swivel chair, asking me questions and writing things down, when in fact everything inside him is screaming 'NO!'?

'Well, we're all parts of a machine, aren't we?'

'A machine?'

'Yes. Like, at my office I'm the part that's supposed to answer the phone to French clients and help them when they can't work our software. Between 9 and 5, I perform my function in the machine. I mustn't allow my real *self* to intrude. I must behave like I don't even have a self. The problem is I can't do it every day to order. I'm not that good an actress.'

'And what would behaving like you have a 'self' mean for you, Sian?'

I looked at him for a long moment. Was that genuine interest on his face? Empathy? Or had he learned how to arrange his features in such a way that I thought he was paying attention? Well, whatever his true feelings, I could see the flaw in my reasoning. I mean, if everyone simply stayed home when they felt like it, how would the world work? But just because I'd identified the problem, didn't mean I had the solution.

'It's like trying to shove cement between bricks,' I said with a sigh.

'How do you mean?'

I looked around the office at the solid furniture, the desk with its closed laptop and leather pen-pots, the pale-wood shelves with their orderly rows of books, the Good Doctor's jacket on its wooden hanger on the coat-stand. I suddenly felt exhausted.

'I mean, we've created a society where routine, discipline... I don't know—consistency are all required in order to make the world function. And we teach people that those are valuable qualities. The problem is, I suspect a fair number of the population don't naturally possess them. In fact, I'm pretty damned certain those qualities aren't 'natural' at all. And you can't just take an inconsistent person and try to shove them into a routine. We'd do better to dismantle the wall and build something else in its place.'

'Go on...'

His questioning had begun to irritate me—was this a game to him? 'A game is when you voluntarily accept obstacles,' I'd once read. I didn't want to play any more

'Look, I've said it before, in my opinion, *I'm* not the problem. It's the way we organise work that is wrong.'

The Good Doctor nodded, somewhat thoughtfully, I felt. Is he actually considering something I have to say? I didn't interrupt his reverie and after some moments he answered:

'Be that as it may, Sian, we have the system we have. Our goal here is to find a strategy to help you thrive within it.'

I was bored with this now, bored and angry.

'It doesn't make any sense though, does it?' I exclaimed. 'The system is wrong, but instead of fixing it, we have to change ourselves to accommodate it. The one's who find that the most difficult to do are the ones we send to doctors!'

This particular doctor wrote something down. Well, at least I'd been honest, although I had no idea what he could do with my honesty, after all he was being paid to 'fix' me, not to redesign capitalism.

'Sian,' he said, turning in his seat to place his pen on the desk. There was an odd look in his eyes and I braced myself for a character assassination. 'Your analysis of why you've been sent to see me is certainly interesting, I'll grant you.' He closed his note book, leant forward and rested his chin on his clasped hands. 'You've spoken about your ambivalence about your marriage, the guilt and loss you feel about your son's way of life, the terrible trauma you endured at the hands of Roger, and…' he smiled at this point, 'your thoughts about the inadequacies of our post-industrial economy. I'd like to pose a question, Sian…' He fixed me with a steady stare, his smile gone. 'You said we'd do better to dismantle the wall and build something else in its place. What would you build in its place? In other words, Sian, how, if you were able, how would you redesign your life?'

Chapter Thirty-two

'You are Sian, yes? My name is Clotilde.'

I'd braced myself for an altercation with Mr Hostile but now, standing at the door of the Delariche house, I falter. I'm not surprised the woman knows my name, her husband will certainly have told her about my complaint. But I hadn't anticipated a friendly welcome and the woman's cordiality is unnerving. The fight has left me. Maybe this Clotilde can at last sort out the problem of the barking dog.

As on my last visit, it is dark inside and I can't fully make out Madame Delariche's features, partially obscured by tendrils of thick black hair. In spite of the lateness of the morning she is oddly attired in what looks like a long, old fashioned night-dress, its cuffs gathered in froths of lace at the wrists, two ribboned neck ties hanging loose over her breasts. I take all this in, unable to help recalling how I'd last seen her, fleetingly but definitely naked at an upstairs window. I open my mouth to speak but Clotilde, seeming not at all surprised to find me on her doorstep, speaks first.

'Please, come in. I was about to pour us an apéritif.'

How odd. Still, I follow Clotilde into the house and we make our way along a narrow hallway into a big dark kitchen where I stand blinking as my eyes adjust. In spite of the warmth of the day, a wood-burning stove is crackling away, throwing strange shadows around the curtained room and, glancing around, I see that it is bigger than my own kitchen and even more cluttered. I take in the collection of ill-matched cupboards and drawers which occupy every available space, some of them open-shelved, bearing stacks of china, jugs, cooking implements of every kind, while ancient fire-blackened saucepans hang from a wooden laundry dryer. Clotilde motions towards a wooden chair and I take a seat at the huge farmhouse table. A heap of men's boots by the door call to mind the surly man of the house and I hope we're not expecting him any time soon.

The woman picks two glasses from a shelf and rinses them at a chipped enamel sink before turning to a cupboard and taking out a bottle containing dark-coloured liquid. I follow her movements, her robe—flimsy in the firelight—shifting and flowing over her curves. How old is she? Thirty perhaps? It's impossible to say. The warmth, shadowy darkness and cosy muddle in which this strange woman moves have an oddly somnambulant effect on me, even though the empty dog basket by the wood-burning stove reminds me of why I am here. I wonder why the woman has lit a fire on a summer day. Clotilde follows my gaze.

'I like flames,' she says.

She pours a good measure of the liqueur into each of the glasses, hands one to me and, smiling, takes a seat at the table. She raises her glass to her lips, all the while maintaining silent eye-contact. I take a quick little nip from my own glass and recoil.

'Wow, this is strong. What is it?'

'It's home-made,' Clotilde replies. 'From herbs and roots.'

I take another sip and then another, each burning my throat a little less than the last, my arms and legs growing heavy and warm. I suppose I ought to get to the point but, looking at Clotilde, I hesitate. The front of her robe is half open, revealing a hint of soft breasts beneath. Clotilde seems unconcerned and still says nothing. She gazes at me, coiling a long tendril of black hair around her fingers. The fire is crackling in the stove and we sip in silence. Finally Clotilde speaks.

'Would you like to see my atelier?'

Atelier? Surprised, I nod.

'Bring your drink,' Clotilde says, ignoring my weak attempt at protest as she pours me another. Having drained what remained in her own glass she sets it down on the table, stands and walks towards a little wooden door in the corner of the kitchen. On opening it, diffuse rays streak across the darkness, highlighting the dust motes. Clotilde, her feet bare, soles black from padding around the tiled floor, stands waiting for me before leading the way up a winding wooden staircase. My head is swimming from the strong liqueur and the sudden light and I follow, acutely aware of the thinness of the woman's robe.

At the top of the stairs a narrow opening gives onto a large space that must run the length of the house. Five roof-windows, two on either side of the slanted ceiling and one in the gable end, allow sunlight to slant in and I stand blinking as my eyes adjust, the dust causing me to sneeze three times in rapid succession. When I open my eyes, I see that I am standing in the middle of a cluttered sculptor's studio. Piles of white stone in all shapes and sizes lie on the floor in jumbled heaps and along one end of the long room, nestled under the rafters which reach almost to the floor, a wooden trestle table holds all manner of tools and implements—points, chisels, hammers, rasps, clamps. Hooks attached to the opposite gable wall hold even more tools and pencil sketches of flowers, leaves, fruits, figures and faces have been tacked to the purlins. One has fallen to the floor and I bend to pick it up—a nude female kneeling, her hands covering her head.

Placing the drawing on a chair, I turn to Clotilde, open my mouth to speak but falter when I see that a shaft of sunlight streaking through one of the windows has rendered the woman's robe completely transparent, the darkness of her nipples and her pubis plain to see. I look away quickly.

'Please...' Clotilde says, holding out a hand to the room.

A more sturdy trestle table holds small sculptures, some on little plinths, some free-standing, many barely bigger than a fist. I walk across the dusty floorboards to look at them, absently taking little sips of my liqueur as I go. Each has been intricately carved with natural motifs; leaves, berries, flowers and birds intertwining with ragged delicacy. I pick one up and turn the cold stone over in my hand before laying it back down. On bigger rocks, strange faces neither male nor female, are surrounded by crowns of flowers and leaves, their expressions oddly alert yet distant, faces in which half-closed lips hint at a smile, blind eyes seem both to see and not to see... The pieces are rough, allegorical, figurative rather than precise, and seen together like this on the long, dusty table, create a disturbing effect.

A low plinth by the gable window is home to what I guess must be Clotilde's current work in progress. Glancing at the woman who stands watching me, I walk over to where the shape—about the height of a person—is draped over with a stained white dust-cloth. I look out of the window and across the meadow—there is a clear view of the bench I sit on each evening, and I imagine myself as Clotilde must see me, a solitary figure in an empty field. Bringing my gaze back to the atelier I reach out my hand and run it over the cloth, the stone of the sculpture hard beneath.

Something makes me look up. Clotilde is walking towards me from the far end of the studio. She has picked up one of the tools that was lying on a trestle, a metal hammer with points at its heads. My hand still resting on the covered sculpture I take a long sip of the strange drink and this time I don't turn away, but watch Clotilde, her body fully visible through her robe as she moves. Coming to stand so close that I can smell her woman's scent, she looks directly into my eyes.

'Would you like to see what's underneath?'

...it falls in a heap of white cotton to the floor, dust rising up around us, a shaft of sunlight falling across cold, hard flesh... the woman of stone; unveiled.

PART TWO

UNDRESSING

Chapter Thirty-three

My dreams that night recreated over and again all that happened in the light-filled studio with the strange woman surrounded by stone sculptures and, in the heat of the night, I sweated and turned, aware through my open window of the scent of dew-covered earth and the ethereal sounds of night-birds calling…

The statue is exquisitely carved but unfinished, the eyes still blank, mouth unformed, the body clearly female, but not yet fully distinct from the great block of limestone it is being hewn from.

'…let me…'

Clotilde moves closer. I feel the heat from her body as she takes my hand and lays it on the face of the statue, the coolness of the stone contrasting with Clotilde's warmth. She moves my hand across one check then the other, over the eyes, the lips, down the neck… shoulders… breasts… stomach… thighs…

I close my eyes…

'This transcendent vision of life which rises slowly from the heavy sleep of stone…'

I flick open my eyes… Clotilde is looking straight at me… straight into me.

'I'm sorry…?'

'…I watch …touch… open a place for the soul … here, transcribed with metal… what lies within, beyond stone…'

The statue, its sagging breasts, thick waist, powerful thighs, bones, muscles, sinew, skin—seem, as I stare, to quiver with emerging life… Clotilde is still holding my hand and with the other she indicates the window, the field, the bench.

'We must discard the superfluous… reveal what is unseen, what is essential—the messy, flawed, living flesh at the core of the stone… expose it, expose it all—the passion, the loves, the heights of ecstasy. And the depths of suffering…'

She drops my hand, raises the metal hammer.

'A *boucharde*—we use it to wear down the stone…'

With a metallic *chink* she strikes the tool against the heart of the statue. Fragments of broken stone fall to my feet ...

'It was me who made you come.'

A different sound invades the moment. We turn. A panting, like someone climbing, is coming from the stairs. A lurch of inexplicable panic pitches in my stomach at the thought of being found here with Clotilde by Monsieur Delariche. But it isn't his gruff face that appears at the opening. It is a skinny Labrador, breathless and wheezing at the entrance to the atelier. The dog looks at Clotilde and gives two half-hearted woofs before shuffling across the room to plomp herself down on a nest of grubby cushions in the corner. Turning back to me, Clotilde puts down the boucharde and picks up a small stone tablet from the table.

'For you,' she says holding out the piece.

I take the sculpture and turn it around. It is slightly bigger than my palm and cut into one side is a woman's face, roughly hewn and like the statue, not fully realised. The eyes are partly closed, creating the effect that the face is turning to stone—or that the stone is coming to life. I nod my thanks.

Without saying more, the woman takes my empty glass, sets it down and leads the way back across the room and down the wooden stairs. I follow, glancing back at the statue silhouetted by the sun at the window. The dog gives a wide yawn and I realise how tired I feel. Downstairs the fire in the stove has burned low and the darkness of the kitchen contrasts starkly with the sunlight in the atelier. I grope along behind Clotilde to the front door. Once open, the light floods in, making me feel nauseous and unable to focus.

'Well,' I falter, grabbing the door-post, '...it was lovely to meet you. Thank you for the drink. And for the sculpture.'

But Clotilde is already retreating inside, a white blur topped by the darkness of her hair.

'I'll do something about the barking,' she says as she fades into the darkness, swinging the front door shut behind her.

It was only when I woke hot and restless the following morning, my heart pounding, my breath coming in shallow gasps, that I realised I had never mentioned the dog.

Chapter Thirty-four

'I made you come,' she'd said. I could no more fathom this Clotilde than I could the silent white clouds that moved over the field. As I went about my days, my thoughts returned constantly to her and to our strange meeting. I placed the little stone sculpture on my dressing table, picking it up from time to time, looking at the face in the stone, trying to recall all the strange things she'd said. But it was just a jumble of words... *expose, passion, loves, ecstasy, suffering, reveal...*

I hadn't returned to the Delariche cottage—not straight away in any case. *Why not?* The ghost said. *You know you want to. Shut up,* I told him. *It's because I have no wish to encounter Monsieur Hostile.* If he'd had an eyebrow, the ghost would have raised it.

And although I sat in the field each evening sipping a cup of coffee, since I'd finished my stock of wine, I'd caught no more than the occasional glimpse of Clotilde at her window, presumably chipping away at her statue. She was as good as her word though. The dog was quieter now.

It was Saturday and at the sound of the bread van, I flung the cloth I'd been using to clean behind the washing machine into the bucket, dried my hands and hurried outside, grabbing a cardigan from the back of a chair as I passed. The season was on the turn, the vines were changing from fresh green to yellow and the weather, although still mild, was getting blustery. I pulled on the cardigan and pushed open the big metal gates which creaked like an injured cat as they swung open. Out in the lane Madame Volt was climbing down from her van as Monsieur Ripaille stooped to pull at some weeds. Madame Clairjo and Monsieur Delariche were nowhere to be seen. Neither was Clotilde.

'*Bonjour* Madame Evans.'

The baker looked me up and down as I arrived at the van, no doubt judging me for the state of my jeans—I supposed they could do with a wash. I resisted the urge to reciprocate since she had my shopping, which she proceeded to haul out of the van.

'It's all here, everything accounted for. Almost. Double cream is not something you'll get round these parts so I got *crème fraîche*. Expect it's all the same.'

She raised an eyebrow at the case of wine as I took it from her and put it down next to the bulging bags.

'Here's the receipt.' She proffered me a long till-roll. 'That wine wasn't cheap, took it over what you gave me with my cut, so I made up the rest. You owe me another four Euros twenty-seven. Expect you'll want the same next Saturday?'

'*Merci Madame*, I'll certainly need the fresh stuff,' I said, wondering, as I reached into my jeans pocket for the money whether she thought I'd drink all that wine in a week.

'Do mine on the internet, I do,' said Monsieur Ripaille, a look of pride on his wizened old face.

Madame Volt smiled and handed him a warm baguette which she'd wrapped in paper. He took it from her with a nod and nibbled the end as he spoke.

'Where's Clairjo, then?'

'Got a nasty cold, she has. Going in after with her medicine. Picked it up from the pharmacy first thing. Soon be on her feet again.'

'And the Delariches?'

The baker turned to me with narrowed eyes.

'Away,' she said bluntly. 'Baguette?'

'I'll take two,' I replied. 'Which one is Madame Clairjo's house?'

Volt nodded towards the furthest cottage in the lane.

'Thanks,' I said handing over my new shopping list and the money for the bread and groceries. Madame Volt shoved my list into her satchel without a glance and painstakingly counted out the change into my waiting hand.

'Good day to you both.'

I nodded at the two locals and, struggling to manage the shopping bags and the case of wine, left them standing by the van, no doubt comparing notes about the alcoholic foreigner. No matter. I'd decided to go on a mercy mission to the ailing Madame Clairjo. She'd told me to someday return the favour of the baguette she'd brought me and, as well as doing that with a good bowl of soup for her lunch, I'd be able to find out about Clotilde.

Back in the cottage, I unpacked my shopping, setting it all out on the kitchen table. All that lovely fresh food—carrots, avocados, courgettes, aubergines, garlic, leeks, apples, pears—had me itching to start cooking, and I felt irrationally happy at the sight so many provisions. Once I'd found homes for all the fruit, vegetables, boxes, packets and bottles, I set about making a big pan of vegetable soup, dipping into my new store of potatoes, carrots, onions and celery in the happy knowledge that it would all be replenished next Saturday. Volt might be a prickly old bird but I needed to stay on the right side of her. I threw a handful of red lentils into the soup for good measure, feeling every bit the considerate country neighbour, despite the ghost's reminder of my ulterior motive.

The soup didn't take long to cook and forty minutes after I began, I poured half of it into a wide-mouthed thermos flask I found in one of the cupboards, grabbed one of the baguettes and set off to Madame Clairjo's.

Hers was a low, stone cottage, probably of the same era as the Duchamp house, but modernised with white UPVC windows and door, framed by a neat wooden porch over which purple lilacs were hanging. The big grey cat appeared from the hedge opposite and, purring loudly, proceeded to wind its tubby body around my legs. I bent to give its head a scratch before pressing the button of the modern call-bell, hearing it ring inside the house. Nothing. The cat caught sight of something in the hedge and darted off to investigate. I pressed the bell again. Still no answer. God, I thought, thinking back to Old-Mrs-Next-Door in Cardiff, I hope the old bird hasn't snuffed it. Just as I was about to ring a third time, I heard Madame Clairjo's grumbly voice coming from the other side of the door:

'Alright, alright, I'm coming!'

She opened the door slowly and peered round it, seeming not to recognise me.

'Yes?' she barked.

'It's Sian Evans,' I said in a voice loud enough for her to hear. 'From along the lane. The baker told me you were unwell so I've brought you some soup.'

'No need to shout, I'm sick, not deaf...' As if to prove it, she broke off into a hacking cough and clutched at the door frame, pulling her arm roughly away when I reached out to steady her. 'Well, I suppose you'd better come in,' she said once she'd regained her composure. 'Can't stand here on the doorstep all day.'

I followed the old woman into a brightly-lit hallway, thickly-carpeted, the walls filled with old photographs, many of them of children of varying ages. She led me into a small salon, where a television was blaring in one corner and, through a wide serving hatch, I could see a modern, fitted kitchen. The smell of cough syrup permeated the air.

'Sit down, sit down,' she said, flicking off the TV with a remote control and pointing at a plaid armchair. 'I'll put some coffee on.'

'Oh no,' I replied, 'please, let me. I'm sure I'll find my way around.'

Madame Clairjo broke into another coughing fit and seemed glad to sink with some difficulty into her chair. She pulled a woollen blanket around her shoulders, although a modern storage-heater beneath the window had the room heated to oven temperature. I went into the kitchen and placed the thermos on the worktop as the old woman blew her nose effusively. *Christ, I hope she doesn't infect me.*

'The soup is ready to eat,' I said through the hatch. 'Would you like some now, or have you eaten already?'

Madame Clairjo shook her head.

'Not had anything since yesterday with this damned cold,' she said. 'I'll try a bit.'

I opened a few cupboards and drawers, located a dish, a spoon and a tray and poured out a bowl of soup. One of Madame Volt's baguettes was on the counter so I put the one I'd brought with me into the freezer. Having placed a hunk of bread and the bowl of soup on the tray I took it through to Madame Clairjo and placed it on her lap.

'Here,' I said. 'Be careful, it's hot.'

I went back to the kitchen and, as the old woman began to eat in big, slurping spoonfuls, filled the kettle.

'Will you have coffee after your soup?' I asked.

'Yes please,' she replied with a grateful nod of her head.

Unexpectedly content at being able to render this small service to a neighbour—*see, ghost!*—I made myself a cup of coffee and returned to the lounge, sitting down in the free armchair.

'Damn nuisance, this cold,' Madame Clairjo grumbled, wiping her nose with a tissue.

I nodded. 'No family nearby?' I glanced at the photographs crowding the mantelpiece and the sideboard.

'Not near enough,' the old woman answered.

I looked around the tidy room.

'Lovely place you've got—you keep it nice.' *Touché*, I thought, thinking back to when she'd said the same thing to me.

Clairjo grunted and dipped a piece of baguette into her soup. I'd imagined a cottage not unlike my own, but this one had been modernised—rather tastefully as it happened—the carpet, furnishings and cushions in shades of cream, taupe and brown. The pale wood dresser and shelves were crowded with nicknacks and photographs and I got up to take a look.

'Do you mind?' I asked, indicating the pictures. Madame Clairjo nodded her assent and, as she continued with her soup, I scanned the pictures of staid-looking brides, severe grooms, laughing children and variously-coloured cats. I picked up an old photo in a pretty silver frame of a young couple in a rowing boat. The man had one arm around the woman and they held an oar each. Both looked happy, smiling widely into the camera.

'Monsieur Chiverny and me,' Madame Clairjo said before I could ask. 'Our honeymoon. Lake Como.'

'Monsieur Chiverny...?' What an odd way of referring to your husband, I thought. And why the different name?

'Dead now,' Madame Clairjo said. 'Over ten years.'

'Oh, I'm sorry,' I replied, replacing the picture and coming to sit down once more. 'You don't share his name?'

'Clairjo I was and Clairjo I am!' the old woman declared. 'Don't see why a woman should change her name for marriage.'

A fair point. I peered at the old bird with renewed interest.

'That's an unusual decision,' I replied.

Madame Clairjo simply grunted. Her soup bowl was still half full but her slurps were slowing down and I decided that I'd better get onto the real reason I was here before the old girl got too tired.

'I met Clotilde the other day...'

Before I could finish my sentence she broke out into another of her hacking coughs and waved me away as I went to steady the tray. I waited a moment for her to compose herself before repeating myself.

'Madame Delariche—I met her the other day. We had an apéritif together.'

'You did what?' The woman scowled at me.

I hesitated, not sure whether Clairjo was outraged by the apéritif or Clotilde.

'...she seems nice... Do you want me to let your cat in, he doesn't sound very happy out there?'

The grey moggy had jumped onto the windowsill and set up a yowling that was impossible to ignore. Clairjo shook her head.

'That's Fripouille. Only get under my feet he will, he can come in later.'

'So anyway, I met Madame Delariche...'

'What are you saying, girl? You met Natalie?'

As I suspected, deaf as a post.

'No, Clotilde,' I said raising my voice. 'I met Clotilde.'

'Don't shout at me, girl. Natalie was Delariches' wife. Ran off to the Île de Ré with some newspaper man years ago, hasn't been back since.'

I stared in confusion as the old woman continued to spoon up the soup.

'Oh, well Clotilde is his daughter then perhaps?' I probed. 'She's a sculptor, I understand.'

'A sculptor?' Madame Clairjo barked. 'Delariche's daughter is no sculptor, lives in Paris she does with her husband. Big shot architects both of them. Never comes here. Here take this.' She nodded her thanks for the soup and thrust the tray at me.

'Well, she must be his partner then—his girlfriend...'

I took the tray as I spoke and went through to the kitchen, rinsing the bowl and spoon under the tap and leaving them to dry on the drainer. Madame Clairjo once more started up a hacking cough and I hurried back into the lounge.

'Hand me my medicine will you,' she said between gasps. She wagged a knobbly finger at the sideboard. 'Supposed to take it after eating, I am.'

I handed Madame Clairjo her cough syrup, which she opened and drank straight from the bottle in two gulps.

'Disgusting stuff,' she muttered, setting the bottle down on a side table. She eyed me with a sly look. A clock on the far wall started up a shirring sound and began to chime three.

'Delariche has been alone for years,' Clairjo said in a voice that indicated the conversation was over. 'Ask Madame Volt. She's had her eyes on him ever since the divorce.'

I peered at the old woman lying back in her armchair, her eyes drooping.

'Well,' I murmured before getting up and slipping out of the front door, 'there's certainly *someone* in the Delariche house.'

Chapter Thirty-five

Told her I did, Clairjo I was and Clairjo I am! Didn't seem to bother her.

I'll tell you something else for free. Sian Evans didn't leave her husband because he wasn't perfect. I'll lay claim he was about as perfect as an imperfect man could be. Nor did she leave him because they grew apart. That's the story the foreigner will tell anyone who asks, I don't wonder. But mark me, the truth is deeper.

My damn cold lingered for a week and the girl brought food each day before my Marie arrived with the grandsons at the weekend. Turns out she can cook. Never stayed long, but we got to talking after a fashion. She's a canny one and it's not just that she doesn't want people to know her business. She doesn't want people to know *her*. Like stone she is. You don't get to see what's on the inside.

'So why did you move here then?' I asked her one afternoon. She'd just washed up after we'd eaten her broccoli quiche and was making coffee in the kitchen.

'What's that?' she called. Like she couldn't hear me!

'Why'd you come here?' I repeated as she brought the tray.

She peered at me, weighing up how much to reveal no doubt, I've got the measure of her.

'To bring you a broccoli quiche,' she shot at me. Thinks she's funny, she does. I raised my eyebrows at her.

'I wanted a change,' she said, pouring the coffee.

'Change from what?'

I took my cup and we both took a sip. Looked as though I'd get nothing from her but she suddenly looked at me with an expression on her face I couldn't place.

'Well, I'm divorced, my son lives abroad and I didn't much like my job.' It was the most she'd revealed since she arrived.

'Fair enough,' I said. 'But you could have got a new job.'

She nodded and picked up her cup. 'I felt like I needed a change,' she said. 'You know—a completely fresh start.'

Ah, now we're getting somewhere.

'Why'd you get divorced, husband didn't treat you well?'

She didn't answer at first, just stared into her coffee. Gave a strange little sigh before she answered.

'He's a good man and he was a good husband,' she said quietly. 'It was me not him. We…we grew apart.'

'Someone else was there?'

She didn't reply and I didn't push her.

I was on my feet by the weekend and on Monday I was fit enough to make my way outside at the sound of the tooting horn. Not the baker—it was Monday—but Jean-Luc and Jean-Paul, the charcuterie men. I'd told Sian to listen out and she was there already, standing by as Jean-Luc let down the side of the van to reveal a counter full of sliced meats, saucissons and patés. Monsieur Ripaille appeared at his gate and hurried along the lane. The two Jeans don't buy his story about being frail, they park outside my place, I'm happy to say. I nodded at Sian and received a kiss on the cheeks from each of the Jeans.

'*Ça va,* Jean-Luc? *Ça va,* Jean-Paul? Good holiday was it?'

'*Ça va,* Madame. Tip-top *merci,* a veritable gastronomic delight,' replied Jean-Paul as Jean-Luc busied himself arranging the saucissons. Love the way he speaks, I do. 'Yes indeed a real foody *vacance.* And the wine…well!' He kissed his fingers and flung them into the air.

'You enjoy it, Jean-Luc?'

'Reckon I did. Here, try this, we bought it while we were away.'

Jean-Luc handed a slice of cured ham to me and one to Sian and we popped them into our mouths and chewed.

'One for you, Monsieur,' Jean-Luc said as the old man arrived, looking anxious that he might miss out.

'Delicious,' I said. 'I'll take six. Got a little party coming up.'

'Your twenty-first, is it?' Jean-Pau winked. I rolled my eyes at him.

Ripaille gave his order of sausage and ham as Sian surveyed the counter. She asked where *'the Delariche's'* were and at her question Jean-Luc and I gave each other a knowing look. As she was pulling her money out of her pocket—don't know why the girl doesn't use a purse—Jean-Paul draped his arm around Jean-Luc's shoulder. I watched to see how the girl would react. She noticed alright, but didn't twitch an inch.

Chapter Thirty-six

The place certainly had its surprises. Not only was one of the neighbours keeping a naked sculptress in his attic, but the charcuterie men were obviously gay. No one seemed to mind. And Madame Clairjo hadn't baulked one bit at the thought of my marriage ending because of an affair. It was a relief to learn that these villagers were not the narrow curmudgeons of my imagination. Even so, I'd stopped short of confiding in Madame Clairjo the real reason I'd ended my marriage. Let her think it was an affair. She'd got enough out of me and I'd got no more out of her about Clotilde.

It seemed that once more Monsieur Delariche was away. Had Clotilde gone with him, or was she keeping to herself in the house? At the charcuterie van, once we'd discussed the men's holiday the talk had been of a man in Pointeusse who'd been sent to prison for poisoning his wife with plant fertiliser. 'Shocking,' Madame Clairjo said, and everyone agreed. No one mentioned Monsieur Delariche or Clotilde.

Clotilde. Later that day, swatting away bees in the jungle that passed as a garden, I pondered, while eating a slice of *jambon*, her deepening mystery and felt surprised but relieved that Monsieur Delariche's business wasn't the talk of the neighbours. It seemed that it was, after all, perfectly possible to lead a private life in this close-knit little community.

A few days later I was startled as I hauled a batch of laundry downstairs to hear the rusty jingle of the door-bell. My first thought was of Clotilde and I dumped the pile of bedding I'd been carrying onto the corridor floor and hurried down the stairs and across the garden. When I opened the gates, I wasn't expecting to see Monsieur Ripaille standing there, eyes screwed up in his leathery face, twisting his cap in his hands.

'Thought you might need your hedges cutting,' he said without preamble.

I smiled at him.

'Why don't you come in for some coffee,' I said. 'I've just made some biscuits.'

I had indeed baked that morning—shortbread fingers—
and I didn't mind sharing them with Monsieur Ripaille, who
nodded his head, replaced his hat and followed me, kicking his
way through the leaves that had begun to fall from the cherry
tree. The look of horror on his face told me the state of my
garden distressed him deeply.

'We can sit out here if you like,' I said, indicating two
wooden chairs and the rickety table. 'Unless you prefer to go
indoors?'

'Here'll be fine, I like the end of summer, I do.' the old
man replied, lowering himself into a chair.

I went into the kitchen and when I came back out some
minutes later, carrying a tray laden with coffee, mugs and a big
plate of shortbread, Monsieur Ripaille was examining a
straggly tree by the boundary wall.

'Wants pruning, this lot,' he said, jabbing a thick thumb at
the tangled bushes. 'Should've been done last winter.'

I poured the coffee and waited for him to make his way
back to the table and take his seat.

'Used to do the garden for the Duchamps,' he said, taking
a biscuit without being asked. 'Can do it for you if you like.
And your hedges. Need to keep on top of 'em, you do.'

I poured the coffee and handed him a mug, which he took
along with a second biscuit, eating it, like the first, in one bite.
Not a man for small talk, I thought. Well, so much the better.
I suddenly had a thought.

'Do you know Monsieur Delariche?' I asked. Stupid
question, of course he knew him. Ripaille frowned.

'I've got all the tools,' he said. 'Do a tidier job than
Delariche.'

'Oh, it isn't that,' I said, concealing a smile. 'I'm just
curious about the woman who lives with him, that's all.'

Ripaille grunted.

'Clotilde. Have you met her?'

'Wife left 'im, she did.'

'I know but there's someone else there now. A sculptor.'

Ripaille took off his hat and scratched his head. 'Knew a
sculptor once. Lived over yonder in Villiers...'

At that moment, Fripouille jumped up onto the garden wall, startling us both.

'Madame Clairjo's cat that,' Monsieur Ripaille said. 'Good mouser, he is.'

Was the sculptor he had known, Clotilde?

'You knew her you say?'

'Who?' Ripaille tutted at a handful of bindweed that was consuming the table legs and bent down to yank at it.

'The sculptor? You say you knew her?'

'Murder this stuff. Strangles everything.'

It was clear I wasn't going to learn anything about the mysterious Clotilde from the old boy. He finished his coffee and, after he'd taken another biscuit from the plate, still muttering about the weeds, I began clearing the things.

'Do your hedges then shall I?' he said, replacing his hat. 'I don't charge much.'

'The thing is,' I replied, 'this isn't actually my house. And I'm on a tight budget. I can ask my Aunt and Uncle if you like? It's their cottage, you see.'

I couldn't see Constance and Jacques agreeing to pay for gardening, but I had to tell the old man something. He was shaking his head.

'Need to keep on top of it, you do,' he grumbled.

I had to admit he was right. We both looked around at the great tangle of garden plants gone wild, straggly bushes and savage weeds, far worse now than when I'd arrived since the flowers of summer had turned to dying stalks and dropping seed-pods. My attempts to tame it had been futile since I didn't have the tools. I held the plate out to Monsieur Ripaille and as he took yet another biscuit the ghost whispered something in my ear. I looked up and smiled.

Ghost, that may be the most useful thing you've said all summer!

'What's that?' The old man jutted out his chin.

'Nothing,' I said. 'I've had an idea. What about if I cook for you in return for doing the garden?

He shoved back his hat and peered at me.

'I mean, I don't have any money to pay you but I'm not a bad cook. If you like, I can make you biscuits, cakes, a good lunch every day—I don't mean forever, it would just be while you're doing the work.'

I left him to consider the offer while I took the tray inside. I wasn't exactly keen on cooking for Monsieur Ripaille, but I'd been thinking a lot recently about how I was going to get the garden in order. *And after all*, the ghost, said, *he isn't exactly a talker*. I returned with the rest of the biscuits in a tin, hoping he'd accept.

'Reckon it'll take a week or so,' the old man said, standing. 'Could work till three most days.'

I smiled and nodded at him.

'Perfect,' I said. 'Here, take these biscuits home with you.'

He took the tin. 'Clairjo says you make a tasty leek tart.'

'Tart for lunch then, tomorrow?'

'I'll start on the hedges first thing.'

And after sealing the deal with a shake of my hand, the old man ambled off at a surprisingly agile trot.

Chapter Thirty-seven

The day Monsieur Ripaille arrived to begin work on the garden dawned with fresh autumn brightness and I got up early to make a start on the baking before he arrived. By the time the rusty old bell clanged at the end of its chain, I'd just popped a sponge cake into the oven. I hurried outside, still covered in flour to let him in.

'*Bonjour* Monsieur,' I said, wiping my hands on the tea-towel I'd flung over my shoulder, before shaking his hand. 'I'm not sure I can match Madame Volt's pastries, but we'll have cake with our morning coffee.'

Monsieur Ripaille, a huge calico bag over one shoulder, picked up the hedge-trimmer he'd leant against the wall.

'A coffee before you start?' I asked.

'Rather get on,' he answered.

Feeling relieved that I wouldn't have to entertain him while he worked, I headed into the kitchen and made a start on the tart. I set about chopping leeks, onions, tomatoes and garlic, as outside the trimmer started up a raucous buzzing and leaves and branches cracked and split, falling into untidy piles. From time to time I glanced out through the kitchen door, standing open in the warm morning sunshine, at Monsieur Ripaille's solid bulk as he wielded the tool with practiced hands, heaving the accumulated debris into a growing heap in a corner by the far wall. Over the course of the morning, the garden began to reveal some semblance of order and I could see that in their day, Aunt and Uncle Duchamp must have cared for it. I thought about planting some kitchen herbs.

It felt oddly companionable going about my chores as Monsieur Ripaille went about his and by 11 o clock the tart was baking in the oven and the newly neat hedges were a fraction of their former straggly selves. Monsieur Ripaille and I stood together surveying his work, him taking off his hat and wiping his sweating brow with it.

'Make a start by the field wall next,' he said.

I nodded. 'Coffee?'

He nodded in turn and sat down at the garden table, freshly relieved of the bindweed around its legs. I returned with a tray of coffee and two large slices of sponge cake.

'Hope this won't spoil lunch,' I said. 'But you've earned it.'

We drank our coffee in silence, Monsieur Ripaille nodding his appreciation of the cake, crumbs falling onto his threadbare shirt. After our elevenses, we made a tour of the garden together, Monsieur Ripaille shaking a bush here, pulling at a clump of roots there.

'Used to be a nice garden this,' he said.

'It will be again,' I replied.

I pushed open the gate in the rear wall and we went through to the field where tall grass, gangly wildflowers and mistletoe-infested trees had Monsieur Ripaille tutting and grumbling. I rather liked the wildness. I told him so and the old man peered at me as though I'd said I liked eating bark.

'Did you hear that?'

A glance at Clotilde's window had already told me that she wasn't there but as Ripaille was examining a clump of trees, I heard it again. I stood still and surveyed the area. There is was again—a mewing sound. Suddenly, out from beneath a thicket darted a tiny grey kitten.

'What have we here?' I said, bending low to move slowly towards it.

The little cat clearly wasn't used to being around people and it shot off into the under-growth—not before I noticed that there was something wrong with one of its legs.

'Won't live,' Ripaille said.

'I'm sorry?'

'Won't live,' he repeated. 'Get a lot strays round here. Injured that one. Won't be able to hunt.'

'Perhaps I could feed it,' I answered.

The ghost, who had been supervising old man Ripaille's horticultural efforts was offended at the idea and wafted off in a huff. Ripaille grunted.

'Better off putting it out of its misery,' he said.

The kitten hadn't looked to me like it was living a life of misery. In fact, it looked suspiciously like Madame Clairjo's cat, making me wonder whether its parentage was only half stray. In any case, I hoped it didn't cross paths with the practical Monsieur. I crept closer to the kitten, who had reappeared by some late poppies, bright red in the afternoon sun, and was pawing at an upturned beetle. *'Puss, puss, puss,'* I hissed, in the international language of cats. Ripaille rolled his eyes and continued with his tree-bothering.

As I bent to stroke the little creature, something else caught my eye and I turned instinctively to the Delariche house. Clotilde! There she was at the top window and yes, she was naked, I could clearly see her breasts bare of her white robe. I went to wave but hesitated, not wanting to embarrass her or Monsieur Ripaille by drawing attention to her nudity. Monsieur Ripaille was, in any case, reaching to pull some mistletoe from a tree. Clotilde looked straight at me before turning and disappearing into her atelier. Had she smiled? I couldn't be certain but I thought so.

That afternoon, after Monsieur Ripaille and I had eaten the tart with a green salad with vinaigrette and hunks of Madame Volt's crusty baguette, I'd left him to get on with the gardening while I paid a visit to the Delariche house. The ghost raised his non-existent eyebrow. *There's no reason I shouldn't make a neighbourly call,* I told him, determining, if necessary, to brave the disagreeable man of the house. I wrapped up two slices of sponge cake in a clean napkin and took them with me.

'I'll be back in an hour or so,' I told Monsieur Ripaille over the noise of his hedge-trimmer.

I had no pretext for visiting Clotilde and, as I walked around the boundary wall and into their lane, my heart beating unaccountably fast in my chest, I wondered what to say. I decided, giving the chain of their bell a yank, that I'd simply invite her over for coffee. I needn't have worried. No one answered. I tried again, pulling harder on the chain, hearing it clang somewhere inside the house. *That's odd. I know she's home.* Perhaps, I reasoned, she can't hear the bell from her atelier. Feeling deflated I trudged back home with the cake.

'Away he is,' Monsieur Ripaille said, once I appeared back in my own garden. 'In Paris half the time.'

'Clotilde is home.' I answered. 'I went to visit her.'

Ripaille ignored me and continued with his work.

Chapter Thirty-eight

I hadn't thought about my sessions with the Good Doctor for some time but that night, instead of sleeping, I'd tossed and turned and remained stubbornly—if involuntarily—awake. I was restless and my thoughts were like butterflies flitting from one flower to the next. *Christ not this again?* I'd got used to sleeping deeply and had assumed I was over my old insomnia. As I lay there staring at the ceiling, following the progress of a drowsy moth, one of the conversations I'd had with Doctor Adebowale came back to me.

'It doesn't matter how much sleep I've had,' I'd told him. 'That isn't really the issue. There are days when I've slept badly but I get through the day no problem. And there are other times when I've sleep well but a great wave of tiredness sweeps over me and I feel as though I just don't know what to do. I mean, I know what I *should* be doing. But it's like I get this kind of paralysis and I can barely move, let alone do anything useful. I end up just staring at my screen at work, feeling bad because I'm not being productive, trying to think up strategies—drink lots of black coffee, go for a walk at lunch-time. But it's odd—it isn't my body that's tired. It's not how much I've slept that's the point.'

It happened at home sometimes, I told him. Just the other week, I'd come back from the supermarket and before I'd even taken off my coat, I dumped the shopping in the kitchen and flopped onto the sofa. I'd sat there, staring at nothing, thinking about all the things I'd planned to do—take a gas-meter reading, renew my TV licence, hang out the washing… It wasn't that I was bored or fed-up with the mundanity of it. I loved pottering around at home and, on a good day, getting domestic stuff out of the way made me feel on top of things.

'It's bizarre when I can't bring myself to start,' I said. 'What is it with me that sometimes I just can't move?'

The Good Doctor was nodding. I looked at him swivelling in his chair, one manically-pressed trouser leg stuck in a Donald Duck sock. I bet he never experienced being paralysed like that. 'It's a choice, Sian,' he could reasonably have said.

'You could force yourself to move.' I knew that. It wasn't like there was anything physically wrong with me. Arwel would have said *'get up, dress up, show up.'* Bastards, both of them.

'Sian, I'd like you to describe your workspace for me,' the Good Doctor said.

Huh?

'Well, it's a call centre, as you know,' I answered, wondering whether he'd been listening to a word I'd said. 'Have you been there?'

'I have but that doesn't matter, I want you to describe it.'

Weird, but okay.

'Well, it's a big, open plan office with desks arranged in 'pods',' I began. 'There are three of us at each pod separated from each other by a kind of partition.'

'Go on…'

'There's not a lot else to say. There're about a hundred of us in the open plan, I suppose. I work in the European section, which mainly deals with clients from France, Belgium and Luxembourg. The rest deal with the UK. There's a lunch-room but I never go there. I usually take sandwiches with me and go for a walk if it's nice—I imagine the others think I'm unfriendly but that's fine by me. And there are small offices around the main open-plan for the managers. That's it really.'

I thought about In-Control Carol's cupboard, with its sad-looking spider-plant and pictures of her spawn.

'I want you to tell me what it feels like to work there. Try to describe this through the use of your senses.'

'My senses? Okay, well as it's a call-centre, we're on the phone all day so it's noisy. We wear headsets obviously, which are supposed to block out the sound of the others, but as soon as you take them off you hear the constant drone of people talking. I'm not sure what other senses I can use.'

'Tell me what you see, Sian.'

Seriously? Had the man never seen an open-plan before?

'Well, we're looking at screens all day. Calls come in pretty much constantly and the computer tells us which customer it is. We enter all the details of the issue and update the account. Other than that…well, let's see…there's strip-lighting on the ceiling, just standard office lighting. Some of the pods are by the windows but I'm down the other end so don't get to see out. And there are people everywhere of course, that goes without saying'

'How close to your colleagues are you?'

I knew he didn't mean emotionally.

'Pretty close. The pod desks are tiny, just room for the equipment. You can't see the others on your pod but you can hear them, talking, typing, moving around. And the other pods are pretty close too, so we hear people all around. I don't know what else I can say, it's just a standard call centre.'

'Okay, that's fine. Now, can you describe for me your ideal workspace?'

'For a call centre?'

'Not necessarily. The kind of place you'd love to work in. Let your imagination go, Sian.'

I'd never given it much thought having worked in offices pretty much my whole adult life. But okay, why not think about it now. The Good Doctor was peering at me in hopeful anticipation, although he didn't look like he was about to write down my every word. I launched in.

'Okay, well, somewhere quiet for a start—sometimes I'm so desperate for some peace that I nip off to the loo and just stand there for a while. Ideally, I'd prefer to work alone. I'm not what you'd call a team-player. Call centre work isn't teamwork but you're never alone. Peace and quiet is what I'd prefer. Not in an office.'

'Go on,' the Doctor nodded.

I nodded back, warming to the theme.

'Well, it must be nice to work outside. And to have a job where the phone isn't constantly going and you have to deal with people's problems all day. Don't get me wrong, I don't blame the clients, they just want their problems solved, after all. It's just that I go mad, sometimes, answering the same questions, dealing with the same issues all day every day. I don't know what job I could do that isn't like that. Gardener?'

The Good Doctor stopped swivelling and leaned forward in his chair, levelling at me an intense look. *Uh-oh.*

'Sian,' he said, 'do you know the difference between an introvert an extrovert?'

I peered back at him. Did he think I was stupid?

'Obviously,' I said, peevishly. 'Introverts like their own company and extroverts like socialising.' Was this his grand theory?

'It's more than that,' he said, leaning back in his chair. He had that look on his face that meant that he was about to impart one of his gems of wisdom. 'Being introverted or extroverted isn't simply a question of how much we like socialising,' he said. 'It's a matter of how we gain or lose our energy. Extroverts gain vitality from the noise, bustle and validation of social interaction. They need it in order to feel energised. With introverts, they spend energy when they are in groups or in a noisy environment or having to talk a lot. They gain energy and perspective when they are alone and quiet.'

Seriously? I thought back to last weekend at the supermarket. The shop had been ridiculously crowded, people jostling each other in the aisles, parents shouting at their screaming kids, pointless tannoy announcements every two minutes, couples arguing in the check-out queues... who could gain energy from that?

'What the research tells us is that introverted people don't do well in noisy, crowded places,' the Good Doctor continued. 'Sure, they can cope for a period of time, even enjoy it. But before long, they need silence and isolation to recharge. Would you say, Sian, that you are an introvert or an extrovert?'

'Clearly I'm an introvert.'

'And a final thought for today's session. Would you say that your work environment is the best kind for an introverted person?'

Chapter Thirty-nine

'You can help out a bit, if you like.'

Monsieur Ripaille was carefully laying out his gardening tools on a bench in the shed. The suggestion had become his refrain and I'd taken to working alongside him, collecting the weeds he dug up and the branches he clipped, raking the leaves, watching, asking the occasional question about this plant or that. 'Delphiniums are hungry buggers,' he'd say, or 'Wisteria will take over everything if you let it.' We got along well enough without the need to make small-talk and, seeing him straighten his back and wipe his brow on his hat or the dirty rag he pulled from his pocket, it seemed as though the old man and I both appreciated this. I baked each day, sometimes biscuits, sometimes cake, and we continued to share lunch together. The day after we'd discovered the injured kitten, he'd raised an eyebrow at the little dish of milk by the kitchen door but said nothing.

The ghost mostly made himself scarce while Monsieur Ripaille was working but the old man had been here for a week now and I suspected the ghost was getting jealous.

'Got a bit of business of my own to see to,' Ripaille said one day.

Regardless of the ghost's intentions, I guessed the old man needed a rest. In any case, he was back two days later, pruning and clipping with renewed vigour. We were often joined now —much to Monsieur Ripaille's disapproval—by the grey kitten who I'd named Pegleg on account of his useless front leg, and who was getting braver—and naughtier—by the day.

On the old man's final day he called me over to the far boundary wall where he'd been attacking a tangle of bindweed that had dared reassert itself.

'Got fruit trees here, you have. Apple. Look. And here's a pear.'

I peered at the gangly trees. He was right, tight little apples dotted the spindly branches of one, and stunted, pock-marked pears were dangling off the other.

'All but choked they were, by the ivy,' Ripaille said. 'Should have a chance now.'

He was matter-of-fact about this marvellous discovery, but I was thrilled.

'But this is wonderful,' I exclaimed. 'Think of all the pies and crumbles I'll be able to make. Not to mention jam.'

'Not with this crop. Need care, they do. Should be alright for next autumn if you tend 'em well.'

My disappointment at missing out on such a bounty was interrupted by Pegleg, who jumped at a fallen apple Monsieur Ripaille had kicked. The old man shook his head.

'Rod for you own back,' he said, frowning at the kitten.

'I haven't exactly adopted him,' I replied. 'He comes and goes as he likes. He's still wild.' Ripaille rolled his eyes.

That afternoon, having finished what remained of a mushroom quiche, Monsieur Ripaille put down his knife and fork and said:

'Reckon the garden's pretty much there. Only needs keeping on top of now.'

I nodded.

'You want to make a start on the field? Bigger job that. Got the tools, I have.'

I'd thought about that but had decided to leave the field alone for now. Despite Monsieur Ripaille's quiet demeanour I was looking forward to going back to my solitary days. In any case, I liked the field the way it was, untamed, with hidden places for wild things to make their homes.

'I think I'll leave it for now,' I said, offering him the last of the buttered potatoes.

Ripaille nodded his head, scraped what remained in the bowl onto his plate, and continued to eat in silence. I went inside to get what was left of the day's cake, bringing it out to him in a tin.

'You can take this home with you if you like. I can bake for myself another day.'

He nodded and took the tin. 'Well then,' he said, wiping his mouth with a dirty rag.

I smiled at him. He eyed me strangely as though he wanted to say something.

I raised my eyebrows.

'Wondering, I was, whether…' he trailed off.

Clearly flustered, he took off his hat and began to twist it between his fingers. *Effing* hell, I thought, he isn't going to ask me on a date is he? I felt myself flush a deep red. The old man's words came in a rush.

'You seen Monsieur Delariche, have you?'

Delariche? 'No, why?'

'Asking questions about you, he was. We all think… I mean, Clairjo said…'

What questions? Why would Delariche be asking about me? The only time I'd spoken to that surly oaf was to complain about his dog. Perhaps my prejudices about nosy country folk were right after all. *Rise above it*, said the ghost. I supposed I'd have to. Fripouille jumped down from a wall and made his slinky way across the garden. Pegleg, in defiance of his father, darted off into the field.

'I haven't seen Monsieur Delariche recently,' I said briskly, starting to clear the table. 'Nor Clotilde for that matter.'

Ripaille gave me a doubting look and bent to stroke the cat which was purring loudly and winding itself around the table legs. Pegleg stared wide-eyed from the back gate, crouched low, ready to run.

'I appreciate all your help, Monsieur,' I said in what I hoped was a polite but final tone.

Ripaille stood up and I walked with him up the path, which was now clearly defined and bordered by little lawns and freshly cleared flower-beds ready for the spring growth. Clairjo's cat followed us and jumped onto the newly bare wall, licking its paw nonchalantly as I yanked open the gates. The sound of rusting metal jarred the late afternoon calm.

'Wants oiling, does that.'

I smiled and gave each of Monsieur Ripaille's whiskery cheeks a kiss. He grinned widely, slung his calico bag over his shoulder and ambled off up the lane.

Chapter Forty

I slept badly again that night but finally managed to drop off in the early hours. I dreamt of Clotilde in her atelier. It was dark and she was calling to me from the window when suddenly Monsieur Delariche appeared by her side. *Who are you*, he was shouting, *who are you?* I couldn't work out whether he meant Clotilde or me. I awoke before dawn, sweating and unsettled.

Then the letter arrived. All the cottages were allocated a small square plastic box a few meters from Madame Clairjo's house and, every morning around ten, the postman stuffed them with our letters and flyers, as well as collecting any we wanted to send. Following a chatty missive from Aunt Constance about a week after I'd arrived, in which she'd asked whether all was fine *chez eux*, I hadn't received anything more exciting than circulars, publicity leaflets and a couple of bills. I'd asked Madame Volt if buying stamps was part of her shopping remit so that I could pay them. Begrudgingly, she'd obliged.

Today was different. On opening my little box I'd seen, lying on top of a pizza-delivery leaflet (interesting) and another advertising an agriculture festival (less so), a slim white envelope bearing a UK postmark. The handwriting was impossible to mistake. I hurried back to the house, tore open the letter and pulled out two neatly folded sheets and a teabag.

Dear Sian

I thought I'd put pen to paper. Since you don't answer your phone or your emails, I couldn't think of what else to do. How are you? I'm guessing all is fine since I haven't had any news. All is well enough here. Work's same as ever. Weather too.

The reason I'm writing is that there's something I want to say. It's not something I could tell you to your face—I don't want you to take this the wrong way but you were never the easiest of women to talk to. I expect you know that yourself. I've started this damn letter four times now and I can't get it right, so I'm just going to say it how it comes and hope you understand.

The thing is, I always thought I'd done right by you and Nate. I still think I did. And I thought we rubbed along well enough as marriages go. Don't worry, I'm not going to say all the things I said when we divorced. You know what I thought then and what I still think now.

What I want to say is that I know there was more to you leaving me than you let on. I've been thinking more and more about it these last months since you've been in France. I know you've never told me the full story. You denied it at the time but my thinking is still that it was an affair gone wrong. I don't know who and I don't want to know. It's okay, I'm not angry or even upset anymore—God knows I was at the time, but now—well, water under the bridge and all that.

Why am I bringing all this up again now? If you were here, I know that's what you'd ask. Sian, it's your life, you'll do as you please, you _are_ doing as you please—new life in France and all that. I didn't say it before you went and I should have—but I do wish you well. I thought at the time you'd soon be back, that it would be an extended holiday. It seems I was wrong. You're good at keeping things to yourself. You always have been. But I want to say this, Sian. It's my thinking that you're over there with a man—a new husband for all I know. I think that's why you went and why you haven't stayed in touch. And like when we divorced, I think it's something you feel you have to keep from me.

And now the point. I want you to know that your new relationship is not something you have to hide. Not from me and not from Nate. At the very least there will be times when we'll see each other—family occasions and the like. Maybe even Nate's wedding if he ever stays somewhere long enough to meet a girl. Plus, I'd like to think if you were over here visiting, that we could meet as friends like we used to, without you having to keep your life a secret.

So there it is. Never said so much in a bloody letter! There's one more reason for writing. I Skyped with Nate last week. He's talking about coming home in the New Year. Wanted to know if you'd come over too. Better than Skyping with him, eh? So I'm inviting you Sian. You and your new man.

Love Arwel.

PS Enjoy a nice cuppa—I don't suppose the tea is the same over there.

Chapter Forty-one

Oh Arwel. I read the letter three times and, I'll admit, I cried. He'd got it all so wrong—the reason I moved to France—and why I left him.

To a large extent I have the Good Doctor to thank for my decision to live in France. I hadn't told Arwel—I suppose I thought it was none of his business—but if nothing else Doctor Adebowale had provided the inspiration for me to hand in my notice at work.

That email to In-Control Carol was one of the most satisfying I've ever written.

Dear Jill,
I take time off work when I'm feeling soft. Thanks to the therapy you paid for, I've come to realise that being soft is simply a way to describe a need. When I feel hungry, I need food. When I'm tired, I need sleep. When I feel soft, I need to be alone. Simple. And what I want now is an extended period of softness. I won't be coming back.

'Sian, now that we've come to the end of our time together, I'd like us to consider what these sessions have achieved.'

Doctor Adebowale, minus his pad and pen, had a suspiciously cheerful look about him at our last session and I'd wondered whether he was pleased to be getting rid of me.

'We've discussed over the weeks a number of facets of your life and work. We've explored your relationships with those close to you, your attitudes towards authority, whether there is anything in your life that triggers a negative response from you that leads to an unsettled work-pattern.'

I'd nodded, thinking back to those early sessions where I'd tried and failed to shock the Good Doctor with tales of dead women and stalkers. I smiled, glad that he'd seen through all that.

'Is there anything in what we have discussed that resonates more strongly with you, Sian?'

I sat for a moment longer, still thinking. It was odd, given how much I fought against him, that I felt something akin to sadness now our Friday afternoon talks were coming to an end.

'Well,' I answered at last. 'It was good talking about Nate. I think I understand more about how I feel—both about him and about myself as a mother, if that doesn't sound too psycho-babble.'

The Good Doctor smiled. 'Not at all.'

'And it was interesting what you said about the needs of introverts. That introverted people get their energy from being alone. That they get drained when they spend a lot of time around others. I certainly relate to that.'

'Sian, I was asked to conduct these sessions with you because of your poor attendance record at your job,' he said, straightening himself in his seat. 'That has been the reason we've explored what we have. I am now required to write a report—which I'll share with you—for your employer, with recommendations for what they can do to help you address the situation. I am not obliged to share with your employer the details of our discussions. Only my recommendations.'

I nodded and sat forward in the armchair, intrigued by what the Good Doctor was about to say.

'Now,' he continued, 'having considered all aspects of our discussions, it is my opinion that the reason you take so much time off work is plainly and simply because you need the space. You need to be quiet and alone in order to recharge, to regain your strength and vitality. I'm willing to guess that there is a direct correlation between how much time you've spent with others and whether or not you take time off.'

He could have a point there.

'Now, here's what my report is going to recommend. Firstly, that you be moved from your current desk as far away from the centre of the open plan as possible, ideally to a corner so that you are able to create a sense of your own space. I'll also recommend that you are placed by a window so that you get fresh air and natural light. I'll endorse regular breaks outside the building and ask that your equipment is checked to ensure it effectively minimises as much ambient noise as possible.'

I nodded, breathing in slowly and rubbing my temples. *So this is all it amounts to?* All that soul searching, all that confiding, raking up past history—and his big idea to 'fix me' was to give me a corner desk and a window? Ah but there was more—it was clear from the way the Good Doctor was leaning forward and tapping his fingers together. I sat back in weary anticipation.

'Now Sian, none of that is going to solve the issue.'

Huh?

'The thing is, what I've learned about you is that even the best managed call centre is unlikely to be able to provide you with the kind of work environment in which you will thrive. My advice—and this won't go into my report—is that you need to rethink your career. Off the record—working in a busy, noisy office simply isn't for you. You'd do well to consider what you can do that will suit your strongly introverted nature—give you the quietness and solitude you need in order to feel well—whilst not isolating yourself to the point of unhealthiness.'

I stared at him. 'You're suggesting I quit my job?'

He levelled me an intense stare back. 'I'm not making any suggestions, Sian. I'm simply encouraging you to think about doing something with your life that will help you come to terms with the kind of adventurous life your son is leading.'

He bent down to pull up a Desperate Dan sock and I swear while he was down there he winked at me.

'Doctor Adebowale, I have one last question before we part ways.'

'Go on…'

'Who buys you those ridiculous socks?'

The Doctor laughed and hesitated for a fraction of a moment before answering.

'My husband,' he said.

I'd thought about all he'd said that night. Fair enough, Doctor Adebowale BSc, MD, OTR/L had done his job, he'd written his report and he'd made his recommendations. But as I thought about the weeks that we'd talked, the way he'd drawn me out gently, pushing me when I needed to be pushed, remaining silent when I didn't, I began to see that he'd done so much more than that. He'd been astute enough to see beneath the presenting issue and encouraged me not just with professional techniques but with human care, to begin to strip away the layers of my defences. Sharing my feelings about Nate had begun the process, I could see that now. And articulating what Roger had done had created a chink in my armour big enough to see that those skeletons in my closet might have overstayed their welcome. And yes, the Good Doctor's parting gem about Nate's adventurous life had certainly encouraged me to say what the *eff*, I'm moving to France.

There was something, though, that I'd never discussed with him, a part of my life, a part of *me* that I'd buried and kept buried. I'd been brave enough to face the other dark corners of my life. But one skeleton remained. Now, faced with Arwel's letter, was it time to admit the truth that lurked in the darkest corner of all?

Chapter Forty-two

There's only so much housework you can do before you begin to look around for the point of it all. Sure, there was nothing wrong as such but the thought that the locals were gossiping about me, the strange Clotilde and the weird things she had said, and now Arwel's letter—all conspired to create a state of underlying disquiet. Perhaps it was triggered by the changing of the season. The last tendrils of summer were reaching into autumn but without conviction and the days were getting cooler. I tried to carry on. The house was now habitable—more than habitable. I'd made it cosy, comfortable and fresh, each room not simply clean, but pretty and inviting, with bunches of wild flowers in little jars and collections of pretty pebbles I found in the field. My Aunt and Uncle would be pleased. However, old cottages don't lend themselves well to modern ideas of cleanliness and I saw that I was waging a constant battle against nature. I began to get sick of the autumn leaves forever blowing in from outside, of floors constantly mucky from trudging in and out of the garden and the damn spiders that didn't desist spinning their *effing* webs. The last straw came when a roof-tile crashed to the ground one windy night, frightening the living daylights out of me. I was fed up.

The ghost pointed out that beyond keeping it tidy, the garden too was a pointless commitment. Monsieur Ripaille had done an excellent job of taming the jungle and I remembered what we'd talked about while he was here—how lovely it would be to have hollyhocks, lilac, begonias and fuchsias for next summer, as well as kitchen herbs—mint, thyme, sage, parsley and marjoram. And the fruit. I imagined the satisfaction of making crumbles and jams, herb bread, tarts, with ingredients I'd grown myself. Except I wouldn't be the one reaping the benefits. The ghost was right, all my efforts were so that the Duchamps could sell the place. Amazed that I'd been at the cottage for nearly six months already—the entire spring and summer—I thought about what the next six would bring; long winter nights, freezing mornings, trying to make a fire in the drafty kitchen grate, fingers numb with cold, mice moving in search of warmer lodgings, leaks from loose roof-slates... What was the point in enduring all that since Constance and Jacques would be putting the house back on the market next spring once my year was up? *I've had my best months here.*

Still, I did my damnedest to shove away thoughts of what it was all for and I swept the leaves, stacked wood, pulled up weeds as they pushed through the newly exposed soil, and watered the fruit trees that had clung on to life through their years of neglect. I thought about what I might have said to the Good Doctor.

'What if I went back to my old life? I could move back into my house, find a new job, pick up where I left off.' He'd nod, swivel a bit on his chair, and use his old silence trick to get me to continue.

'But then, what if going to some office all day is just a way of filling in time, no more meaningful than collecting wood or gardening? I mean, we all need to earn a living, but that doesn't make the work meaningful, only the means to an end. And since I'm not about to retrain as a surgeon or go off and save orphans, I'd be left with the basic question: How to live a meaningful life.'

'Does life have to be meaningful, Sian?'

I could imagine Doctor Adebowale saying those words. And it's not only psychiatrists who are obsessed with the question. The French in general are pretty hot on the topic. I'd written a mediocre essay about it at university.

'It discussed Camus' view that the most important philosophical question is why we don't commit suicide.'

'And did you conclude anything helpful?'

'No, not really.'

I replayed this fantasy conversation on one of my afternoon ambles. In the absence of suicide as an ideal solution to the hours I had to fill, I'd taken to going on long walks. The cool autumn afternoons that stretched into fresh evenings lent themselves perfectly to this and even though winter was nipping, it was pleasant weather to walk in. I started to enjoy exploring the lanes and tracks around Saint

Vey and further afield. The first time I'd gone on such a walk, I'd been amazed at how vast the sky was, how dramatic the clouds. The gently undulating countryside made for easy walking and I'd discovered vine-bordered lanes, fields packed with the last of the heavy-headed sunflowers, little streams where Willow trees—*saules pleureurs* in French—*crying souls*—dipped their branches as bright blue kingfishers darted in and out of the water. Occasionally I'd pass isolated cottages like mine, their creamy brickwork glowing warmly in the evening sun, gardens still bursting with colour. Rarely did I pass another human being and if I spotted a hamlet of houses I'd take another route if I could, rather than walk past them.

There was one time I did encounter someone else—two people in fact, within moments of each another. I was thinking about Arwel's letter and composing a carefully worded reply in my head. My indecision about what to say, plus a broken night had made me tetchy and not able to settle to anything, had made me think a walk might at least tire me sufficiently to sleep well. I'd locked the front door of the cottage, clanged shut the screeching gate—*I really must oil the effing thing*—and made off down the lane. On a whim—or perhaps not—I turned left past the Delariche house and paused outside, peering into the courtyard. A big silver Audi was parked there. I looked up at the windows but could see no sign of Clotilde—or Monsieur Delariche for that matter. I hesitated, my hand on the bell-chain, but the thought of the nosy Monsieur who certainly was home sent me hurrying past.

On a previous walk I'd discovered a pretty little lane bordered on both sides by vines—their leaves turning orange now—which led to a small wood. I decided to see what lay beyond. I'd been walking for about half an hour and, having exhausted my store of tact in my imagined letter to Arwel, was contemplating what I'd do if I moved back to Cardiff. The thought didn't inspire me.

A sudden honking of a horn had me leaping onto the grass verge. Expecting to see a boy-racer speeding into the distance, I was surprised to see the car slowing to a stop a few meters ahead. A man leaned out of the window, evidently waiting for me to catch up. What's this about, I thought? A lost tourist wanting directions? He should drive more *effing* slowly.

'*Bonjour*, Madame.' The man's gruff voice told me straightaway that this was no tourist. It was the nosy Mr Hostile.

'*Bonjour*, Monsieur,' I said warily, stopping by the car, which I now saw was the one that had been parked in his courtyard. His mangy dog was sitting on the back seat and it gave an obliging woof when it saw me. I scowled at it.

'You came to my house a while back...' *Hell of an opener.* I cut him off mid-sentence so I didn't have to be subjected to more of his boorishness.

'Yes,' I said, 'but don't worry, if it's about your dog, I've spoken to your wife, and...'

The thought of Clotilde in her studio, her body visible beneath her transparent robe, made me falter and I felt myself flushing deeply. *Damn this weird couple.*

'In any case, I'd better...'

'You've spoken to my...'

Our words collided and neither of us finished our sentence. Delariche narrowed his eyes and seemed about to say something more but evidently thought better of it.

'Good day, Madame,' he said, and with that he put his car into gear and drove off.

How rude! I was so flummoxed that I didn't hear a second vehicle speeding along behind and I jumped out of the way as a white van screeched to a stop. It's like busses, I thought with irritation, nothing for ages then two at once.

'*Bonjour*, Madame Evans. Lost are you?' It was Madame Volt the baker and her tone wasn't friendly.

'Not exactly,' I replied. 'I'm taking a walk. Or trying to.'

She looked me up and down with an appraising eye, clearly unimpressed by my jeans, trainers and the 1970's sunhat I'd found in a wardrobe. I appraised her right back.

'That Monsieur Delariche, was it?' She nodded her head up the now empty lane.

'It was,' I replied.

'Just being neighbourly, was he?'

Good grief, do these people need to know everyone's business?

'He stopped to say hello, that's all,' I said, wondering why the man *had* stopped.

'I'll have your shopping Saturday, good day to you, Madame.'

The baker sped off up the lane and I was left standing there with a fledgling headache and a mounting set of prejudices against country folk. Indeed, I thought, giving up on my walk and heading back to the cottage, aside from Clairjo and Ripaille, who each had their own reasons for being civil to me, only Clotilde had shown me any genuine friendliness.

Chapter Forty-three

I sat out that evening much later than I usually did, tired from yet another restless night but determined to stay up late in the hope of falling asleep before the early hours. The last rays of the setting sun had lost what little warmth they'd had and were casting long shadows over the field, while little pipistrelle bats flitted occasionally past. The ghost pointed out that the good thing about autumn and winter is that there aren't many flies. I wasn't interested. Pegleg was keeping me company and he managed to make me smile as he jumped after various peepings and rustlings in the undergrowth, his twisted leg no hindrance. *He'll grow up to be a hunter, despite the odds.*

I was thinking about Arwel's letter. I needed to send him some kind of reply, it would be mean not to. *You're good at keeping things to yourself,* he'd said. He'd got that part right. But he thought I'd moved here to be with a man. How wrong could he be? *Dammit Arwel.* I was perfectly happy before. Pegleg purred loudly at my feet and I reached down and gave him a scratch behind the ears. I'd surely feel more settled if I got my reply out of the way. The problem wasn't what I'd say to him—I had no issue with telling Arwel I was in France alone—not that it was any of his business. The problem was what I *didn't* want to say. Should I tell Arwel, after all this time, the truth about why I divorced him? I turned the dilemma over in my mind, my single nightly glass of wine turning to two as a rosy dusk faded to a rich, dark night. The temperature fell further as a half-moon rose with the stars and I pulled my cardigan closer around my shoulders, sipping my wine as starlight flicked the windows of the Delariche house. I looked up in hopeful anticipation, but all was dark.

Something in my peripheral vision made me alert. Pegleg darted off into the undergrowth and I peered out across the field. In the darkness I could see nothing that might have startled him. The big walnut trees along the border were silhouetted by the half-moon and were throwing twisted shadows across the field, while the tall grass murmured in the breeze. Sitting perfectly still I maintained my gaze, hoping to catch a glimpse of the hares that sometimes loped across the field. For a few long moments, nothing stirred and I'd decided that there was nothing to see, when—*there!* Down by the far boundary, I could just make it out among the trees. I held my breath. Hare's are majestic creatures and, being shy, all the more mysterious. I'd come to regard them as a good omen.

I took a sip of wine, all the while focused on the boundary wall, a gentle breeze stirring the rising scent of night-moist earth. All I could discern was a vague shape in the shadows. A large shape. *That's one big hare.* I stared. For a moment nothing moved. But there it was again, undeniably something was there, a blur of movement against the darkness of the hedge.

'Where are you Pegleg, it's only a hare?' I said out loud, wanting the comfort of his now-familiar company, but the kitten was nowhere to be seen. I squinted into the night...

...*that's no hare*...

I froze. Whatever—or *whoever* it was, was making its way slowly up the border of the field. A burglar? Or worse? What should I do? *Calm down, Sian, it's probably nothing.* Strangely, although I could imagine danger, I did feel calm. I kept up my stare. The figure continued to move closer and, peering through the shadowy trees, I now saw that it was stooping every now and then. To hide? Still I didn't move and still the figure came closer, seemingly unaware of being watched.

Doubting the wisdom of such a move, I nonetheless stood and was about to creep closer to get a better look when I began to hear an irregular 'clink, clink' sound. Not moving a muscle, I didn't take my eyes from the figure, the clinking getting louder until I realised in a shock of astonishment what it was that I was watching...

Barefoot in the moon-shadowed trees, dressed in nothing but her white night-gown, she bends to pick up stones, throwing them into a basket by her side.

'Clotilde?'

It's clearly her. I wave but she seems unaware of my presence and continues to make her way up the edge of the dark field, bending to pick up stones as she goes. Fascinated as much as confused, I watch, the *clink-clink* as the stones land in

174

the basket breaking the silence. The breeze is sharp in the autumn night, the thickening clouds scud over the half-moon but Clotilde, her white robe flapping, doesn't notice or doesn't care.

'Clotilde!'

She stands suddenly still, silhouetted in cold-fire moonlight. *Has she seen me?* Motionless as a frightened animal, she looks at me but shows no sign of recognition. Her face is half-hidden in shadow and her dark curls and face are wild—eyes watchful, body taut as though ready to run. *What are you doing, Clotilde?* I take a step forward and two bats startle me and perhaps her. She makes a jerky movement that seems at odds with the fluid drape of her gown. And then...

'*Sian...*'

I'm rooted to the spot. We stand, eyes locked. Neither of us moves.

'...Sian...'

Should I go to her? What is she doing? Standing there among the trees, she is easing her robe over first one shoulder then the other... white cotton falling...

...undressing...

I stare... she stares...

Undressed.

She and I in the dark field. We stand still. I notice I'm holding my breath and I let it out slowly. Run towards or run from? *I am at the point between.* I close my eyes.

'*...Sian...*'

Eyes snap open, ready to run... I look this way and that...

'...Clotilde..?'

The only response is the barking of the Delariche dog.

I covered my mouth with my hand and sat down heavily on the bench. Staring out into the field, I scanned the boundary wall, the far hedge, the trees—*where had she gone..?* I rubbed my hands together, shivering with cold. It's late, I told myself, she's gone home. But a glance at her house revealed no sign of life, all was dark and silent, even the dog was no longer barking. *What to do?* Surely I should check she was okay, that nothing had happened to her, naked in the dead of night? I stood once more and took a few steps into the field, narrowing my eyes, trying to make her out among the shadows. But Clotilde was definitely no longer there.

Heading back into the garden, my empty wine glass in hand, I tried reason. Whatever the woman chose to do at night, however strange, it was none of my business. Even so, perhaps I ought to see that she was safely home? I hesitated at my front door. *Effing hell.* I had no inclination to go to the Delariche house at that hour, but I turned, placed my wine glass on the garden table and marched up the newly cleared path. Cringing at the great squealing that ripped the night-calm as I heaved opened the gates, I paused a moment in the silence, looking up and down the lane, hoping to catch sight of Clotilde, fully dressed and on her way home. All was deserted, the only sound the wind whistling in the electricity wires. The first spots of cold rain strengthened my resolve and I hurried out.

The Delariche house, shuttered and dark, revealed no evidence of occupation. The gate was half-open though, swinging slightly in the wind, which was picking up pace. Perhaps that was a good sign. I peered through. The silver Audi wasn't there and I hoped that meant the Monsieur of the house wasn't there either. I gave the chain a firm yank before I could change my mind. The bell clanged loud and ugly in the wind and the dog started to bark once more. No one came. Shivering, I buttoned my cardigan—it was very cold now—if Clotilde was still outside, she'd be freezing. I pulled the chain again and was about to go, set on looking for her in the field, but just as I turned to leave, the front door opened. I swung round full of relief, but it wasn't Clotilde standing there. It was Monsieur Delariche.

He was dressed haphazardly in a wrongly buttoned shirt, trousers drooping and no socks, as though he'd thrown on his clothes in a rush. His hair looked wild and he pushed it back from his face.

'Madame Evans... what is it? It's late... has something happened?'

'I'm so sorry to wake you at this hour,' I faltered. 'But it's Clotilde. She was out in the field. I was worried and I came to see that she'd come home safely.'

Delariche didn't move from his doorway.

'…Clotilde…'

'Yes. She was looking for stones.'

He stared at me. 'She was looking for stones?'

'She was in the field just now,' I repeated, turning to point. 'I wanted to make sure she'd come home because…' His scowl made me hesitate—I certainly didn't want to tell him that she'd taken off her clothes. '…because it's cold.'

'It's late,' Monsieur Delariche said. 'Go home.'

'…but… can you just tell me if she's back?'

'Go home, Madame Evans.'

Chapter Forty-four

The note was written in a scrawled hand on thin paper and had been delivered by hand into my mail-box.

'I am expecting you at 1.30 on Sunday for a cocktail dinatoire, to celebrate the occasion of my birthday'

I'd slept in late after my exertions of the night before and although I was pleased I had slept, I was nonetheless feeling fragile. The last thing I felt like doing was going to a party and my initial response was to politely decline.

It might shake you out of your malaise, the ghost said. *You find the housework irritating, the gardening pointless, baking a waste of time since you have no appetite. Even your nightly glass of wine in the field is interrupted by thoughts of the elusive—and if I might say it—the downright weird Madame Delariche. Perhaps being with people might jolt you out of it.*

What a speech! Jesus ghost, what are you, a shrink?

Regardless, however, of the ghost's good counsel, I knew the real reason I accepted Madame Clairjo's invitation. It was because Clotilde might be there.

With this in mind, I set about finding my one good dress and the matching shoes, neither of which had seen the light of day since Cardiff. Setting them out on my bed, I looked at myself in the long wardrobe mirror. I barely recognised the androgynous human staring back at me in shapeless and grubby jeans and jumper. Her hair was greasy and straggly, long lank tendrils escaping unflatteringly from a scruffy pony-tail. When had I stopped showering? *Effing hell—I smell rank!* And make-up? I couldn't remember the last time I'd bothered.

It's the 'real' you, the ghost said.

Well the fake me is going to the party, I replied.

Get up, dress up, show up! Oh the irony.

If I were going to attend this function, there was more to consider than my appearance. I was growing increasingly fed-up with having the baker do my shopping, but mindful of my tight budget and my lack of inclination to get the bus into town, it was clear that my birthday gift to Madame Clairjo would have to be home-made. And given that my crafting skills were on a par with my skills as a particle-physicist, it would have to be of the edible variety. So on Saturday afternoon I lit the oven and set out the ingredients—or the best approximations I could get in a country that doesn't use cream—for a Victoria sponge cake, handed over by a suspicious Madame Volt.

A little after 1.30 on Sunday, I was scrubbed, coiffed, made-up and dressed in my best dress and shoes. My hair smelt of apples and my make-up looked harsh. I stared once more at the woman in the mirror and once more barely recognised her—although not for the same reason this time. Feeling inexplicably nervous, I turned this way and that—was I over-dressed for a country party? I could no longer see myself. I mean, there I was in the mirror, a middle aged woman in a blue dress and high heeled shoes. But I couldn't connect with what I was seeing. *Who am I, ghost?* The ghost took great pleasure in reminding me that this wasn't the first time this had happened but I told him to pipe down and bugger off.

Reasoning that it is better to be overdressed than underdressed, I made a final tweak of my hair, walked downstairs—hobbled more like, more accustomed now to wearing wellington boots than heels—and, having collected the cake, left the house. As an afterthought, I went back in and grabbed my cardigan. Although the sun was shining in a cloudless sky, autumn was resolutely here and the weather was as changeable as my mood. *Effing hell*, I muttered as I stumbled on a stone, just managing not to drop the tin. Standing on Madame Clairjo's doorstep, I took a deep breath, rang the bell and waited for the birthday girl to let me in.

But it wasn't Madame Clairjo who opened the door. It was Monsieur Delariche who, after the briefest of starts, gave me a curt shake of his hand. I too was momentarily flustered and I mumbled something inaudible at him.

'We're on the terrace,' he said, with no hint of recollection of the events of the other night and I wasn't sure whether to feel relieved or not. He led the way along the brightly-lit hallway, out through the back door and down a little flight of stone steps that led to the garden.

The terrace was warm and pretty, receiving the full force of the autumn sunshine, and I took in a blur of beautifully attired guests. Relieved that I hadn't worn jeans, I straightened my dress and looked around. Two tables, both decked out in pastel green table-clothes and little glass vases of michaelmas daisies, had been set out between wooden tubs bursting with late roses, dahlias and asters, which I now recognised, thanks to the ministrations of Monsieur Ripaille. The larger table bore a range of bottles and glasses, which no one had yet taken, as well as plates loaded with charcuterie, rounds of baguette spread with tapenade and goat's cheese, dishes of olives and cornichons, cherry tomatoes stuffed with pesto, and an impressive cheese board. The smaller table had been reserved for birthday gifts, and a number of exquisitely wrapped parcels of different sizes and shapes stood in front of a magnificent bouquet of roses. I felt awkward about placing my old cake tin there, so I kept hold of it, hoping that no one would ask what it was.

A quick scan of the guests revealed, in addition to Monsieur Delariche, a frail-looking old lady dressed in a yellow two-piece, orange pashmina and enormous matching flower in her hair, as well as two olive-skinned teenage boys, who kept taking sneaky peeks at their mobile phones. I couldn't see Clotilde. Standing by myself feeling disappointed and out of place, I felt reluctant to barge into the group who seemed to be engaged in earnest conversation. Monsieur Delariche disappeared back into the house, perhaps to open the door again, or maybe to avoid having to talk to me. Fidgeting in my uncomfortable shoes, I stood clutching my cake tin and eying the Champagne longingly, cursing the fact that in typical French fashion no one would be offered a drink until all the guests had arrived. As one of the teenage boys bent to hear something the old lady was saying, I was relieved to spot Monsieur Ripaille, who was sporting a smart jacket and a dark green necktie. He was talking to the most perfect woman in the world who, to my horror, came wafting over to me in a cloud of floral perfume.

'Ah, you must be Sian,' she said in perfect English, placing an air-kiss on each of my cheeks. 'I'm Marie—Jeanine's daughter—I'm so glad you could come.'

After a fraction of a second's confusion, I realised this vision of elegance must be Madame Clairjo's daughter. I felt myself flush deeply.

'*Enchantée*, it's lovely to meet you,' I mumbled in French. The vision seemed happy to continue in her native language.

'Ah, but your French is excellent,' she exclaimed. 'I gather you were of assistance to my mother when she wasn't well?'

'Oh, it was nothing, I took her lunch a few times.'

As she spoke, Marie placed a manicured hand on my arm and led me into the group of people who were regarding us with curiosity. *Here goes*, I thought taking a deep breath, knowing that, following French etiquette, I'd now have to greet them all one-by-one.

'Now then everyone, this is the English lady who lives across the way. Her name is Sian.'

'Welsh,' I said, and immediately wished I hadn't. Marie looked confused. 'I'm not English, I'm Welsh,' I muttered.

'Yes, yes,' she said. 'Well, this is Aziz, my husband...' A dark-skinned, bespectacled man shot out a plump hand and pumped mine rigorously.

'*Enchanté,*' he said with a heavy Algerian accent.

'...and this is Madame Fontenay, a long-term family friend...' The old lady in yellow proffered me first one and then the other pinkly powdered cheek. '...these are my sons, Olivier and Dominique...' The boys came forward one after the other and dutifully kissed my cheeks. '...you already know Monsieur Ripaille of course...' I kissed the two whiskered cheeks he thrust at me with a wink of his eye. '...and I'm sure you know Monsieur Delariche.'

Delariche had materialised once more and he nodded at me, offering neither a hand nor cheeks. I supposed he considered the perfunctory handshake at the front door to have been sufficient. As if on cue, the doorbell rang and he left the group to open it. I was dying to knock back a glass of Champagne but stood there looking expectantly at the back door, hoping to see the arrival of Clotilde.

'Such a helpful chap, my mother is lucky to have such caring neighbours,' Marie gushed. 'Ah Madame Volt, Messieurs so good to see you.'

The baker, escorted on each arm by the two Jean's, was making an entrance in a bright fuchsia dress nipped in at the waist, set off by red high heels. Her hair, normally shoved under her starched baker's hat, was tumbling in pretty curls around her shoulders, and from her neck hung a delicate silver shell pendant which rested at her amply displayed décolletage. I barely recognised her, so different was this stylish woman from the dowdy, overall-clad baker. The two Jean's were dapper and debonair by turn, Jean-Luc sporting a rather jaunty flat cap. Madame Volt extricated herself from them and began an extravagant round of cheek-kissing, including mine, which with a furious look at my dress, she skimmed fleetingly before turning to Monsieur Delariche.

'Been hiding from us he has, the naughty boy,' she said in a teasing voice.

Monsieur Delariche looked bashful and was about to say something but Madame Clairjo chose that moment to make her grand entrance. All eyes turned to the door and Aziz rushed over to help his mother-in-law down the steps. The old woman was wearing a long, flowing two-piece in pale mauves and creams, trimmed with lace at the high neck, where a sparkling broach had been fastened. Her hair was newly white and freshly fluffed and, instead of her usual sensible leather lace-ups, she was wearing lilac rhinestone pumps. I marvelled at how these French country ladies could transform themselves from drab-dowdiness to stylish-elegance at a moment's notice. I certainly didn't feel over-dressed anymore and I thought with regret of the clothes I'd discarded in Wales as being too dressy for the French countryside. Madame Clairjo chapped her hands together in child-like glee.

'Oh, you're all here,' she cried.

Joyeux anniversaire!' the guests responded.

I hung back and watched as Madame Clairjo proceeded to make the rounds, kissing her guests extravagantly and exclaiming with delight at the display of gifts.

'I never did let being born in October get in the way of a good garden party!' she said. Indeed, the late autumn sunshine had managed to summon up enough strength for the ladies to discard their pashmina shrugs, hanging them delicately over the backs of chairs. Checking that no one was watching, I chucked my old cardigan under the drinks table.

'*Alors*,' Aziz said, 'now that we're all here, what about a little glass of bubbly to toast the occasion?'

Thank god! There was a murmur of approval as Madame Clairjo's son-in-law picked up one of the bottles of chilled Champagne, popped the cork with an expert hand and proceeded to fill the assembled flutes.

'*Santé*,' Aziz exclaimed once we were all clutching our glasses. 'To your good health,' we all repeated.

I took a deep, grateful sip of the cool liquid and, as the buzz of conversation resumed, moved towards Madame Clairjo, kissed her on each cheek and held out the cake in its tin.

'Happy birthday,' I said. 'I'm sorry it isn't anything more sophisticated.'

To my embarrassment, Madame Clairjo handed her Champagne glass to one of her grandsons and proceeded to prise off the lid of the tin while I was still holding it. She narrowed her eyes and stared at the cake before taking a long sniff. I braced myself.

'I wondered when you were going to bake me a cake. Monsieur Ripaille has had plenty, so I hear!'

There were murmurs of 'delightful,' 'how lovely,' and 'what a nice idea', and I relaxed but not without noticing the piercing look Madame Volt gave me.

Smiling at Madame Clairjo, I replaced the lid and put the cake on the table with the other gifts. The party began to get underway and, with the awkward preliminaries out of the way, I chatted with the friends, family and neighbours, popping the occasional olive or goat's cheese delicacy into my mouth and accepting a second glass of Champagne from Jean-Luc.

'So,' he said. 'How's French country life treating you? Not missing the big city too much?'

'Cardiff isn't so big,' I replied. 'No, I'm a fairly solitary type, so the isolation suits me well.'

'Isolation?' Jean-Luc laughed and indicated the party-guests. 'You might well *feel* isolated, but there isn't much that gets past this lot, I can tell you.'

'Oh, I'm sure it's possible to have a private life,' I said, glancing around for Clotilde who, it seemed, still hadn't arrived. 'How do you and Jean-Paul find rural life?'

On hearing his name Jean-Paul turned, a bottle of Champagne in one hand, which he thrust before him. 'Not taking the name of a barer of the nectar-of-the-god's in vain, are you?' I smiled and shook my head at a top-up. 'I know someone who never says no,' he said with a wink at Jean-Luc, as he refilled his flute.

'To answer your question,' Jean-Luc said, 'the best way to get on here is not to expect to have secrets. Live your life as though you have nothing to hide. Because you're not going to be able to hide anything anyhow.'

'That's not an empty glass I see in your hand is it?' Jean-Paul exclaimed to Madame Fontenay, and the pair drifted off to talk her.

After a while, I found myself standing next to Monsieur Delariche and we both went to speak at once:

'About my dog…'

'I see you've come alone…'

'After you,' he said.

On quick reflection, I decided that my initial opener seemed somewhat rude, so I changed my tack.

'I met Clotilde,' I said. 'She's lovely. Will she be joining us for the party?'

'No,' he said. 'She won't.' He peered at me with a strange expression on his face. 'And I hope Coco is quieter now. My dog is called Coco. I've started taking her with me when I'm away.'

'Yes I've noticed that, thank you.'

I wanted to ask him about Clotilde, why she wasn't coming to the party, but Madame Volt chose that moment to bustle up to us and, laying a proprietorial hand on Delariche's arm, waved her glass at him.

'Now then, you promised me you wouldn't let my glass get empty, and look. Naughty boy.'

Monsieur Delariche gave me a little half-shrug and allowed himself to be steered away to the drinks table.

I'd begun a headache and now that I knew Clotilde wasn't coming, decided it was time to go. I grabbed my cardigan from under the table and sought out Madame Clairjo, who was holding court on a wooden chair, a grandson at each side like two princes.

'Thank you for a lovely party,' I said. 'I'm going to slip off now.'

There were murmurs of 'oh, so soon', and 'so nice to meet you', and in spite of my entreaty not to get up Madame Clairjo, with the aid of the olive-skinned princes, heaved herself out of the chair.

I did the rounds of goodbye kisses, Madame Volt taking my head in her hands as soon as Monsieur Delariche had kissed me on each cheek.

'No monopolising the handsome men,' she said, planting two frosty kisses on my cheeks.

Madame Clairjo took my arm and led me towards the stone steps leading up to the back door. 'You're a good girl to come to an old ladies party,' she said, clinging to my arm and hobbling up the stairs.

'Nonsense,' I replied, 'I've enjoyed myself. But please, I'll see myself out. You go back to your guests.'

Clairjo ignored me and followed me into the hall.

'Don't you mind Volt,' she whispered when we were standing by the front door.

I glanced at her in surprise.

'Oh come on, you're no blushing bride. Competition, is what you are. For Delariche. We all know he likes you.'

Chapter Forty-five

Clairjo I was and Clairjo I ...*oui oui*, if you haven't got the picture by now you never will. Came to my party she did, the foreigner. I'd have been put out if she hadn't—but even so I don't mind admitting I was surprised. Not one for small talk, Sian—hard to get to know. And I know her better than any round here. I've said it before and I'll say it again; distant. That's what she is.

She scrubbed up well enough. First time any of us had seen the girl in a dress—wouldn't have surprised me if she'd shown up in jeans and those giant gum-boots she insists on wearing. And she brought a cake—English it was, named after some queen of theirs if my memory serves—ate a slice before bed. Not bad at all.

I watched her at the party. Oh, she was at ease enough. Chatted with my Marie and the grandsons—lovely boys but much too interested in their wireless phones. Asks questions, does Sian. Gets along by getting the other talking. No one notices she isn't saying much because folk like talking about themselves. I've got the measure of her now. It's how she manages to seem like she's being social but in reality no one learns anything about her.

Overheard her talking with the two Jeans. '*...you're not going to be able to hide anything...*' Jean-Luc said. What does she want to hide? '*Got to be a story there,*' Ripaille remarked when she first arrived. Happen he's not far wrong.

One person who wasn't keen to talk to her was that sassy bird, Volt. Ah, she's a canny one. Soon as she saw Sian, she ran her eyes up and down her like she was some manner of creature crawled out of the River Vey. Does it every time she sees her. Sian didn't flinch. Ha! Just looked right back at her. And Volt kept her beady eyes on her, following Sian around the garden, jumping in the way if ever it looked like the foreigner and Delariche might cross paths. Volt would do well to back off and look somewhere else for a husband. You mark my words, for all her persistence Delariche is no more likely to make eyes at her than he is at me.

Volt and me weren't the only ones watching Sian. Paul Delariche led Volt a merry dance, making himself busy with the drinks so that he didn't have to talk to anyone. Just like Sian but with a different technique. But he kept his eyes on the foreigner all the same. Volt knows it and I've remarked on it to Ripaille more than once—I'll wager I'm not wrong. There's a flame there. I know Delariche of old—since the day he was born in fact. Always was the same. If he wants something he'll make out like it's the last thing in the world he cares about.

I remember years ago, about eight years old, he was. Old ma Delariche told me he wanted a fishing rod for Christmas. All the local boys had hatched up a plan to ask their parents for one so they could fish for tiddlers in the Vey—heard it from the Sunday school teacher, had Madame Delariche. But her tight-lipped son—admit it he would not. Asked for everything else, his ma told me—football boots, a penknife, the latest Jules Verne novel. '*It's like he thinks if he tells anyone what he really wants, it might put the jinx on it,*' she said. Perverse if you ask me. He got his fishing rod, though. Paul Delariche usually gets what he wants in the end.

Chapter Forty-six

Here it was, that old feeling, the disconnected reality, the emotionless emotion... The night after the party and the next day I couldn't think, couldn't function... I knew exactly what it was. I was *soft*. Sitting on the edge of the bed, I stared at the wardrobe for several long minutes as though the answer to my stupor might leap from the doors. *Get up, dress up, show up?* I would have laughed out loud had I had the energy. *Just feel your way through it,* the ghost said. Much better advice. I spent the rest of the day wrapped in a blanket, crying on and off, drinking hot chocolate. I couldn't even read. Was it because I'd spent the afternoon socialising? That's what the Good Doctor would have said. 'You're replenishing, Sian, that's all.' Whatever the cause, the fact that I didn't have to lie about how I felt was hugely liberating and by that evening a subtle shift had taken place—enough for me to string a few coherent thoughts together. What I thought about was Monsieur Delariche—or more accurately what Madame Clairjo had said about him.

In what possible world could Mr Hostile's mean-spirited rudeness be considered amorous? I hadn't heard anything more ridiculous since Arwel announced one summer that he wanted to buy a sports car. I'd dismissed Arwel's hankering as the desperate yearnings of a middle-aged man whose youth was receding as fast as his hairline. Now I dismissed Madame Clairjo's comments as the ornate imaginings of a bored old lady.

A few days later, I had cause to wonder whether the old bird might be right. Another note had appeared in my mail box:

'Madame Evans, I feel we've got off on the wrong foot. I'd like to make amends by taking you for a meal. Would you be free this Saturday?'

It was signed *Paul Delariche.*

Not 'Clotilde and Paul' or 'Monsieur and Madame Delariche.' Just 'Paul Delariche'. *The brazen cheek of the man.* At least he realised how rude he'd been to me, but regardless of that, the man wasn't at liberty to ask me out for dinner. Clotilde—who no one wanted to talk about despite the fact that she posed naked at her window and ran around fields in her nightclothes in the middle of the night—was quite clearly living in Paul Delariche's house.

Outraged on her behalf, I took the note into the field and peered up at the Delariche cottage. All was quiet. Was she in there, chisel in hand, chinking away at her statue? I sat on the bench to reread the note and to ponder the mystery of this strange couple. *So much for Jean-Luc's insistence that there are no secrets here.* Of course, I reasoned, she might not be his lover at all, in which case he's at liberty to invite who he likes for dinner. She could be his sister, I supposed. Or a friend. But as the ghost pointed out, the way she moved around his home wearing nothing at all or nothing but a transparent robe suggested otherwise. Was she some kind of mad Mrs Rochester he had hidden up there? I snorted a laugh, but it wasn't beyond the realms of possibility.

The most obvious solution to the mystery, I told the ghost, was that it was a love affair that hadn't worked out, and Clotilde was simply no longer there. Staring hard at the attic window, which as if in confirmation of my idea, remained empty and dark, I fantasised about my reply:

'Monsieur Delariche, before I consider your invitation, I'd like to know exactly what your relationship is to Clotilde.'

Or maybe:

'Paul, I'd love to accept your invitation to dinner, will Clotilde be joining us?'

The following morning, I woke feverish and sweating, my head aching and my nose congested. *That's just wonderful, a head-cold.* I turned over and tried to go back to sleep but the sneezing and my thumping head got progressively worse. What are you supposed to do, feed a fever, starve a cold or feed a cold, starve a fever? And what's the difference between a fever and a cold anyhow? Thoroughly miserable, I knocked back a couple of paracetamol I found in my bag and dozed on and off until lunchtime when I dragged myself out of bed and dosed myself up again before heading to the bathroom. There I stood in the steaming shower for a good twenty minutes, the comfort of the hot steam keeping me there until my finger-tips wrinkled.

The next day was worse. Shivery, headachy and streaming with the full force of the cold, I'd barely slept, my dreams fractured and indistinct.

...I'm in the moonlit field, watching Clotilde's statue, a letter in its stone hand, dancing between the trees... the woman of stone... moving closer... I'm trying to run but I can't, trying to scream but no sound will come... she's standing in front of me, bearing down over me, I'm on my knees, her hand outstretched, blind eyes boring into me, mouth opening... I cover my ears but it's too late, it's too late... go home Madame Evans... Go home.

For the first time since arriving, I felt lonely. More than lonely —I felt alone. No one knew I was ill, no one was here to help. I supposed I could have asked one of the neighbours, but to do what? Bring me food? Call a doctor? It wasn't that I needed anything, I realised—I just wanted someone to care. I dragged myself downstairs, downed two Paracetamol and threw together a tomato soup, wishing mightily that I'd stowed a few tins of Heinz in my suitcase when I came. I imagined Clotilde arriving with a thermos of something nourishing, as I had for Madame Clairjo. But of course no one came. Day and night blurred into one and for the next three days I tried to keep warm in my bed, tried to sleep. Each morning I woke to Delariche's parting words the night I'd seen Clotilde in the field. *Go home.*

It was the day before my rendezvous with Paul Delariche and I hadn't yet accepted or declined his invitation. I'd woken early, the fug of illness finally beginning to lift and I'd thrown open the bedroom window and stripped the bed of my sweat-damp sheets. I was still sneezing, but less now, and my head was no longer thumping. Downstairs I set the washing machine going and looked at the big kitchen inglenook—I hadn't made a fire since I'd arrived. I could think of nothing better than to curl up in front of blazing flames with a hot chocolate and a good book. I carefully laid scrunched-up newspaper in the grate, topped by a heap of twigs and a couple of logs. Thank goodness the Duchamps had left a huge stack of wood, it was perfectly dry and soon the twigs were popping and cracking, flames curling round the logs.

I sat with a hot-water bottle in my lap, a blanket round my shoulders and a mug of steaming chocolate. Maupassant's *Bel Ami* lay unopened by my side. *I really ought to tell Paul Delariche whether or not I'm going to dinner.* I thought about it. I could use the cold as an excuse to decline. Or, I could accept and finally find out who Clotilde is…

A pad of paper was propped up on the hot-water bottle and I tapped it with my pen. Rereading the words I'd written, I hoped I was doing the right thing. I signed my name, folded the sheet and slid it into the envelope. This letter wasn't to Paul Delariche. Neither was it to Arwel. It was to my letting agent in Cardiff asking them to give my tenants notice to quit.

Chapter Forty-seven

It was still early and, having hung the bedding out to dry, I was back by the fire, a fresh cup of hot-chocolate cooling by my side. I still hadn't opened my book. I was rereading Arwel's letter for the thousandth time. *'You're good at keeping things to yourself.'* I'd never argued with him about that. Stone-faced, he used to call me. To me, keeping your own counsel had never seemed like the wrong thing to do. He wasn't asking for the truth. But my withholding of it had enabled him to draw his own mistaken conclusions. The problem with truth is that it can get you into all sorts of hot water. I'd learned that from my mother.

When I was a little girl we lived near a big common where once a year the fun-fair set up camp. For three magical days the sounds of organ music, shouts of coconut-shy men and the shrieks of children would assail the ears of anyone within a half mile radius, the kids in my school talking of nothing else.

'The fair's here, will your Mam give you money for the rides?'

'My Mam gave me three quid.'

'Mine gave me two, meet you by the cut at eleven, big wheel first.'

My own mother, not prepared to let her only daughter loose where gypsy-boys tempted young girls with their wild looks and their barely concealed intentions, would never let me go to the fair with my friends.

'If their mothers are content to fling their daughters into harm's way, then more fool them,' she'd say, ignoring my pleas to be allowed to go with the other girls in my class. 'You'll go with me or you'll not go at all.'

The prospect of missing out on being able to compare our candyfloss-gorging, fish-winning, bumper-car injuries and the gypsy-boys who'd winked at us was too much to bare, and each year I'd relent and go to the fair with my Mam. Sometimes Aunty Sue and Penny came too. They'd come with us *that* year.

'Come on, Mam, I've been ready for *ages.*'

'Sian Evans, you behave yourself or you'll not go to the fair at all.'

'Maaaam, come *on.*'

'We're off, love, back at five,' she called to my Dad.

Aunty Sue—who wasn't really my aunt—and her daughter Penny, were meeting us by the big wheel and I was *desperate* to get there first so that Penny didn't get more rides than me. We were first to arrive, but Mam made me wait and that was worse. *Here they are!* Penny was dragging her Mam by the hand through the hordes of excited children and at last we were let loose on the waltzers, roller coasters and helter-skelters, dizzy within half an hour from candyfloss sugar and gypsy testosterone. Mam and Aunty Sue wandered after us forking out money with indulgent tuts and talking about grown-up things. By half past three I'd cried when a boy from my class pinched my bum in the ghost train, blaming it on a gypsy, and Sue had been sick round the back of the coconut-shy.

'Time to go home,' Mam declared.

Aunty Sue concurred and Penny and I, having made the prerequisite pleas for just one more ride, were happy enough to run ahead comparing ideas for naming our goldfish.

'Not that way girls, Aunty Sue needs to do a bit of shopping.'

'Aw Mam, we can't take the fish to the shops. They need to go in the bowl.'

'She's right, Sue, I'm not having them sloshing dirty fish-water all over Finefair's. Girls, you run on. Tell your father to put the kettle on, we'll be back within the hour. And mind you go straight home.'

We didn't need telling twice. Penny and I ran off, our fish-bags slopping water onto our jeans. I'd never been allowed to be what my Mam called a latch-key kid so there was no need for me to own a key. Penny and I ran up the path to the house and I pressed the bell.

'Mine's called Minnie,' I said with the superiority that my two months seniority conferred.

'You can't call a fish Minnie.'

'Yes I can. That's her name. And yours is Mickey.'

'That's stupid.'

I pressed the bell again.

'Where's your Dad, Sian? I'm starving.'

'That's because you sicked up your hot-dog.'

Still no answer. Where was Dad? I opened the letter-box and peered in. I was only eight years old but somehow I knew I was seeing something I shouldn't be. My Dad was coming down the stairs tucking his shirt into his trousers. Behind him was my Mam's friend Jo. She was buttoning up her blouse.

'Come on, Penny, my Dad's not in, let's go and wait for our Mams by Finefair's.'

The two of us and our pet fish went off to find our mothers.

'You little bitch, do you think you're clever telling me that?'

Penny and Aunty Sue had gone home and, as Mam and I were walking back from the shops, I'd made the monumental mistake of telling her what I'd seen.

'It's the truth, Mam.'

The slap across the face she dealt me was all the more shocking for being unexpected and I dropped my fish-bag to the ground. She grabbed my hand and dragged me up the street, ignoring my cries to rescue the goldfish which was flip-flopping pathetically in the gutter.

'Leave it, it would have died within the week anyhow.'

I was still sobbing when, at the gate, Mam yanked me round, bent down and shoved a finger at my face.

'Sian Evans, if you think for one moment I don't already know what your father is like, you are sorely mistaken. You will not mention this ever again, do you hear? Now stop your snivelling and go straight to your room.'

I nodded hard, wiping away tears and snot with the back of my hand.

'And Sian? The next time you think to enlighten anyone with the *truth*, you think good and hard.'

The truth. I don't know how long I'd been sitting there by the kitchen fire, Arwel's letter in my hand, but a sudden clanging of the bell made me drop my pen. I glanced at my watch—it wasn't yet ten. *Who could that be at this time of the morning?*

Probably Paul Delariche wanting to know if I was going for dinner with him or not. The bell clanged again and, irritated, I scraped back my chair and hurried out to see what the fuss was. On screeching open the gate I was confronted not with Monsieur Delariche but Madame Clairjo's daughter. She looked worried and my first thought was that something had happened to her mother. But that wasn't it.

'Come quickly,' Marie said. 'There's someone on the phone for you. I don't want to alarm you, but it sounds urgent.'

Chapter Forty-eight

It's strange how we become so calm in these moments... like we know the tornado is blowing things to bits but we're at still centre of it. I guess something like autopilot kicks in. I handed the phone back to Marie and didn't move. She took me by the shoulders and steered me into the salon. 'Coffee,' she said to Aziz. I don't recall the detail of what happened after that. The day passed in a blur of activity. Aziz made all my travel arrangements while Marie and Madame Clairjo made me sip strong coffee and eat something, I don't recall what. Marie came back with me to my cottage, washed the dishes and collected the laundry drying on the line while I packed a small suitcase. All the while my mind was lurching from blank numbness to fragments of incoherent thought. I replayed his words over and over in my mind but still I couldn't believe it.

I'd followed Marie up the lane to Madame Clairjo's cottage, my mouth dry, not knowing what to expect. Who could it be? My first thought was that it was Aunt Constance or Uncle Jacques and I hoped that nothing had befallen either of them. When we arrived, Aziz was standing in the hall with the phone receiver in his hand. I knew it was him before he spoke and although his voice at the other end was clear enough, I nonetheless couldn't comprehend a word he was saying.

'Slow down,' I said. 'First of all, are you okay?'

'I'm fine. I mean... no... I mean...'

'Where are you? Are you alright? Has there been an accident?'

'I'm home, I'm in Cardiff, and I'm fine... it's...'

'Come on, take a deep breath, that's it...' I heard him doing as I'd said. 'Now then, what is it? Tell me what has happened.'

I listened to him holding back tears, already knowing what he was going to say...

'It's Dad... he had a heart attack... Mam... he's died.'

*

'Pegleg!' I cried as I climbed into Aziz's car. 'Who will feed Pegleg?' Marie assured me that her mother would take care of the kitten. Aziz drove me to the airport and we spoke very little during the two hour drive. He seemed content to leave me to my own thoughts. I was grateful both for the ride and the silence.

'Will you come back?' Marie had asked as I'd locked up the cottage.

I hadn't answered. Two letters still lay on the kitchen table, both of them sealed and stamped. The one to my letting agent. And the one I'd written to Arwel.

Nate was there to meet me at Cardiff International, and as soon as I reached him, I hugged him so tightly he had to tell me to stop. It was the first time I'd seen him in over a year.

'You look well,' I said, although he had dark shadows under his eyes like he hadn't slept in days. It was clear he didn't know what to say.

'Mam...' he began.

Busy travellers rushed past us, bumping us with their luggage.

'Shhh,' I said. 'All in good time.'

Nate nodded, took my case and steered me through the crowd to the exit. He had a taxi waiting and the driver jumped out of his seat, opened the door and hauled my bags into the boot. Nate and I climbed into the backseat. I was surprised that he started talking as soon as I'd given the driver the address.

'I was in Frankfurt when I got the call,' he said. 'I was on my way to surprise you in France.' I looked at him in astonishment and Nate flicked me a fleeting smile. 'But Uncle Bernie called me on my mobile and told me to get home quick —it was lucky I hadn't boarded my plane. He said Dad had a heart attack at work and was in Cardiff Royal, so I got the first flight I could back home...'

I nodded and Nate paused, seemingly reluctant to say more. I understood and didn't push him, staring ahead as the taxi crawled through the rush-hour traffic. I wanted to hold his hand but I didn't. Eventually Nate continued.

197

'He seemed alright when I got there, he was talking normal-like, sitting up, eating—he even made a joke—said it was like a holiday, the service and the food were better than being at home. And the Doctor told me he was doing well...' Nate tailed off once more. It was clear that he was close to tears. It was like my little boy was sitting next to me in the car, not a twenty-eight-year-old man. I glanced at the taxi-driver who couldn't fail to hear us but was tactfully showing no signs of interest in our conversation.

'Do you want to wait till we're alone?' I whispered. Nate shook his head.

'I wanted to get a message to you,' he continued 'but Dad said not to worry you, said there was no point since he'd be out in a few days. But then...' his voice cracked and I squeezed his hand while he composed himself. His Adam's apple rose and his jaw tensed as he glanced at the taxi-driver who kept his eyes on the road.

'Mam... he had another heart-attack. The hospital called me, and I went straightaway, but... but it was too late...'

'Oh, Nate,' I said, 'Nate, why didn't you call, I'd have come.'

'Dad said not to, Mam, I thought I was doing the right thing...'

We went directly to Nate's father's house where Arwel's sister Lynne and her husband Bernie were waiting for us. As the taxi-driver took my suit-case from the boot of the car, I watched Nate straighten his shoulders and tense his jaw. 'You take care,' the driver said giving me a pat on the shoulder.

'Sian, we're so pleased you could come,' Lynne said, her cordial words not masking the cool reserve that lay beneath them. 'Such a pity it was too late. Do sit down.'

Bitch. 'I came as soon as I could,' I said, flicking a glance at Nate, who thankfully didn't seem to have noticed his aunt's dig. 'Nate love, put the kettle on would you,' I said to him. 'I think we could both use a nice cup of tea.' Nate loped off to the kitchen seeming pleased to have something to do.

I sat down in an armchair and looked around. I hadn't been to Arwel's house very often. He'd bought it following the divorce and I'd never felt fully comfortable visiting. I saw that among the pictures of Nate and his father's side of the family there was a picture of me on the sideboard—an old one, taken on some holiday—young, smiling and tanned. I looked away.

'We'll take care of all the arrangements, of course,' Lynne —or Cruella, as I was more accustomed to thinking of her— said. 'Nothing for you to do, you'll be pleased to hear.'

What did she mean by that?

'Well, if there's anything I can help with I'd be pleased to,' I said.

'No need,' Cruella replied. 'Staying close by are you?'

I looked from her to Bernie. 'Well... I assumed...'

'My cousin and his wife are arriving tomorrow. Of course they'll be staying here.

What had I done to *eff* this woman off other than divorce her brother?

'I'll give you a lift soon as you're ready,' Bernie said. 'Take your time, no rush.'

I was relieved in a way. Tolerating more of their unnecessary frostiness was beyond me and I didn't want Nate to have to see it. He arrived carrying a tray and began to hand out mugs of steaming tea.

'What do you mean a hotel?' he exclaimed when I told him I'd need to book one. 'You're staying here!'

'Honestly, Nate, a hotel will be fine,' I said. 'There'll be other family coming for the funeral, it makes more sense for them to stay here.

'Well I'll stay at the hotel with you then,' he declared.

Cruella sipped her tea and watched us through narrowed eyes. Finally Nate relented and used the internet to book me into a bed and breakfast and, after finishing my tea, I prepared to leave.

'I'll come and stay when it's just us two,' I said.

Chapter Forty-nine

Cruella and Bernie continued to insist that I needn't concern myself with the funeral arrangements, and consequently I had very little to do. I spent as much time as I could with Nate but as well as being involved in the formalities following his father's death, he was in demand with the rest of his family.

'I'm really sorry, Mam,' he said. 'We'll get some time together after the funeral, I promise.'

With the letter I'd written to the letting agent still on the kitchen table in France, I decided to go to their office in the centre of town and arrange the notice to quit in person.

'No manager today. She back Wednesday,' a heavily-accented young man told me. 'It necessary you talk to her. I appoint you to inspect the property?'

I thought about that. I did want to see the house, but why? Was I curious about my tenants? Concerned for my property? Or did I want to imagine myself living there once more? In any case I allowed the young man to 'appoint me' and as luck would have it, the tenants were happy for me to come that afternoon.

I'd never met the couple who'd rented my little end-terrace, the agent having taken care, at my insistence, of all the arrangements. It felt strange having to make an appointment to visit my own house and even stranger after all these months to be walking up the little path. It all felt so familiar, so natural, as though my move to France had never happened, like I could take out my key, walk in and pick up where I'd left off—which I supposed was exactly what I would be doing soon. For now though, I rang the doorbell and waited to be admitted. The sound of a vacuum cleaner ended suddenly and moments later the door was opened by a shy-looking woman in her late twenties, I guessed. She was carrying a fretful baby.

'Come on in,' she said. 'Me fella's at work.'

The first thing I noticed was the smell. It wasn't bad, but it wasn't mine. Was six months all it took for a life to dissipate, to be replaced in the most visceral sense? I followed the woman along the hallway, where a big modern pushchair took up most of the space, and into the lounge.

'Well then, I'll make a cup o' tea, shall I?'

I could tell she was nervous—the woman didn't quite make eye-contact and she spoke too quickly. I expect she thought that the sudden arrival of an absent landlady didn't bode well for her security. She wasn't wrong. But I smiled at the Britishness of our interaction and without waiting for an answer (because of course I'd want tea) the woman bustled off into the kitchen still balancing the baby on her hip.

I looked around the room. There was evidence of hurried tidying—the recently-used vacuum cleaner had been shoved behind an armchair and a pile of toys had been pushed to the corner of the room. But the place seemed clean enough—I was reassured given I'd arrived at short notice. The furniture and the décor were the same as when I'd left, but the sofa—now covered with a navy throw—had been moved so that instead of facing the fireplace, it occupied the space in the bay window. And on the opposite wall was a big television that hadn't been mine. I didn't much like the way they'd organised the room but then, I reminded myself, I didn't have to. A row of birthday cards lined the mantelpiece. *Number One Mum*, proclaimed a big pink one.

The woman popped her head around the door. Her baby was crying now and she looked flustered. 'I need to change 'im,' she said. 'They said you wanted to look round. I don't mind. I keep the place nice, like.'

Arwel and I had raised Nate in this house and, after the divorce, we'd agreed that I'd be the one to keep it on since I'd paid off the mortgage with my parents' legacy. 'It's only fair,' Arwel had said. In the fallout of a divorce he couldn't understand, his decency had both impressed and humbled me. Since then I had come to think of this as *my* house—I'd lived there not just with all the accumulated memories of my life with Nate and his father, but for some years on my own. It was Nate's childhood years that came back to me vividly as I walked around the house.

Upstairs I peeked into the bathroom, which was much the same as it had been when I lived here, but for a new yellow shower curtain and the bath-full of plastic toys. The woman hadn't had a chance to clean in there and there were toothpaste stains in the sink and a soap scum tide mark in the bath. I resisted the impulse to lift the lid and peer into the toilet. The room was grubby but not filthy. At least it meant they were using the bath. Nate used to hate bath-time as a little boy and I remembered how I'd have to coax, cajole and bribe him—*But Mam, it's not fair, I had a bath yesterday.* Later, once his teenage hormones kicked in, demanding near-lethal levels of *Lynx Africa*, I'd have to yell at him to get him out. *Nate, have you taken up residency in there, you're going to make us all late.*

Nate's old bedroom was now a neat little nursery, freshly painted in pastel lemon, and I took in the Ikea wardrobe and drawers, an open stack of disposable nappies and other baby-necessities on a changing table, and a cot full of soft toys. I picked up a teddy-bear, a big blue fluffy thing sporting a white bow-tie. When Nate was here, there'd been Power-Rangers wall-paper, which he'd chosen himself and had been so proud of—I remembered the two of them decorating the room together, Arwel pretending to hang the paper upside down, Nate shrieking *'not like that, Dad!'* The Power-Rangers had remained until Nate left, after which Arwel had stripped it off, replacing it with magnolia paint. I pictured Nate sitting on the floor surrounded by Star Wars toys, his little face screwed up in concentration as he made them act out adventures. He was acting out his own adventures now. I put the teddy-bear back feeling an ache in my throat, as though I was mourning not the loss of his father, but of a younger Nate.

I opened the door to the bedroom which had been mine, first for twenty-odd years with Arwel and for the rest of the time by myself. That sickly-sweet smell of someone else's sweat told me I shouldn't be there—but it still looked like my bedroom. The big sleigh-bed we'd splashed out on after Arwel had a bonus from work, the matching wardrobe and drawers exactly where they'd been when I lived here. The pale blue wall-paper, bedspread and curtains—a compromise, I'd wanted lilac, which Arwel flatly refused—had been replaced with cream and chocolate brown. Arwel would have approved.

I picked up a tube of hand-cream—'*Pretty in Pink, Rose*'—part of a Christmas gift-set no doubt. Nate must have given me dozens over the years. With a glance down the hall, I opened it and squeezed some out, rubbing the creamy liquid into my skin and taking a deep sniff. It did indeed smell like roses. Truth in a plastic tube.

I couldn't name what I felt. Someone else's intimate mess in my most private space—their clothes hurriedly shoved into drawers, gunky-topped pots and bottles cluttering the surface, the wicker washing basket, its frayed cover toppling off the laundry inside. I lifted it and was confronted by another woman's dirty knickers and grubby teeshirts.

I'd known none other than Arwel in this room, the most intimate parts of our married life unfolding here in this bed, the sticky, gamey, bitter, comfort of all that we were and were not, reassured and repelled by familiar otherness—the warmth of his soft belly against my back, the smell of his sour morning-breath, his stubble scratching my cheek as we made love, his ejaculation grunt, blood and semen stains on countless sheets, snotty tissues on the floor, a bed-full of toast-crumbs, laughter, arguments, tears, planning, pleading, sulking, forgiving—talking in whispers so as not to let Nate overhear. It was in this bed I learned to cry in silence. And where Arwel and I finally agreed to part.

'You live in France then?' We were sipping tea in the lounge, the young woman's baby content now, gurgling away in a bouncy-chair which the woman twitched absently with her toe.

'Yes I do,' I said.

Guilt made me reluctant to say much more. I'd decided to take the cowardly route, letting the agent manage the notice to quit, and as the young woman looked at me warily, I doubted the wisdom of coming here. Still, something—perhaps the need to be in a familiar space—made me linger and I looked at her as I drank my tea.

'Must be exciting, living abroad,' she said, more out of politeness than envy, I felt.

'I guess it sounds exciting but in the end, living is just living, wherever you are.'

I picked up a custard cream from the plate on the coffee table wondering, as I took a bite, why the British like them so much.

'Your family over there, are they?'

She made 'over there' sound as though I lived on the moon. I shook my head.

'No, it's just me.'

Her look of incredulity made me smile.

'I'd miss me family,' she said with conviction. 'Can't imagine not being close to them.'

I looked around the room at the toys scattered here and there, the photographs lining the shelves, the birthday cards crowding the mantelpiece. *Number One Mum* was jostling for space with three *Best Sister*, a couple of *To My Cousin*, a *Darling Wife*, two *Daughter* (she must have nice in-laws), a *God-daughter*, various assorted *Aunts* and *Nieces* and innumerable *Special Friends*. '*Superstar Ma*' proclaimed a little porcelain bear. It made me think of my '*Mam Gorau yn y Byd*' mug. How strange that we switch our lives from house to house. Is it no more profound than putting on a new dress? I'd soon be stepping back into my life here. Faced with this woman's total colonisation of the place—her *enmeshment*—imagining this as my home once more felt unreal, like the kind of fantasy you have on holiday. My gaze came to rest on one of the pictures on a shelf—the woman tired-looking but smiling, holding her baby in a hospital bed surrounded by those I supposed were the card-givers, family and friends, old and young, grinning into the camera. This woman had strong roots here. Did that constitute 'home'?

'This is Geraint,' the woman said. 'My partner.' She took another of the pictures down and handed it to me. Two happy faces smiled out from a sunny beach. I was sure I had an identical one of Arwel and me. 'This here is little Geraint.' She picked up the baby who was gumming away at a plastic giraffe, and held him out to me. I put the picture down and reached out my arms but little Geraint screwed up his face and began to cry. The woman took him back and kissed him on the forehead.

'He's at that age,' she said apologetically. 'Only wants his Mam.'

'You enjoy him,' I answered, standing up to leave. 'They grow up far too fast.'

Sometimes clichés are the best way to express immutable truths.

Chapter Fifty

Arwel. My grieving was complicated. No longer being married when he died, I wasn't mourning the loss of a husband, but of a man I'd once loved. I was grieving the man I'd spent the biggest part of my life with and who had given me a son, but whose significance in my life had nonetheless changed. It suddenly struck me how utterly callous it must have seemed to him that, after years of marriage, followed by years friendship, I'd left for France and not spoken to him again. Why had I done that? And why had I taken so long to reply to his letter? Guilt and regret kept me awake in my hotel bed and I cursed myself over and over for being a coward. The fact that he died believing there had been another man in our marriage weighed on me like a penance for what the truth actually was.

I was grieving for Nate's loss, too. I watched him, pale-faced and tired, going through the motions, doing what had to be done but all the while suffering, and I learned what a terrible thing it is to see your child brought so very low and being able to do nothing to fix it.

I barely remember the details of the funeral, except how strong Nate was. Most of Arwel's family came, some of whom neither Nate nor I had seen for years and it was hard to think that this handsome, suited, young man shaking people's hands, accepting their condolences with such gracious poise was my little boy. In spite of his composure, I could see what perhaps only a mother could see. The way the corner of his mouth twitched while the priest gave the eulogy. How his Adam's apple bobbed three times in succession before he gave his tribute to his father. How tightly he held on to my hand as the coffin was lowered into the grave. I didn't know if pride was an appropriate emotion, it was certainly more than just my mothering that had given Nate his strength, but nonetheless, as I said my tearful goodbye to Arwel, I felt honoured that he'd given me this son.

'Are you happy in India?'

It was the day after the funeral and now that Cruella and Bernie and their clan had gone home, I was staying at Arwel's place with Nate. Nate's place now, I supposed. That evening, he and I were sitting on the living room floor having eaten a takeaway pizza while looking through old photographs, which Nate had hauled down from the loft. He kept exclaiming; 'Oh my god, I remember that!' or 'wow, how did you get me to wear those!' or more quietly 'I really loved going camping with Dad.'

'Yes I'm happy in India,' he said now.

I looked at him. Lamplight was carving shadows into his cheeks and from a certain angle, he looked like Arwel had when I first met him, gauntly attractive, his big grey eyes serious yet soft.

'Tell me what you like about it,' I said.

Nate didn't respond straight away—he seemed to be weighing his answer in his mind. I didn't rush him. We both took a sip of hot chocolate.

'Well, it's a different sort of life,' he began. 'There's a different rhythm there. It can be crazy, so fast and loud and crowded. The cities are mad, so much traffic and poverty, kids begging... I think it's all that the tourists get shocked by... '

'It sounds delightful!' I said. Nate laughed.

'Well, living there isn't the same. There's a lot that still does my head in. The bureaucracy is as bad they say it is, it can be impossible getting stuff done... but you know what, Mam? Once you've been there for a while, fallen into the rhythm of the place... you see a humanity there that's hard to find here. People are less bothered about *things*—you know, like consumerism. Even the richer families don't fill their houses with junk. I used to visit the house of two doctors—I was giving their kids extra English lessons. Their place was nice, really big—marble floors, beautiful gardens. They had money. But you know what, in their house they didn't have much more than what they needed—hardly any ornaments or paintings, only the basic furniture. It's like what's more important over there are the connections people have. I really appreciate that way of thinking.' He'd been speaking fast and with conviction, but now his face softened and he seemed no longer aware of me listening. 'It's not only that though... in the hills where I live... you can see the mountains opposite reflected perfectly in the lake... there's this mist over the water in the mornings... the smell of incense comes out of nowhere and you hear the sound of chanting from the temple... it's a peace like nowhere else...' He looked at me cautiously, as though unsure whether I'd take him seriously. I nodded. 'I feel at home there, Mam.'

The beauty of what he'd described and the fact that I was absent from the connections he'd found hurt. I swallowed hard, fighting the urge to cry. *I can't imagine not being close to them,'* the woman in my house had said of her family.

'Really?' I said quietly, 'You feel at home so far away, even though you don't have any roots there?'

Nate looked at me for a long moment.

'I'll always feel comfortable here,' he replied. 'I mean Cardiff, Wales. It's really easy to be here... I mean I know how it all works, the food feels like comfort food—like I don't miss fish and chips in India but it's the first thing I want when I'm here. I understand exactly what people are saying without having to concentrate... All that creates a kind of a homely feeling. But I think... it isn't really enough—those things for me at least, are kind of superficial. I think ultimately, home isn't necessarily where you grew up. It's where you feel connected.'

He'd never spoken to me like this before. I stared at him, not knowing how to respond. *Don't you feel connected to me, Nate?* He must have read my mind.

'And family will always be family. But—Christmas dinners and Sunday lunches and living in each other's pockets are only one way to do it. Those things don't necessarily equate to love, same as living apart doesn't have to mean you don't care. Me, I feel more free knowing you and Dad *set* me free... I'll always be grateful my whole life that you supported the fact that I'm doing my own thing, living my life in a way that makes sense to me...' He paused and raised a quizzical eyebrow. 'Of course it helps with keeping in touch when your mother doesn't throw her phone in the sea.'

My relief must have been palpable. The tears broke and I laughed and cried at the same time, so hard that I started to cough and Nate had to thump me on the back. Once I was calm again, he hesitated for a moment and, in that instant, as so often happens with Nate, I knew exactly what he was going to say.

'Mam... there's... there's a woman. In India. Swati. She's very special to me. I'd love you to meet her one day...'

Unable to speak with such a mix of love and pride rising in my chest, I simply grinned at him like a loon.

'So you've finally found yourself then?'

'Found myself! Don't be daft, Mam,' he put both hands on his heart. 'I'm right here, where I've always been.'

I wondered how Arwel and I had managed to produce such a wise young man.

'So will you go back to France?' he asked.

I hadn't yet told him about my intention to return to Cardiff and I hesitated, surprised by his question.

'You don't seem very sure.' He took a sip of his chocolate. 'You know, you can live here if you want to move back. What with our place rented out. I'll be going back to India.'

I looked around at my late ex-husbands house, at the photographs spread out before us of our life together, of Christmases, birthdays, holidays, happy times spent with one another and with our boy. Of course our life together hadn't been one big holiday. Looking at Nate, I felt a complex mingling of relief and guilt that his father had never known the truth. I picked up a photograph—the two of them by a tent, grins as wide as their faces, rain plastering their hair to their heads. It was true what I'd told the divorce solicitor, Arwel had been a good father and a good husband. Seeing this grieving yet strong young man before me, our beautiful, imperfect, wise son, I felt more settled than I had in some time.

'I'll go back to France for now,' I said. 'And then we'll see.'

Chapter Fifty-one

This time, rather than a boat I took a plane to France, and instead of Arwel seeing me off it was Nate. And this time I let myself cry.

'Are you sure you're going to be okay?' I asked, realising how silly I sounded saying this to a grown man.

'I'm alright, Mam,' Nate insisted. 'You're the one crying! Besides, I'll be over before you know it.' We hugged each other fit to burst.

'I'll text once I'm back,' I said, patting the new iPhone in my pocket.

We'd agreed that once he'd finalised his father's estate and organised the letting of the house, assisted—quite unnecessarily—by his Uncle Bernie, *'don't you worry Sian, I'll see him right,'* Nate would fly out to France in time for Christmas.

'But what about work,' I'd asked. 'Won't they miss you?'

'I'm a yoga teacher, Mam, not president of the Bank of India.' He laughed. 'They'll do without me for a while.'

Aziz was waiting at the airport to meet me. Winter had arrived abruptly in France and I almost didn't recognise him in his big black overcoat and scarf.

'You really are so kind,' I said, accepting a kiss on each cheek.

'Just being neighbourly,' he replied, although of course he wasn't technically-speaking my neighbour.

In spite of the rain, which was coming down in sheets, it didn't take us long to get onto the AutoRoute, the villages, fields and vineyards flashing past in a sodden mass of grey as Aziz sped along. We stopped only for the péages, the toll-payment booths whose lights loomed in front of us from time to time, and at the Carrefour where I did a food shop as Aziz sipped an allongé in a café. Once more we spoke very little and, as when he'd taken me to the airport, I was grateful. The rain hadn't let up and back in the car, my coat steaming in the heat, which Aziz turned to maximum, I wiped the fogged-up window with a glove and stared out at the passing countryside. An idea had started forming in my mind.

I hadn't gone back to the letting agent in Cardiff, phoning instead to say that I was no longer sure of my plans and that I'd call or write soon. *'I tell manager,'* the boy had said. Being back in Wales, seeing my house and the life the new family had created there, talking to Nate about India—even saying goodbye to Arwel—it had all helped me to see my options more clearly. One thing was sure—Constance and Jacques would be putting the cottage back on the market in the spring. I'd narrowed my choices down to two possibilities: I could either go back to Cardiff. Or buy the cottage.

At last the rain began to clear and as we sped along I thought about the first possibility. My choices in Wales were moving back into my own house or I could continue to rent it out and live in Arwel's—now Nate's place. Either way, I'd have to find a job. Thoughts of long hours in open-plan hell presided over by some In-Control Carol convinced me that my previous employment wasn't an option. But what else I could do?

On the other hand, I could stay in France. I did the sums in my head. If I sold my house I could certainly afford to buy the cottage. I had no idea of my tenant's circumstances, whether they'd be in a position to buy my place or even want to. In any case, would a sale give me enough money to replace the roof? And install some kind of heating system, the open fires would surely not be enough in the long term? I'd have to get a job here. *Back to the same problem.* I stared out at the French countryside flashing past in a blur of rain. Could I call this home?

'What sort of industry is there around Saint Vey?'

Aziz started, having been deep in his own thoughts. Frowning, he pushed his glasses further up his nose.

'*Pas beaucoup,*' he said. 'Not much. Mainly wine.'

The life of a *vigneron* sounded appealing—I pictured myself in a big, floppy hat, tending the vines all summer, grape picking in the autumn, sampling the wines—for quality purposes, of course. Something told me the reality wouldn't be quite like that.

'What about in the towns?' I asked. 'Is there much business in the region?'

Aziz shrugged. 'The usual. Tourism in the summer.' He flicked a look into the rear-view mirror and sped up to overtake a lorry. 'There's a nuclear power-plant over by Rochfourchelle. And a military base a bit further.'

I nodded. I could work as some kind of clerk I supposed. But what made me highly employable in the UK—my French fluency—clearly was of no interest here. Besides, who'd employ a foreign woman in her mid-fifties when they could get a young French graduate? In any case, I thought, remembering my talks with Doctor Adebowale, I'd rather eat my own head than work in an office again. I laughed at my own joke and Aziz raised an enquiring eyebrow.

'It's nothing,' I said.

I could always set up in business with Monsieur Ripaille, as a gardener. The idea made me chuckle again.

Darkness had begun to fall by the time we arrived at Saint Vey and even though it was raining steadily again, I was surprised by how relieved I felt at being back. I stepped out of the car to the tang of wood-smoke and wet leaves, the cold air sharp and clear in spite of the rain. Aziz insisted on carrying my suitcase inside as I managed my shopping bags and I thanked him profusely once more, insisting that he take the petrol money I was pressing into his hand. He finally relented, stuffed the Euros in his pocket and hurried off to Madame Clairjo's, pulling his coat over his head as he ran. 'Be here for the week,' he said. 'You be sure to call on us if there's anything you need.'

Inside, the cottage was dark and cold and smelt like old soot. I shivered, keeping my coat on as I heaved my shopping onto the kitchen table. The unhappiness I'd lived with here for the last few weeks... had my time in Wales changed it? Suddenly I was tearful, so very tired... I held onto the back of a chair and let the tears fall, not sure what they meant. But something—either in me or the cottage—seemed to have lifted. A subtle change in the quality of the space or how I fit into it, a deepness that was more protective than sad... the cottage wrapped around me, it's now familiar winter smell comforting, and all I wanted to do was fill the place with warmth.

Bonjour, ghost. I made myself a mug of hot chocolate and set about stacking scrunched paper, twigs and logs in the kitchen inglenook. The ghost—glad that I was back—saw my relief that the shape of my softness had changed, and before long I was rubbing my hands together by a cosy fire.

The wood crackling and spitting in the hearth, flames flickering in the jars on the shelf, I set about putting away my shopping, thinking, as I found home for the vegetables, packets, bottles and jars, about the first time I'd arrived here. And like that first evening, I dispensed with the idea of cooking in favour of a glass of chilled wine and a cheeseboard of Brie, Cantal and creamy Bleu de Bresse—not under the stars this time but watching the flames.

I wonder where Pegleg is. I hoped the kitten had found somewhere warm to sleep during my absence—and enough to eat. I glanced at my suitcase, which was sitting by the front door where Aziz had left it. *The unpacking can wait.* I smiled—again reminded of the first time I'd arrived. Instead I grabbed a pen and a pad of paper from a drawer in the salon, finally took off my coat and settled myself in the old armchair. Taking a long, deep breath, I looked around the kitchen. The fire was hissing and cracking now and shadows from the flames were dancing around the walls. The thought of Clotilde popped into my mind and I wondered whether she was sitting in front of her own fire enjoying a glass of her strange liqueur.

Lying where I'd left them on the kitchen table were the two letters I'd written before going to Wales—both sealed, stamped and waiting to be posted. I picked them up and looked at my handwriting on the envelopes, neat and precise. Had what I'd written in each represented a new start or a cowardly end?

What do you think, ghost?

A burning log rolled out of the fire onto the hearth and I trapped it with the poker and flipped it back in. I nodded and took a sip of my wine. *You're right.* I threw both letters into the fire. The paper curled and blackened and I watched as the flames devoured my words. I had a new letter to write.

Chapter Fifty-two

I dropped the letter into the post-box with a good-luck kiss, willing my Aunt and Uncle to look favourably on its contents. The baker's van tooted its horn just as the letter left my hand.

'Ah, Sian, you're back, we all wondered if you'd decided to stay in England.'

'Wales,' I corrected with an indulgent smile. 'Well, as you can see, I'm back.'

Clairjo, Ripaille and I huddled in our winter coats around the van breathing in a sharp north wind which was blowing smoke from our chimneys down the lane. Madame Clairjo seemed to have forgotten it was her son-in-law who'd picked me up from the airport. She smiled and pecked a kiss on each of my cheeks. Smiling once more I turned to Monsieur Ripaille who winked at me as I planted a kiss on each of his bristly jowls.

'Those hedges want trimming again,' he said, as though I'd been away for months.

A tubby youth with a pockmarked face had climbed out of the bakers van and was bagging two pains au chocolat.

'Where's Madame Volt?' I asked.

'Terrible thing,' Clairjo tutted.

'Nasty fall, she had,' Ripaille muttered.

'Tripped on her stairs.'

'Christ! Is she okay?'

Clairjo and Ripaille shook their heads.

'Broke her leg,' said Madame Clairjo. 'Been in hospital since you left, only just out. Marie took me see her. Right sorry state she was in.'

'Oh no,' I exclaimed, surprised to find myself concerned in spite of the old bat's sour nature. 'I'm sorry to hear that.'

'Oh she'll mend alright, silly fool. Shouldn't leave things lying around at the tops of stairs. Dangerous, it is.'

'The thing is,' Ripaille said, 'who's going to do the bread run now?'

I looked enquiringly at the boy who was wrapping a baguette to within an inch of its life.

'Got to go back to college,' he mumbled. 'Can only do up to the end of the week. Sorry.' He thrust the baguette at Madame Clairjo who took it and handed it to Monsieur Ripaille.

'Never mind the bread, what about the shopping?' she declared. 'There's no-one to do it. Marie can't run over here for me every week. Poor Madame Fontenay is at her wit's end, no family at all to help. Right before Christmas too.' She jabbed an accusing finger at me. 'It's alright for you young things, you can jump on a bus, but it's not so easy for us. Madame Volt did the weekly shop for all the old folk hereabouts.'

'Do mine on the internet, I do…' the old man began but Clairjo cut him off.

'Oh be quiet, Ripaille, we can't all be doing with that.'

We were silent for a moment while the chastened Monsieur paid the young man for his bread.

'No Monsieur Delariche?' I asked suddenly.

The two old folk exchanged a knowing look.

It was strange to imagine Nate being in the house, accustomed as I'd become to no other company than the ghost. But I was overjoyed at the prospect of sharing some of my life here with my son and I hadn't spent a Christmas with him in years. I hoped he wouldn't get bored. We can always get the bus to town I thought, and I set about sprucing the place up, paying particular attention to the room that would be his.

One thing did present itself as a problem though. I'd planned to buy all sorts of nice food for Nate's stay. The shopping I'd done at the Carrefour on the way from the airport wouldn't be sufficient and with Madame Volt indisposed for the foreseeable future it looked like I'd have to get the bus into town. I thought of lugging back bags full of bottles, tins and packets, fruit, vegetables, potatoes, loo paper, flour, sugar, pasta, cheese, wine, cat food … *Yes I know what I said ghost, but Pegleg needs to eat.* I supposed I'd have to get a taxi. Pegleg, as though he'd heard us talking about him, limped over, wound himself around my legs and—his stomach already bulging—mewed at me pathetically until I poured him some milk. I wondered what Madame Clairjo would do about her shopping. And Madame Fontenay. As prickly as she was, I had to admit Volt provided a valuable service for us isolated folk.

I returned to the question of the shopping on and off that afternoon as I replenished my stock of wood from the garden shed, the great pile of logs covering my jumper in sawdust as I heaved them inside. It occurred to me as I dumped them in a heap by the fire that now I had an iphone I could order what I needed on the internet. But a sudden thought put paid to that idea. I hadn't checked the gas bottle which powered the cooker since I'd arrived. Six months' worth, my Uncle had said. I'd completely forgotten until now. I went to the store room and tilted it up. The bottle was suspiciously light. *Imagine running out of gas in the middle of cooking the Christmas dinner.* I'd have to buy a new one. For this reason I'd resigned myself to ordering a taxi and set about googling local services on my clever new mobile. I decided that I'd go into town on Saturday, spend the morning at this farmers market—it had reached mythical proportions in my mind by now—and stop off at the supermarket on the way back. Surprisingly enough, I was looking forward to it. *Perhaps ask Madame Clairjo if she needs anything?* Good idea, ghost, I'll do that.

I was considering whether I ought to get Nate something for Christmas. *I wonder if you can buy yoga pants in St Cloud?* Chuckling at the thought of some wizened *paysanne* explaining the merits of stretchy leggings, an idea flashed into my mind. Flopping into the armchair, I gave the fire a poke and turned the thought over, doing a few quick sums in my head. *Is this brilliant or crazy*, I asked the ghost? The ghost didn't have an opinion and I took that as a good sign. I thought about it some more. *It's a long-shot but it could work.* Before I could change my mind I put the fire-guard in place, grabbed my coat and hurried off to Madame Clairjo's.

Chapter Fifty-three

Clairjo I was and Clairjo I am, although for how much longer given my state of health, I couldn't tell you.

'*Ah, Madame Evans, bonjour, ça va?*'

Marie opened the door and I heard her greet the foreigner. In she came wearing a sweater bristling in twigs. That notwithstanding I kissed her cheeks and told her to sit down. She did, not before remarking how hot it was in the salon.

'Well it is December,' I retorted, 'Got to keep the chills at bay.' I pulled my shawl tighter around my shoulders.

She joined me at the dining table as Marie went to the drinks cabinet to pour us an apéritif.

'What's Pegleg doing here?' Sian pointed at the kitten.

'Pegleg? Who's Pegleg? This is Poufpouf. Nearly time for his dinner, isn't it *ma puce*?'

Poufpouf cast me a haughty sneer—ungrateful animal—jumped down from my lap and limped off to the kitchen.

'Any news of Madame Volt?' Sian asked when the three of us were sitting at the table sipping little glasses of Beaumes-de-Venise.

'*Ah, c'est très difficile,*' Marie said, shaking her head. 'I've stocked up for Mother, but it's hard, I live two hours away. What with the boys, I can't come every weekend. What will she do about the fresh food, the bread?'

She's a good girl, Marie. To illustrate the gravity of her question she threw up her hands in supplication.

'Where does Madame Volt live?' Sian asked.

'Lives above her bakery in Duroque sur Vey,' I eyed her sharply. 'Why? Thinking of taking her flowers?'

She didn't tell me her plan. I'd have laughed at her if she had but credit where it's due, the girl had it all figured out. Feisty. That's what she is. Volt told me all about it when I visited, and what she didn't tell me I could well imagine. I told Ripaille what the baker told me.

Went with Aziz she did, the next morning, him insisting he didn't mind since he had to go to the hardware shop in any case. No doubt Sian thought about how she'd approach her idea as they sped along the lanes. Happen she wasn't convinced the baker wouldn't dismiss her out of hand.

Duroque sur Vey is a pretty village—nicest in the region if you ask me, dominated by a huge church. It's a twenty minute drive from our little hamlet. The young woman in the bakery in the tiny cobbled square showed Sian upstairs to Madame Volt's living quarters while Aziz went to the hardware shop and no doubt to have an allongé at the café opposite.

Volt was propped up on her sofa reading a magazine, her right leg plastered from thigh to ankle stretched out in front of her. She wasn't pleased to see Sian.

'Can't make you a drink,' she said. 'Can barely move at all.'

'That's okay,' Sian replied. 'Would you like me to make you something?' She looked around the apartment—it's what they call minimalist, devoid of nicknacks and photographs, not to my taste but there we are—but all the doors were closed so Sian couldn't see which one led to the kitchen. There was a huge bunch of flowers on the sideboard and I bet the girl cursed herself for not bringing anything.

'Don't suppose you'll be staying long,' Volt snapped, but then thought better of it. 'Sorry, I get so tired.'

'How are you managing?' Sian asked, sitting down on an armchair.

Volt made a noise of exasperation and indicated her plastered leg.

'Ridiculous is what it is. Be months before I'm walking again. Months! Even more before I'm driving.'

She sighed hard and Sian shook her head in sympathy.

'What happened?' She asked.

'Tripped,' the woman spat, as though it should be obvious to all but a fool. She flung her magazine onto the coffee table.

'What will you do about the business? Are you able to bake?'

'No, I'm not!' Volt moaned, 'Lucille and Pierre are going to have to do the best they can. With some help down the stairs I'll at least be able to supervise.'

'And the bread runs? The boy said he had to go back to college.'

It was clearly a question that had been vexing the baker and her voice rose once more.

'Six months it'll be before I can drive, the Doctor told me. Six months. The boy's going back to college this week and neither Lucille nor Pierre will do the runs. Big part of the business that is. I supply bread and the pastries for everyone round here—and the hotels. Now they'll all be off into St Cloud, buying supermarket bread. *Pah!* She threw up her hands in disgust. 'Don't know what I'm going to do. Then of course there's the old folks shopping.'

Sian nodded. 'Actually, it's that I've come about,' she began. 'The shopping and the bread runs...'

'Well, I can't help it, can I,' the woman snapped, cutting Sian off mid-sentence. 'You'll just have to find a way to do your own shopping.'

'Madame Volt, I think I have a solution to the problem.'

'Solution? What solution?' The baker peered at her dubiously.

'Well,' said Sian, 'why don't I do the van runs?'

'You?' Volt snorted, as though Sian were the last person who could do such a thing.

'The thing is,' Sian said, 'we'd be helping each other. I'm going to have to look for a job pretty soon. And I'm...well, let's just say I'm not looking for nine to five work. You need someone to do the van run three times a week, plus the shopping for the old people. Well, I can drive and I can shop.'

Volt peered at her, clearly not sure what to make of the suggestion. Most likely the first time Sian had seen her lost for words.

'I tell you what,' Sian said. 'Why not give me a try? I can do the runs for a week after the lad goes back to college, and we can see if it works out.'

Volt was silent for a moment more. She narrowed her eyes and thought the idea through. Sian didn't interrupt.

'Couldn't pay you much,' she said eventually.

'I don't need much,' Sian replied. 'And I assume what I'd get for doing the old folks shopping would be mine.'

Madame Volt grunted. 'Need a good driver, I would.'

'Had my licence for twenty-three years, never an accident.'

'Think you could find your way around? It's a big area I cover, all tiny lanes.'

'My iPhone has GPS.'

'My leg won't be broken for ever, you know.'

'I realise that. But this job would be a start.'

Volt regarded her long and hard. Downstairs, the bell on the shop door tinkled and they heard muffled voices. Madame Volt was suddenly surprisingly business-like.

'Well, I suppose there's no harm in a trial,' she said. 'You can go out tomorrow with the boy. He can show you the ropes as best he can. I'll sort things out here and get the boy to pick you up again on Tuesday and give you the van. 6am sharp, no later, you hear? 6am sharp. I don't abide lateness. Come up and see me after the run Saturday and, if you've done well, we'll discuss terms.' She narrowed her eyes and regarded Sian for a long moment. 'I hear your baking's not too bad...'

She stopped speaking as someone tapped gently on the open lounge door and they both turned. Sian no doubt expected to see Aziz, but instead a rather stocky man of about sixty was standing at the threshold, a huge bunch of calla-lilies in his liver-spotted hands.

'*Mesdames!*' he said, no doubt delighted to find not one but two women in front of him. 'Lucille said you had a visitor.'

'Come on in, Marcel,' Volt said, fluffing her hair and straightening her dress. 'Madame Evans here is my new driver.' She drew herself up proudly. 'Madame Evans, this is my very good friend Marcel Blanchard.' Happen she emphasised the word 'very'.

'*Enchantée,*' Sian said, standing and shaking the man's hand.

'Been looking after our invalid, have you?' he said, taking off his coat.

'Yes, well, thank you very much, Madame Evans, I'm sure you want to get on.' Volt said before Sian could reply. She thrust out her hand for her to shake. 'The van will pick you up tomorrow as agreed. Good day to you.'

Chapter Fifty-four

I hadn't seen Clotilde since I'd arrived back from Wales and what with preparing for Nate's arrival and getting to grips with my new job, I'd had little time to give her or her husband (if that's who he was) much thought. Winter was in full force now, the swallows had long since left for warmer climes and the days ranged from bright and sharp to wet and windy. Whether the sun was out or not, it was always cold. I now had my nightly tipple—or more often than not a mug of hot chocolate—in front of a roaring fire—often joined by 'Poufpouf' who would purr loudly and let me tickle his fat little belly. I noticed a light in the window of Clotilde's studio a few times as I went about my days, and I imagined her up there, *boucharde* in hand, chinking away at her statue. I hoped she was dressed in something warmer than a nightgown.

The baker's van was parked by my cottage now and three times a week, on Tuesday's, Thursdays and Saturdays, I put on my warmest coat and my gloves, left the house early and drove the twenty minutes to Duroque sur Vey. There, with Madame Volt shouting directives at us from the upstairs window, Lucille and I, our breath condensing in the cold air, loaded the van with big square baskets piled high with fresh, warm baguettes, breads, croissants and pastries before I set off into the lanes to make my rounds.

'Women,' Arwel used to say, 'no sense of direction and can't read a map to save their lives.' Contrary to his bizarre conviction, I had no problem at all reading a map and, rather than the GPS app on my phone, enjoyed the challenge of using one to find my way through the lanes, villages and hamlets to the places that Madame Volt had circled in red marker pen. 'I don't expect you to finish as fast as I did,' she said. 'You go steady, I can't be affording a new van.' I took great pleasure in pulling up at the designated spots and tooting the horn, whereupon a little huddle of locals would emerge from the nearby cottages to gather round the van, rubbing their hands and stamping their feet against the cold.

I soon learned my way around the district, which roads were likely to be muddy, where the lane narrowed so much I'd need to back up if I encountered another vehicle, at which hotels I'd be given a tip. Madame Fontenay took to inviting me in and I fell into the habit of spending a contented twenty minutes drinking coffee in her warm little kitchen. Generally I was home by two, except on Saturdays when, having picked up the bread at the bakery and made the hotel deliveries, I'd drive on into St Cloud.

Having avoided going into the town for months, I began to look forward to Saturdays and wondered why I'd closeted myself away all summer. Each week, all year round, the Farmers Market took over a broad, cobbled square bordered on all four sides by handsome half-timbered buildings. The first time I went, I parked the van in the municipal carpark and followed the hordes up a winding street bordered by Linden trees and into the square. The market was alive with activity. The stalls were ranged under covered awnings so that whatever the weather the doyennes of the region could take their time choosing the best of the abundant produce. Ruddy stall holders in flat caps called their wares, doughty matrons prodded and sniffed, families filled wheeled caddies with enough vegetables to strike horror into the hearts of British children. The whole vibrant panoply was suffused with the smell of warm pastries, cooked meats, fresh fish, cheeses... I wandered through the market, accepting little tasters of sliced pears, walnuts, goat's cheese, olives... from smiling proprietors who rubbed their hands together in their fingerless gloves. I soon learned that on Saturdays I didn't need to bother with breakfast.

I discovered that an aged Michel did indeed still run the end stall, aided by Michel Junior who helped me to pick out the firmest potatoes, the sweetest sprouts, juiciest pumpkins, crunchiest apples—only fruits and vegetables of the season, all of it fresh from the soil. Old Michel took to handing me a bunch of fragrant herbs which he told me he grew himself in his greenhouse—*pour la jolie étrangère,* he'd say, winking. I'd thank him and move on to the next stall where I'd take my time choosing ripe Bries, St Féliciens, Fourmes d'Amberts and

Chèvres, followed by fresh fish, big pats of butter, speckled eggs, tangy Crème Fraîche, local wine... I took to allowing myself the luxury of drinking a *noisette*—a tiny cup of milky coffee served with a slither of chocolate at *Café Dominique*, where the portly waiter—possibly Dominique himself—chatted to the stall-holders and never stopped smiling.

After the market I'd load my bags—each one labelled with the name of its owner—into the van, and head off to the big supermarket on the edge of town, where I'd whiz around filling even more bags with household necessities. Then, the back of the van heaving with shopping for myself plus eight or so old people, I'd leave the bustle of the town, head back into the countryside and start my round. I learned a new-found respect for Madame Volt—this amount of shopping, followed by the delivery run was no mean feat.

As I sped along the lanes one bright and blustery Saturday afternoon, I thought back to my imaginary conversation with the Good Doctor. *'Does work have to be meaningful?'* Was I feeling more settled because I was doing something that could be considered worthwhile? Or was it simply because I now had some structure in my life? Perhaps it was nothing to do with my work, but because I'd made a decision to make this my home—or maybe it was because I was looking forward to the arrival of my son. I wondered, as the vines flashed by, whether we ever truly know the cause of our feelings. Whatever the answer, 'the foreign baker's assistant' soon became a hit with the country-folk and I enjoyed the little interactions I had with them as they bought their bread and cakes. It was clear that the locals valued it too. Only Madame Clairjo grumbled. 'Means I always get mine last,' she said.

Nate's visit was growing closer. 'I'll be there just before Christmas,' he'd said when I'd left Cardiff. Knowing Nate, that could mean anything. I was delighted to receive his text with the date and time of his flight. I texted back straightaway to say I'd pick him up from the airport. With so much happening, Clotilde took a back seat in my thoughts. That was, until another note arrived in my post-box.

Chapter Fifty-five

Well, he was certainly persistent, I'll give him that. I took the note from the post-box to the cottage and reread it.

Dear Sian,
I was so sorry to hear about your loss. If there is anything I can do don't hesitate to ask. I'd be happy if you'd do me the honour of allowing me to renew my invitation. Would you be free for dinner this Saturday? If so, I'll pick you up at 19.30h.
Paul

I really couldn't be bothered, as I had last time, to agonise for days about the man's absence of morals. There were plenty of reasons to decline his invitation. But in a fit of sheer audacity that I hoped matched his, I decided to accept. At the very least I might be able to finally solve the mystery of Clotilde. So I wrote a note and dropped it into his post-box.

In Cardiff I'd bought three dresses. A black one for the funeral, which I'd since shoved to the back of my wardrobe hoping never to wear it again. And, with the memory of Madame Clairjo's party in mind, another two which I'd hoped —should the need arise—would exude the kind of understated sophistication that the local dames managed to command. Paul Delariche's invitation proved to be the first such occasion.

At 7.15 on Saturday evening I was standing in front of my dressing table mirror, regarding my taupe, knee length dress, fitted at the waist, with a neck line that showed just a hint of cleavage. I turned this way and that not sure I was completely happy. *What do you think, ghost?* The ghost demanded to know what on earth I was doing, going out for dinner for this man, and wasn't interested in my outfit. *Oh don't get your knickers in a twist,* I said and, opening a drawer, rummaged around for a scarf, found a deep pink one and tied it at the neck. Much better and very French. I was still arguing with the ghost while fiddling with my hair, which I'd attempted to style into a chignon, when I heard the bell. Grabbing my good shoes, I ran down the stairs in my stockinged feet, almost tripping on the way. *It's not an effing date*, I muttered as I forced myself to walk more calmly, grabbed my coat and closed the door behind me.

Yanking open the gate—*dammit, why have I never got round to oiling this thing?*—I was confronted with Paul Delariche who clearly *did* think this was a date, having dressed up for the occasion in a smart fawn-coloured ensemble. I eyed the open neck of his pristine shirt which revealed just a hint of dark hair and leaned in to kiss his cheeks just as he held out his hand and, both blushing, we settled for a fumbled peck.

'There's a nice place in town,' Paul said once we were seated in the big silver Audi, which contained neither Clotilde nor the dog. 'Auberge St Juste. Do you know it?'

I'd seen the place, it was in the same square as the market and it looked pleasant.

'I've never been,' I replied.

Some people might be surprised to learn that house-ghosts sometimes go out. Mine does and on this occasion he wasted no time wafting into the car where he spent the next twenty minutes annoying me. I was glad Paul had the radio on.

What exactly do you think you're doing?

Isn't it obvious? I'm going out for dinner.

Very drôle. Why?

Because I want to find out about Clotilde.

Madame Clairjo thinks he likes you.

Madame Clairjo is a nosy old lady.

Aren't you worried you're leading him on?

Look ghost, bugger off and leave me alone.

Okay, but on your head be it.

Damned ghost, always has to get the last word. Delariche, oblivious to the conversation, kept his eyes on the road ahead.

We left the car in the same car-park I used on Saturdays and walked past the sand-coloured buildings with the stalky remnants of purple and red geraniums still tumbling over balconies, along the winding cobbled street which opened out into the little square, empty now that the market wasn't here. Three or four cafés—including Café Dominique—had their striped awnings out, their lights shining invitingly, and couples and small groups were walking in the chilly evening calm. The ghost had at last buggered off and I allowed Paul to steer me towards a tall, half-timbered building in the far left corner of the square.

'I've booked a window table.' he said—pretty much the first he'd spoken since we left Saint Vey.

'Lovely,' I replied.

Inside, the restaurant was warm and cosy with a fire crackling in a huge hearth, low beams and wooden furniture giving the place a relaxed, rustic feel in spite of the well-dressed diners. I was pleased I'd worn the taupe dress. A waiter rushed over. 'Messieurs, Dame,' he said, with a look that suggested that Paul was an habitué. *He's probably been here with Clotilde.* The waiter led us to a quiet table by the window and took our coats. 'An apéritif to begin?' he said once we were seated.

'A coupe of Champagne?' Paul looked at me with a raised eyebrow.

And I—*oh my god*—I panicked.

...effing hell, the ghost was right, what am I doing here, I should never have accepted...

All the clichés were running riot in my body, pounding heart, nausea, rush of blood to my face... *Calm down, Sian, it's just dinner!* I took a deep breath and forced a smile.

'Just wine for me,' I mumbled, hoping I didn't sound love-struck. Paul didn't seem to notice anything amiss and I marvelled at how outward appearance can be so misleading.

'The local white is excellent,' he said. And to the waiter, 'We'll take a bottle of the 2009.'

Two glasses, no more. I attempted to keep my anxiety firmly on the inside by consulting the menu. The waiter returned, showed the bottle to Paul who nodded his approval, and proceeded with a well-practiced hand to squeak the corkscrew into the cork and draw it out neatly. He poured a drop into Paul's glass and looked politely away as Paul gave it a swirl and a sniff.

'Fine,' he said.

The waiter poured us a small measure each and I was dreading Paul proposing a toast like *to getting know you better* or worse, *to our budding friendship.* I was hugely relieved when he took a sip from his glass and picked up his menu. I stared blankly at the words for what felt like an age. *God, is one of us going to say something soon?* I half-wished the ghost was here to distract me and I realised I was clenching my jaw. Unclenching it, I glanced around. The restaurant was buzzing with the murmur of happy diners enjoying a Saturday night meal. Some of them looked distinctly romantic and panic threatened to grip me once more. *For god's sake relax, you're an adult.*

It occurred to me that Paul and I had barely spoken to one another—not just this evening but ever. We'd hardly exchanged a civil word, never mind small-talk. I had no idea how to begin and the silence was becoming embarrassing so at last I ploughed in. But my *I've never tried rabbit before* crashed into his *the duck is always good here* and I cringed, not knowing whether I had the will or the heart to carry on with this.

'It's a lovely menu,' I said eventually.

'Have you chosen?' Paul replied.

I had and Paul waved the waiter over once more. I wondered whether he was the old family friend my aunt had mentioned in her letter but was in no mood to ask. He took our order with a little bow and returned almost immediately with a basket of bread.

'Did the funeral go well?'

'How is your dog?'

Christ almighty, can we not just communicate like normal human beings?!

'I'm so sorry.' I attempted a laugh.

Paul didn't speak and I took a sip of wine, sorely tempted to break my two glass rule and knock back as much as necessary to get through this torture.

'Yes thank you,' I said. 'The funeral went as well as these things can. And it was good to spend some time with my son.'

'*Mais oui,*' he said, 'Madame Clairjo told me you have a son.'

'Yes, he's called Nathan. Everyone calls him Nate. Actually, he's coming out to visit me in a few days. He's spending Christmas here.'

227

'That will be nice. I have a daughter.'

At last an actual conversation. I wondered whether it was too soon to mention Clotilde.

'Does your daughter live with you?' I asked.

'No, no, Gabrielle lives in Paris,' Paul replied. 'And she isn't a lover of the countryside so regrettably she rarely visits. But I visit her often. My work takes me to Paris a lot.'

Not his daughter then.

'Do you have many visitors here?' I asked.

'Er, not really, no.'

Stupid question. Paul's look of confusion reflected how odd it sounded—the natural thing would have been to ask him about the job that takes him to Paris. Thank god our starters arrived and we could focus our talk on the delights of the soup à l'oignon and garlic escargot. Now that I'd warmed somewhat to the occasion, I got the work-conversation out of the way.

'I'm an architect,' Paul said in answer to my question. 'Semi-retired. My practice is in Paris—my daughter runs it now. I help out from time to time.' We'd moved onto the main course and Paul took a large bite of his steak.

'You'll have heard that I'm doing the bread run for Madame Volt,' I said, shoving carrots around my plate. As good as my côte de veau looked, I found that I had very little appetite.

'Ah yes, commendable of you,' Paul replied.

'Well it's not pure altruism. I needed to find a part-time job and this suits me. Madame Volt has talked about me keeping it up once her leg has mended. Says it's about time she delegated some of the work. We've talked about me baking British cakes for the bakery as well. She thinks the locals might like that, as long as she continues with the French patisserie as well.'

Paul nodded and took a sip of his wine. 'Word has got around about your cakes,' he smiled. 'I seem to be the only one who hasn't had that particular pleasure.'

Feeling myself blush, I swallowed the potato I was chewing and decided it was time to ask about Clotilde.

'Paul,' I said, taking a fortifying gulp of wine. 'There's something I've been meaning to ask you. It's about Clotilde...'

but before I could go any further the waiter arrived to refill our glasses.

'Would you like some more water?' he asked.

Paul nodded and we sat in silence while the waiter brought a fresh water jug and poured some into the two waiting glasses then, having clicked his fingers at a colleague to clear out plates, handed us the desert menus. Paul once more took his time consulting his. I on the other hand was desperate to get back to the subject of Clotilde and chose the first thing I saw.

'You were about to say... about Clotilde...?' I prompted, once the waiter had taken our order. I was trying—and I suspect failing—to sound as nonchalant as possible. By this point though I'd decided I no longer cared and I levelled Paul a knowing stare. He frowned, went to say something and seemed to think better of it. He clearly felt uncomfortable talking about her. *I knew it—the conniving philanderer.* Eventually he shook his head and said:

'Yes sad, very sad.'

'Sad?' I repeated.

'Yes, I'll miss her terribly.'

So I was right, it was a love affair that went wrong. I thought about Clotilde in her studio, barefooted in her transparent robe and wondered who had left who...

'Do you mind me asking... what happened?'

'Well, she was sick, you see.'

'Sick..?'

Did this effing waiter have some kind of bad-moment radar? He chose that very point to bring our deserts and took an age setting them down, rearranging our spoons and asking if we needed anything else. *No we don't, now bugger off.*

'I'm sorry, Paul,' I said, unable to take the suspense any longer. 'What exactly happened to Clotilde?'

'Clotilde...' Paul repeated the name as though it sounded strange on his tongue. He frowned, picked up his spoon, put it back down again and looked at me for a long moment. 'She had a tumour, you see...'

'Oh God...'

'I'm sorry, Sian. I'm afraid Clotilde is no more.'

Chapter Fifty-six

I hadn't laughed so much in years, especially over someone's dead companion! Paul sat there staring at me while the other diners flicked curious glances at us. Once I'd calmed down, I hastily re-arranged my face into an expression of concerned sympathy, conveyed my regret and attempted to explain my reaction.

'You're talking about your dog, aren't you? You've had to have your dog put to sleep.'

'Yes, my dog. As I say, she was sick. It was a hard decision but the kindest in the end.'

'Paul, I was asking about Clotilde.'

'The thing is, Sian, I never understood why you insisted on calling my dog Clotilde. I assumed you were simply forgetful. Her name was Coco.'

Paul continued and over our mousses au chocolates. The first time I'd been to his house he'd expected me to introduce myself as the new neighbour and had been taken aback when instead I'd complained about his dog.

'I'll admit, I did think it rather…abrupt, shall we say, but I put it down to you being foreign.'

Paul gave me a shy smile. The next time he'd met me was when I came to his house in the middle of the night, having seen Clotilde in the field. He explained how he'd found it bizarre in the extreme that I thought his dog had been out collecting stones.

'I must admit, I was so embarrassed standing there half-dressed and half-asleep in the middle of the night. I thought I must have misunderstood your French. After that, I saw you walking in the lane. I stopped to ask if you were lost—I was going to offer you a lift and invite you in for coffee—sort of start the acquaintance again so to speak—but blow me, you told me you'd spoken to my wife about my dog—well I was so perplexed, I didn't know what to say.'

'And at Madame Clairjo's party, when I asked whether Clotilde would be joining us, you thought I was asking whether your dog would be coming?'

'Exactly. I'd begun to suspect you were obsessed with her.'

We laughed at the absurdity of the misunderstanding and were once more the focus of attention of curious diners. It did cross my mind to wonder why on earth, given the fact that he clearly thought I was mad, he had asked me to dinner. *Perhaps he likes eccentric women.* The thought of Clotilde naked in the field flashed into my mind. Regardless of the hilarity of the confusion, the mystery remained. If Paul thought I meant his dog when I spoke about Clotilde…then who *was* Clotilde?

'Paul,' I said growing serious, 'There was a woman. I saw her a number of times at your upstairs window. She told me that her name was Clotilde.'

Paul shook his head. 'You must be mistaken, Sian, there is no woman.'

What is he playing at?

'Paul,' I said carefully, 'we drank a liqueur together in your kitchen. She told me about how she makes it from herbs and plants.'

Paul looked utterly mystified and shook his head.

'Really, Sian,' he said. 'You can't have been in my house like that. There hasn't been a woman there since my wife left, four years ago.'

I told him about my visit to the studio in the loft room, the strange faces, the tools, the covered sculpture on the plinth…

His voice took on a sharp edge. 'Sian, I can assure you there is no such room in my house.'

Suddenly, I remembered the little sculpture Clotilde had given me. 'I can show you one of her sculptures, it's of a face, she gave it to me when I was in the atelier. I can show it to you tonight.'

Paul nodded and glanced at his watch. It was clear he was tired of all this, that he thought I was crazy or making it all up or both. I pushed away what remained of my desert, refusing a coffee, noting the look of relief in his eyes. We drove back to Saint Vey in silence and once Paul had pulled up outside my cottage, I planted two hasty kisses on each of his cheeks, thanked him for dinner and scurried off inside. Neither of us mentioned the sculpture.

Chapter Fifty-seven

Nate arrived a few days later looking barely older than the day he'd left for his first adventure, his battered old backpack slung over one shoulder. I picked him up from the airport in the bakery van. 'Take it if you want, but you pay the petrol,' Madame Volt had warned.

'What's this, Mam,' Nate said when he saw the white van waiting for us in the short-stay car-park.

'Company car,' I said.

'You got a job as a handy-man?' He laughed.

Nate was still looking pale and more gaunt than usual, which didn't surprise me. I wondered whether he'd lost weight. I didn't comment on it but resolved to feed him up with plenty of home cooking. He talked the whole way back, telling me what he'd been up to since I saw him in Cardiff and updating me on his father's affairs. I look that as a good sign.

'He left me everything, Mam. He didn't have much, but the house is mine now.'

We'd both known that this would be the case and we'd talked about it when I'd been in Cardiff.

'It isn't a bad idea for you to keep a base in the UK,' I'd said, and I repeated the words now. 'I know you're happy in India and with your travelling, but it can't hurt to keep a place back home.' I didn't mention the possibility of selling my house—quite contrary to my advice to him. Nate isn't daft though.

'Why?' he said, 'You got plans for our place?'

'I'm looking at my options,' I answered, not sure how much I wanted to share at this point. After all, I hadn't yet heard from my Aunt and Uncle about buying the cottage—for all I knew they had a buyer lined up for when I moved out. 'How would you feel if I sold our house?'

Nate looked at me with a curious expression.

'Not sure,' he answered. 'I s'pose it would feel a bit strange. Lots of memories there. But then, it's rented out now anyhow, so it's not like we can use it.'

He'd said 'we'. I loved the fact that he still considered it to be his home—and that his memories were important. But I knew I couldn't make my future plans based on my son, especially now that he owned a house of his own.

'Let's get to the cottage and we can make time to talk about it all before you go.'

Nate was fascinated as we drew up outside the house. I screeched open the big red gates—*I'll oil those for you, Mam*—and he hauled his backpack up the path, staring around the garden as I unlocked the door.

'Wow,' he said, gazing up at the cottage. 'This is great.'

I felt his enthusiasm like a relief and it made me see that I'd been hoping for this as a validation. Nate's opinion, I realised, was the only one I cared about. Once inside, he dumped his backpack and after quick glance around the kitchen poked his head around the lounge door.

'Cool,' he said. 'I'm dying for a cup of tea.'

I put the kettle on and followed Nate upstairs where he opened each door and peered into the rooms. I smiled broadly loving the fact that he was so at ease.

'This is your room,' I said, opening the door to the little spare bedroom.

'Great,' Nate replied. He opened cupboards and drawers and peered out of the window before throwing himself onto the bed, hands behind his head. I grinned, resisting the urge to tell him to take off his shoes.

'You like the place then?' It was more of a statement than a question.

'It's brilliant, Mam,' he replied, springing up, loping out of the little room and back down the stairs. 'Not haunted is it?'

'Don't be daft.'

The ghost had agreed to make himself scarce during the visit and I was happy to note that he was keeping his promise, even if he did show up and whisper to me every now and then.

'You're very relaxed with your son,' he said that night after we'd both gone to bed.

'Shhh,' I replied, 'He'll hear you.'

We agreed that Nate would come on the bread runs with me and help with the old folks shopping on Saturday.

'Are you sure?' I said. 'Won't you be bored? The locals don't speak much English.'

'Nah, it'll be fun, I'll get to see a bit of the area. And I can practice my French—not spoken it since school.'

I was pleased—it was more time to spend with my son. With his help we got the shopping done in half the time, Nate hauling the heavy bags into the van like they were full of air, not vegetables. We had a coffee at Café Dominique—*ton fils? Eh, bien!*—before spending the next hour exploring the town, wandering through the cobbled streets and looking in the shop windows full of extravagant Christmas displays.

'Is there anything you want as a present, Nate? I haven't wrapped anything up—there'll be your Christmas money as usual, of course.'

Arwel and I had been putting money into Nate's bank account each Christmas and birthday for years. I'd hated that at first, it felt so impersonal. I remembered the Christmases when he was a little boy, staying up late wrapping toys, trying to think of new places to hide them before Santa delivered them on Christmas Eve. *He's been, Mam, he's been!* The wrapping would be ripped off twice as fast as it went on, Arwel and me grinning at each other at Nate's elation over plastic Superheroes and Tonka Toys and Lego. Even as a teenager I'd put his presents under the tree at the last minute so he didn't get a chance to peek. That all changed when he went away, of course. But, as Arwel had said, the money was what Nate preferred so why not give him what he wants.

'Not really, Mam,' he answered now. 'You know me, travel light, live lighter.'

'I tell you what,' I said glancing at his hands, red raw from the cold. 'I'll buy you some gloves. You can leave them here for when you visit again.'

After choosing a pair of blue thermal gloves in *Monsieur Chic*, we ate a lunch of crepes and dashed round the supermarket. 'I don't know how you manage all this on your own,' Nate said. We then headed out of town to begin the round, which involved much fussing, cheek-kissing and cooing from the ladies.

'Bet your father was a handsome man,' Madame Fontenay said.

It had been more than two weeks since I'd written to the Duchamps and I was beginning to wonder whether I ought to call them when a letter arrived. I knew immediately it was from my Aunt and Uncle since the only other post I received was bills and junk mail. I considered calling Nate who was inside checking his emails on his phone, but thought better of it and took the letter into the field. Sitting huddled in my coat on the bench, I ripped open the envelope and, with great anticipation slid out a single sheet, written in a wavering hand.

'Ma chère Sian,
Your Uncle Jacques and I were not at all surprised to receive your letter. Indeed, we had spoken already about the possibility of offering to sell you the house once the initial year was over. You would be doing us a great favour as the money will certainly be useful, plus we'll have the joy and pleasure of knowing that the home we cherished for so long is in loving hands. You adored your visits when you were a little girl and we have fond memories of you playing in the garden and in the field behind the house. What better than to pass its care to you, our niece. Your Uncle and I are well aware of the house's shortcomings. The roof will need attention before long and you may want to modernise in other ways. For this reason we are willing to offer the house to you at a price which we think you will find more than favourable. We realise that you will have to sell your house in Wales in order to afford the price. If that doesn't take too long, we are willing to wait, but in any case you are free to remain at the house for the year as planned. If you can come to Paris after the Christmas festivities we can talk about the finer points of a sale. Wishing you all the joys of the season.
Your loving Aunt and Uncle, Constance and Jacques.

Chapter Fifty-eight

'It's time,' he whispered.

The ghost was watching me. A new start. A new country. A new home. Even though I'd been at the cottage for almost nine months, that's what it felt like now. That night, standing at the sink washing up after an early supper of macaroni cheese, I considered how my Aunt and Uncle's letter had the effect of shifting my life here from theory to practice. I thought about the arc of emotions I'd been through since I arrived, from excitement, to euphoria, to despair and back again. I was sure. My future was in France. There was much to be done—the sale of my house in Cardiff, finances to organise, a solicitor to find. I didn't savour the bureaucratic formalities to come. But looking around the kitchen, at the fire dancing in the hearth, the homely old furniture, the weird cooker which hadn't blown up—I was ready to commit. The ghost nodded sagely and, placing the last plate on the rack and drying my hands on the tea-towel, I pondered the fact that I didn't feel a sense of loss for my old home.

I looked round as Nate burst through the door hauling an armful of logs.

'Don't know how you cope without me.' He winked.

Smiling at my son I saw that, as Nate had said that night in his Dad's house, our most profound connections aren't necessarily with where we were born.

But Nate was preparing to leave. Christmas was almost here and he was flying back to India soon after.

'I can't tempt you with your Mam's home cooking to stay?' I'd joked.

'I'll visit again,' he'd replied. 'Maybe not on my own next time.'

Once, I'd have badgered him about when, hectored him to Skype more often, demanded to know when he'd be done with travelling. But I felt no inclination to do any of that now. Was that down to Doctor Adebowale and our talks? I don't know but it felt as though there was something of a new bond between Nate and me. Perhaps not new, but different. I watched him stacking the logs in a neat pile by the chimney, smiling as he brushed the sawdust off jeans. It was so easy being with him. I felt I was more myself with my son than with anyone else. Do we all feel like that with our children? 'It's time,' the ghost had said. I knew he was right.

'Nate, make us some hot chocolate will you, and come into the salon. There's something I want to tell you.'

Nate raised his eyebrows but didn't say anything. I went through to the salon and got a fire going, stacking the grate high with paper, twigs and logs. As I stood regarding my handiwork, Nate came in carrying two steaming mugs.

'I remember buying you this,' he said, nodding his head at my *Mam Gorau yn y Byd* mug.

'I reckon I'm still the best mam,' I smiled, hoping he'd still think so too after what I had to tell him.

Comfy in the deep old armchairs by the roaring fire, our mugs warming our hands, I looked around the room. The curtains were pulled and the flames were throwing gentle light onto the books lining the shelves and the twin paintings of the young Constance and Jacques, whose smiles seemed animated by the flickering shadows. Pegleg had eschewed being Poufpouf for the night and was purring softly by the hearth. It was exactly how I'd imagined it when I first arrived at the cottage, when I'd felt so overwhelmed by the task of making the house a home but had vowed to try.

'I'm not a bit surprised, Mam, it's fantastic, I mean who wouldn't want to stay here.'

I'd told Nate about Constance and Jacque's letter and he swept a hand around the room, taking in the cosy scene.

'And after all, you are part French, even if it's only a small part. Me too for that matter. I suppose you're discovering yourself.'

I laughed and took a sip of my chocolate. 'But seriously Nate, you're okay with me selling the house? I mean, I'm guessing it's fine since you've got your Dad's place…'

'Of course, Mam, there's nothing keeping you in Cardiff. Besides, you should do what's best for you, it's your life.'

Was this my son giving me permission to have a life of my own? I watched him as he gave the fire a poke, less skinny now after my hearty meals, the day's stubble showing through, eyes alert yet dreamy. He replaced the poker and took a sip of chocolate, leaving a milky moustache on his lip which he licked off with the tip of his tongue. He's like a wild kitten, I thought, watching Pegleg attack Nate's foot with his tiny claws —I want to nurture him while knowing I can't contain him. Was this how his Swati saw him too?

'What, Mam?' Nate smiled.

'What what?'

'You're looking at me, I can see you out of the corner of my eye.'

He turned to face me, giving me a playful wink. 'There's something else, isn't there?'

I didn't reply but picked up Pegleg and settled him in my lap, stoking his soft fur.

'It isn't just selling the house, is it? I mean, I as good as knew that anyhow. You called me in here to talk about something else didn't you?'

It had always been like that with him and me. When he was a boy I could tell by a single twitch of his mouth if he was upset. I still can. So often, I know what he is going to say before he says it. And he can read my moods like an open book. More so than Arwel could, if truth were known. I took a deep breath and looked at him. He was right of course. There was something else. *Okay, here goes.*

'Nate—you're right it isn't just about selling up and moving here permanently…'

'Okay…'

That feeling when your heart is audibly pounding in your chest and your mouth goes dry.

'The thing is… the thing I want to tell you…'

How on earth am I going to explain?

I stopped, took a sip of hot chocolate and stared into the fire, using my toe to stub out a cinder which had popped out with a snap. Nate didn't rush me and Pegleg's loud purring and his soft fur beneath by hand calmed me enough to continue. This was going to be one hell of a conversation.

'Okay. What I want to tell you… it's something big. And it explains why me and your Dad got divorced.'

238

Chapter Fifty-nine

'Get yourself to the quack's, Sian, sleeping tablets never hurt anyone, and you tossing and turning all night keeps me up as well.'

Unkind? No, Arwel was fed up, that's all. I'd been having sleepless nights for weeks. He was right there's only so much insomnia you can take before the cracks begin to show. I was a wreck. So the next morning after Nate had left for school I'd rung for an appointment. The receptionist wasn't helpful.

'Today? Goodness me, no dear, I've got nothing at all before Friday.'

Well stuff her. I'd resigned myself to having to go work and was about to leave the house when the phone rang.

'If you can get here by ten this morning, we've had a cancellation.'

An hour later I was sitting in the crowded waiting room flicking through back issues of *Cosmo* and hoping the ailing folk hacking away like consumptives wouldn't infect me.

Dr. Golstein was new to the practice, no older than me and unsurprisingly wanted a full account as to why I thought I wasn't sleeping. Lovely eyes… lovely smile… I acknowledged these, but thought nothing more. Still, I'd been happy to talk.

We don't like prescribing these long term. I'm giving you a week's worth. Come back and see me next Monday and we'll see how you're getting on.

That was the start of it. Such an innocent start. Weekly visits where I'd talk more each time, share more—first about my insomnia, then about Arwel, Nate, my job... It wasn't like with the Good Doctor—there was no analysis, no therapy. It was more like chatting with a friend. I began sleeping well even after I stopped taking the pills. But I kept going back.

I'm not sure these appointments are really necessary any more, Sian. There are lots of other patients who need my time.

I'd been shocked by the extent of my disappointment. But then…

…what say we meet after surgery for a drink?

Meet for a drink? I leapt at the idea. There was no reason why not I told myself, it's friendship, nothing more. Every Monday at 6.30 we met at the Caldwell Arms on the edge of town. It's because it's a nice pub I told myself, not because it's discreet.

I love talking with you, Sian.

Getting closer…

You're not like anyone I've met before…

Just a friendship…

It's more than friendship, you know that, don't you…

Resisting…

Don't pull away from it, Sian…

Relenting…

You know what you feel. Let's be together, it's what we both want…

And Nate…?

Bring him, we'll make it work.

It's too hard…

I love you, Sian.

I love you too, Catherine.

Chapter Sixty

'Are you telling me what I think you're telling me?'

I started, suddenly aware of Nate's presence, and Pegleg jumped off my knee. He sat licking a paw by the fire which had burned low as I spoke. Nate leaned forward to throw on another log. Sitting back in his chair he looked at me for a long moment. I nodded.

'I am, Nate.'

'I mean, have I got this right, Mam... this doctor, this friend of yours—Catherine—you're telling me that you and her...'

'We were in love with each other, Nate.'

'So... you left Dad because... because...'

I left the question hanging and a log rolled forward out of the fire onto the hearth, startling Pegleg. Nate leapt up and hoisted it back in with the shovel.

'Bloody hell,' he said. 'This isn't a conversation I expected to have with my mother.'

'I don't suppose it is.'

Neither of us said anything and the silence deepened as we stared into the flames. I didn't know what I felt. But I knew I'd been right to tell him.

'You didn't go and live with her though—this Catherine.' His voice was quiet, careful. I breathed in deeply.

'No I didn't. I couldn't. I knew it would break your Dad's heart if I left. And more to the point, yours. I couldn't leave without you. And... I was a coward. I was scared. Scared of what people might say if I took you to live with another woman, scared for you, scared *of* you, of what you would think of me, that you might never forgive me... We argued, Catherine and me. For weeks, months. She said we'd work it out, you'd come to accept it, that we had nothing to be ashamed of... in the end I just couldn't do it. I left her. It was one of the hardest decisions I've ever had to make. And I couldn't tell anyone. I was in so much pain... so very much... and I had to hide it all. Your Dad knew something was up, something serious... but of course I couldn't tell him and, in any case, I'd left her, it was over, so what would be the point in hurting him? I'd never felt so alone.'

'Aw, Mam…' Nate's voice was low with a different kind of softness now.

He got up, knelt by the side of my chair and put his arms around me. I don't know if he was crying, but I was. When he broke off he smiled sheepishly and we both sat in silence watching the flames. A few moments later he spoke again.

'But I don't understand, since you decided to stay with Dad, how does… how does you being… you know—in love with Catherine—explain why you divorced?'

I nodded. I'd been expecting this question.

'The thing is, Nate, I found out later—it was a few years later… I found out that she'd… that Catherine had died. Of cancer. I was devastated. Even though I hadn't seen her for years it was like I'd lost her all over again. And again I couldn't tell anyone. I had to grieve for her in secret.'

I broke off. There is only so much you can share with your children after all. I stopped short of telling him how I'd never stopped questioning my decision, never known whether I'd been right or wrong not to leave Arwel for her, the pain of living with the fact that if I hadn't been such a coward, Catherine and I could have been together, if only for a few short years.

'In any case, Nate,' I continued. 'It was then that I decided I owed it to her—no I owed it to myself—to leave.'

He'd have to make of that what he would. Nate nodded and didn't ask any more, until:

'But you've never come out as being… well, as being gay—not until now I suppose.'

I winced but it was a fair point.

'I was so confused—I mean it had never occurred to me before meeting Catherine that I could be attracted to another woman. After I divorced your Dad, I even went out with a man I met at a speed-dating thing to test myself, to try to work out what I am—who I am.'

There it was, what I hadn't told the Good Doctor—the test I'd set myself, the real reason I'd gone out with Roger.

'And?'

'And… the labels don't fit. I think for me it's not about being gay or straight. It's… it's a matter of attraction. I loved your Dad. Believe me, Nate I *loved* him. But I fell in love with Catherine and I loved her. I think for me it's more about the person than their gender.'

Nate nodded slowly and smiled. 'Wow.'

Here at last was the relief at having shared this. The fact that Nate seemed to have taken it well was even more reassuring than I'd imagined and I smiled back at him.

'One thing though, Mam?'

A frown creased his brow and I was suddenly nervous again.

'Why now? I mean, it's been years since you and Dad divorced. Why are you telling me this now? Is it because Dad isn't here anymore?'

Perhaps it was. But I was thinking of Clotilde naked in the field, her hand outstretched…

'It was time,' I said.

Chapter Sixty-one

That night... the night I saw Clotilde collecting stones in the field... it hadn't ended when I got back from the Delariche house...

'Go home, Madame Evans,' Paul Delariche had said. I'd done as he'd bid, returning to the cottage and once inside went straight to bed, where I fell almost immediately into a fitful sleep. I woke to moonlight, feeling hot, damp, *soft*... I grasped after my dreams... Clotilde—barefoot on the wooden stairs... Clotilde smiling in her atelier... her hand on mine touching the woman of stone... *I open up a place for the soul to flow in...* I'd curled into the warm quilt and reached back into sleep to find her...

When I woke again the imperfect moon had almost set, the sun had yet to rise and I saw that everything was blurred at the edges. That there were no edges. I sat on the side of the bed and stared, dust motes barely visible in the gloom... I cried. I opened the window to cold night, black trees, milky clouds over the morning star...

...I stared. At the sky—at some point between—not dark and not light, at the wall-paper, faded floral-pink rinsed grey by the night, bare patches where pictures used to hang... I stared at the dressing table—the jumble of little-used morning things, hairbrushes, make-up, moisturisers, magic... I stood, walked, picked up Clotilde's sculpture from where I'd placed it. Turning it over in my hands... holding it against my cheek, cold stone against hot flesh. Held it out to the glimmer of dawn. Woman turned to stone... Stone becoming woman... *expose it, expose it all...*

...I moved barefooted through the shadowy cottage, my nightdress brushing my thighs, acknowledging the spirits of the past and the future... downstairs in the darkness, touching objects, jars, cushions, books, picking things up, putting them back, their colours bleaching out, textures no longer solid escaping from their mass. I couldn't focus or concentrate, couldn't fix on anything.

I picked up the little onyx egg, a birthday gift from Catherine, the one thing I had that she'd touched... *the passion, the loves, the heights of ecstasy. And the depths of suffering...* I closed my eyes and put it to my lips...

...I let myself think...

...let myself feel...

...let myself be...

...door creaking in the night, walking barefoot into the garden, one star winking, bushes black, hedgehog startled, through the gate, into the field of grey-green darkness, taint of sunrise, cold air on skin. Two hares silhouetted against the wall, long ears twitching. I stood stock-still, watchful animal. One loped off slowly towards the east, a dark shape moving. The other followed, both disappearing into the vines...

I turned. She wasn't at her window but a light was shining... Like the hares, I cocked my head, but I was listening for a different kind of danger: the chink of metal on stone...

...the sleeve of my nightdress slipped... Smiling, easing the other sleeve over my shoulder, cotton falling to grass exposing flesh the colour of stone... sharp breath of wind on skin, I breathed in the scent of damp earth and my body's musk. Stepping out of my gown, I walked into the waist-high grass, brushing the tips with my palms; walked on into the grey-dark field, bats flap-fluttering, dry grass scratching, lone owl swooping, clouds scudding, body shivering, rat scurrying, half-moon sinking, tease of sun to come... I began to run...

...I ran....

...nettles stinging skin, grass-stalks grazing feet, cold air on sweat, running...

...through the field, along the hedge, panting hard, into the copse, around the trees...

...running ...stones cutting flesh, breath in gasps, arms and eyes wide open...

...running...

...pounded, chiselled, pared back, emerging... flood of sensuality, glut of viscerality...

I stopped.

Stood.

Heart fast, skin sweating, body raw. I peed standing up at the foot of a tree. Dropped to my knees. Breathed air into pumping lungs. On my back in the pre-sun glow, gazing up through branches, ...all is moving, stars, clouds, moths, birds, bats, moon. On the earth, a body, nettle-stung, feet bloodied, legs scratched, pee drying on thighs, twigs tangled in hair, insects crawling on skin... a woman. Undressed.

Chapter Sixty-two

'Well, son, are you ready to meet the neighbors?'

Nate had met most of them already in his capacity as assistant to the baker's assistant but we'd decided to have a little Christmas party in his honour.

'You'd better get changed,' I told him, emerging from my bedroom in the second of my new dresses, a mid-blue fitted shift, over-printed with an emerald-green swirling leaf design.

'Seriously?' Nate said, eyeing my outfit. 'This is the middle of nowhere, not Paris.'

'Trust me,' I said.

We'd decked out the salon with pine cones and bunches of holly, which Nate collected from the field—our concession to Christmas decorations—and I'd spent the morning baking for our *dinatoire*. I'd had the idea to have a traditional British themed party complete with Christmas cake, mince pies and cucumber sandwiches but, in deference to my newfound Frenchness, I'd changed my mind. 'No one likes mince pies anyhow,' Nate had said. In the end we settled on a somewhat eccentric combination of cheese puffs, mini-pizzas, sesame snaps—which were almost cremated when I was called upstairs to deal with a minor spider crisis—*Oh Nate, she's only a little one*—plus crusty baguette, Cantal, St Albray and Camembert cheeses, and dishes full of stuffed olives and tomatoes.

'What do you think of this, Nate?'

I proudly unveiled the crowning glory of the feast, a Bûche de Noël which I'd spent the morning making using my Aunt's old recipe.

'You going to serve that?'

We both looked at the chocolate log. To be fair it had collapsed at one end and the icing sugar 'snow' had sunk into the chocolate cream, creating the effect of slush more than snow.

'Isn't it supposed to have some kind of Christmas scene on top?' Nate said. 'It looks like the remains of a plumbing disaster.'

I could hear the ghost cackling somewhere.

'It's fine,' I said, proceeding to lop off the sunken end with a carving knife. 'You get on with your *vin chaud.*'

Nate was in charge of the mulled-wine and by three o' clock the scent of warming Burgundy, cinnamon, cloves and orange was wafting through the cottage.

Madame Clairjo was the first to arrive, tapping on the kitchen door and opening it without waiting for an answer. 'I let myself in,' she said, handing me her coat. She wafted into the room resplendent in a flowing pink gown, complete with pearls at her neck and ears, pink diamanté studded pumps, her hair fluffed to candy-floss perfection.

'Bloody hell, it's Barbara Cartland,' whispered Nate.

'Your gate's rusty,' Clairjo tutted. 'Should get that son of yours to oil it.'

She winked at Nate, kissed us both on each cheek and thrust a bunch of crimson poinsettia at me.

'Look lovely on your table, those will,' she said raising an eyebrow at the jar of mistletoe I'd placed there.

Monsieur Ripaille was the next to arrive, sporting his good hat and a navy necktie. He kissed my cheeks and thrust a dirty calico bag into my hands.

'*Joyeux noël,*' he said. 'Christmas gift for you. Just a few of my old gardening tools but they'll get you started.'

Having greeted Madame Clairjo he shook Nate's hand heartily and insisted on taking him off for an impromptu winter-gardening lesson. 'He never could abide to be indoors,' Madame Clairjo said. While they pottered around outside I showed the old woman into the salon where she took a confused double-take at my Bûche de Noël before getting comfortable by the fire. The bell clanged and I went to let the next guests in. The two Jean's were quickly followed by Madame Volt with a dapper looking Monsieur Blanchard behind her wheelchair. 'He has a beautiful car,' she said, pointing at a Blue Peugeot parked in the lane. I led them into the salon—Monsieur Blanchard most solicitous of the invalid —where Monsieur Ripaille and Nate joined us.

'Now, Sian, this is a rather cheeky little red we've been hiding away for an occasion just such as this.'

Jean-Paul presented the dusty bottle with great ceremony before turning to Madame Volt, who had taken off her coat to reveal a tangerine trouser-suit set off by a lime green scarf.

'Oh, my dear, you look lovely,' he cried. He himself was sporting a rather fetching fedora.

'Steady now, slowly,' Volt said as Monsieur Blanchard and Jean-Luc lowered her into an armchair. Nate brought up a stool for her plastered leg and she clucked her approval. 'Now,' she said, glancing at my butchered and bald Bûche de Noël. 'I've brought a small contribution to the party. Marcel? Marcel, where are you? Get the tin.'

Marcel Blanchard did as he was told and produced a cake tin which Madame Volt took great pleasure in prising open to a chorus of 'ooo's' and 'aaahs'. Out came the most exquisite Bûche de Noël in France, complete with a forest of coloured marzipan pine trees, perfect little pine cones, bunches of holly, and a smiling, present-bearing snowmen, all amid sumptuous snow-frosted chocolate cream. I took it from her and placed it next to my attempt, where, to Madame Volt's evident satisfaction, it demonstrated my total inadequacy when it came to French patisserie. She beckoned me forward.

'I'll show you a trick to get the snow just right,' she whispered, kissing me warmly on each cheek.

'Are we waiting for anyone else? I'm as parched as a priest at Lent.' Jean-Paul had no interest in the duel of the Bûche de Noëls but was eyeing up the bottle of chilled Champagne I'd set out on the sideboard.

We were. Last to arrive was Paul Delariche. I'd hesitated, but I couldn't leave him out.

Je suis désolé,' he said with a wink as Nate led him in. 'Clotilde can't make it.' He kissed me on each cheek and handed me a bottle of Cognac.

'Well then, what about a drink,' I said once we were all assembled in front of the roaring fire. 'We've got mulled wine for later, but I thought we'd start off with a glass of bubbly. Perhaps Nate, you could do the honours.'

'Avec plaisir,' Nate said, picking up the bottle of Champagne.

I handed round the glasses and Nate made a great show of untwisting the wire, easing up the cork and popping it open to a chorus of 'oooh', and '*trés bien*', and 'such a nice young man.' I'd never loved him more.

'What shall we drink to?' he asked.

'To friends and neighbours,' said Paul Delariche.

'To friends and neighbors,' we all chorused.

'So, what's it like having a foreigner for a neighbor?' Nate asked once we'd all taken a sip.

'Her baking's atrocious.'

'She'll never fit in.'

'Barking mad.'

'Needs to keep those hedges trimmed.'

Monsieur Blanchard nearly choked on his Champagne but the rest of us laughed so much we scared Pegleg, who leapt from his place by the hearth and limped out of the room.

Chapter Sixty-three

It was Christmas day and Nate and I had decided to cook a feast and eat at home, just the two of us.

'Wouldn't you prefer to go out to a restaurant in town?' I'd asked.

'No, I'd rather stay here and enjoy my last day in the cottage,' he'd replied. I was pleased.

He'd packed his battered rucksack ready for his flight the next day. 'Sorry it's so soon, Mam,' he'd said, 'it was the cheapest ticket.' Now he sat at the kitchen table fiddling with his mobile just as he had when he was a boy while I sliced potatoes. 'Have you finished your homework?' I wanted to ask.

'What's that, Mam?' I turned to find Nate pointing at the tall, narrow cupboard in the corner of the room.

'That son, is what's known as a cupboard,' I quipped, going back to the potatoes.

'Yes, very drôle,' he replied. 'What's behind it?'

'I've no idea,' I said without looking up. 'The wall?'

Nate got up, went over to the cupboard and opened the door.

'It's practically empty,' he said. 'Nothing in here but bottles of some weird-looking home brew.' He held up a half-empty bottle, swirled the contents and popped out the cork.

'Wow, this smells lethal. You haven't drunk any I hope?'

'As if,' I replied, 'You know me, two glasses of wine and I'm done.'

Nate took the bottles from the shelves and placed them on the table.

'Hey, what are you doing?' I said.

'Come and look.'

I put down my knife and joined Nate in front of the cupboard. He pointed to the top.

'Look at that.'

I peered up. Above the cupboard was a wooden panel and below it what I supposed could possibly be a frame.

'That looks like it could be a door. Haven't you noticed before?'

'No, I haven't,' I replied, watching as he grabbed hold of one side of the cupboard.

'It isn't very heavy, reckon even you could move it,' he said, heaving it to one side. 'Look!'

Nate was right. There, behind the cupboard was a little wooden door. As we stood there looking at it, I felt the strangest feeling.

'This is great, let's see what's in there,' Nate said, giving the handle a tug. The door swung open with a long, slow creak. 'Spooky!' Inside, a wooden, cobweb-strewn staircase wound to the right, thin shafts of light coming from somewhere above. 'Wow, this is amazing! You coming, Mam?'

I stood rooted to the spot.

...would you like to see my atelier...?

'Come on,' Nate called, already half way up the stairs. 'Don't you want to know what's up here?'

I followed him up the curved, wooden staircase, each step heavier than the last, a feeling of deep trepidation making my breath come fast.

'Wow, look at this place,' Nate cried, ducking his head under the rafters. 'It's a bit low but you could make a whole other room up here.'

I stood at the top of the stairs, my eyes adjusting while shafts of sunlight slanted through gaps in the roof, crisscrossing the dusty floor. An empty bird's nest lay forlornly in the middle of the space. Nate shoved it with his toe.

'Not much up here, is there?' he said.

I couldn't name what I felt. Currents of nausea rose inside me in intoxicating dizziness. I grabbed hold of a beam to steady myself.

'You okay, Mam?'

'I'm fine, just adjusting to the light.'

'What's this?' Nate loped off to the corner and I followed him over the dusty wooden floor, barely knowing what I was doing. Nate was pulling at a large, stained sheet which covered something roughly person-height.

'*...would you like to see what's underneath..?*'

He threw the sheet to the floor and stood back.

'Well, look at that!'

We both stared.

'It's just a big block of stone,' Nate said. 'But look here, if you look at it in a certain way, it almost looks like a woman. What do you think?'

I couldn't think.

'And what's this?' He reached down and picked up an empty glass, giving it a sniff.

'Have you been up here before?'

'No,' I answered, a little too quickly.

'Well, you don't seem very surprised by it all. I mean, come on, hidden door, secret room, weird rock-thing—I'd have thought you'd be amazed.'

'It's just a loft, I said. 'Let's go down.'

After dinner, we wrapped up warmly and took a glass each of Monsieur Delariche's Cognac out to the field. 'One won't hurt you,' Nate had said. 'It will be my going-away drink.'

The cloud was low and we sipped our Cognac in silence, the liquor providing warmth as we watched the lines of mist hanging over the field. The sky was just beginning to blush.

'I can see why you love it here,' Nate said.

I glanced at the window in Paul Delariche's house where I remembered seeing Clotilde. The reddening sun was dancing over the glass, the reflections milky and fluid in the dusk. *Light and shadow*. I turned to look across the field where I'd seen her collecting stones. *A few glasses of wine, the field in darkness…* Had I seen only shifting shadows among the trees, heard only the rustling of nocturnal creatures? And the strange liqueur… the atelier… her sculptures…

'Projection,' the Good Doctor had said. 'When someone unconsciously transfers her own feelings onto another person instead of owning them herself.' Had I transferred my feelings onto a phantom I'd named Clotilde?

'Do you remember asking me what I like about living in India?' Nate asked, stirring me from my reverie.

I nodded. 'You talked about the lake and mountains…you said you feel at home there.'

'So what do you like about living here?'

I breathed deeply. The sun had not yet dipped and the field behind the clump of trees in the far distance was receiving the full force of its rays, glowing a bright, verdant green. I let my eyes move along the gently undulating horizon, just beginning to turn a darker, almost black-green, like the walnut trees would be in springtime. In the field the grasses, ranging from almost yellow to deep emerald, swayed in the breeze.

'I never knew there were so many greens,' I murmured.

Nate laughed. 'You moved to France for the colour green?'

I laughed with him. 'Well, let's see,' I said. 'What do I like about living here? I live a quiet life, I suppose what people call a simple life. That suits me well. I like looking after my little house and my garden. I sit here in the evenings drinking a glass of wine and watching the sun setting. I like the fact that I can be alone while surrounded by life. I've met good people who are close but keep their distance. I can talk to no one for days if I choose, without feeling guilty or lonely. No one here wants to change me, to fit me into a mold.'

I peered at Nate and hesitated, but of all people I felt sure that he would understand.

'Here, I feel... I feel like I'm no longer a block of stone... it's like I'm finding my shape—a bit like that statue in the loft. I'm...emerging... Does that sound weird?'

Nate shook his head while gazing out over the field.

'It was me who made you come,' Clotilde had said.

'I suppose I could have found all this somewhere else. But whether by chance or design, for me it happened to be here.'

Nate nodded. 'I know exactly what you mean, Mam.'

Something made me look up. There she was at the window, naked and smiling, her dark hair falling over her face. I smiled back.

'Thank you, Clotilde.'